# To Catch a Leaf

Mary B.

*To the memory of my beloved
husband and soul mate,
who will be in my heart forever.*

# ACKNOWLEDGMENTS

From the bottom of my heart, I want to thank my editor, Ellen Edwards, for her patience and understanding through these most painful, difficult months; my agent, Karen Solem, for her support and guidance; my sister, Nancy, for traveling the road with me; my best friend, Barb, for her voice of wisdom; and my dearly beloved family — Jason, Julie, Tasha, Kerry, my cousins, my stepmom, Bonnie, and my many kind friends. A special thanks to my fellow cozy mystery authors for their help — Deb Baker, Lorraine Bartlett, Maggie Sefton, Leann Sweeney, and Jennifer Stanley.

And a special shout-out to my uncle Lyndon and aunt Pat for always being there for me.

# CHAPTER ONE

*Monday*

Happiness oozed from every cell in my body. No, wait. Ooze sounded bad, and what I was feeling was definitely not bad. Not by a long shot. I was in a zone. I *radiated* bliss. As my assistant Lottie pointed out, I had a certain glow about me.

The best part of a glow of this magnitude was that nothing could dim it, not the ding in the paint on my refurbished yellow Corvette, not the snarl of traffic from a stoplight malfunction, not even the knowledge that my mother had completed a new art project and was going to deliver it after school let out for the day.

The reason for my blissful state was that after weeks of having to keep my news under wraps, the secret was out at last. I was officially engaged to the sizzling-hot man of my dreams, my sexy neighbor, former Special Ops Army Ranger–turned-owner of Down the Hatch Bar and Grill, Marco Salvare. Yes, the very male who turned the heads of women all over town, the pragmatic, enigmatic, charismatic, and, yes, sometimes autocratic Marco, my Italian American hunk, was now engaged to little ol' *moi.*

Added to all that joy, my flower shop Bloomers was operating in the black for the first time since I'd bought the business from former owner Lottie Dombowski. Poor Lottie had been drowning in debt from her husband's ginormous medical bills, while I was up to my freckles in failure, having flunked out of law school and having been unceremoniously cast off by the man I thought I wanted to marry. Instead of succumbing to despair, I took action.

Scraping together the remainder of my inheritance from my grandpa, I plunked down enough money to ensure my servitude to the bank forever, hired Lottie to teach me how to be a florist, put in a coffee-and-tea parlor, lured the foremost British authority on tea in Indiana, Grace Bingham, out of retirement, and attempted to make a go of it.

Needless to say, with the national economy in the tank, it had been a struggle. But a recent spurt in business had pushed my checking account into positive territory at last, giving me even more reason to ooze — I mean radiate — happiness.

Horns honked around me. People were getting impatient. In a small town like New Chapel, traffic jams were fairly uncommon. But I merely cranked up the volume on my CD player and sang along until I was able to turn off the main road and escape the congestion.

It was a gorgeous, sunny May morning, business was up, and I was engaged to the most wonderful man in town. Nothing on earth could dim my happiness.

Then I hit a cat.

Jamming on the brakes, I threw the car into PARK and jumped out, horrified at the thought of what I might find. I ran around to the front and saw a ragged yellow tabby cat crouched on the macadam a few feet in front of my car, staring at me in fright. I hadn't run it down after all!

Seeing that I wasn't about to do it harm, the tabby rose unsteadily and attempted to limp to the curb, dragging its right hind leg behind it. The leg was bent at the wrong angle.

"Oh, no! I did hit you," I cried, blinking back a sudden rush of tears. "I'm so sorry.

I'll make it all right, I promise. Please don't try to run away from me. I want to help you."

The cat meowed pitifully, gazing at me with fearful golden eyes, ready to attempt to flee. I glanced around for assistance, but I'd turned off Concord Avenue onto a side street that had no houses and only a few businesses, none of which were open yet. Would an ambulance come if I called 911? Probably not.

The cat was in terrible pain, and so was I, the pain of horrendous guilt. I took off my jean jacket and approached the poor animal cautiously, talking to it in a soothing voice. "I'm going to take you to the vet, okay? I'm really, *really* sorry. You don't know how sorry I am. I'm just going to pick you up gently now, so don't scratch me."

The cat either understood or was too injured to fight. I wrapped my jacket over it and picked it up, careful not to touch the damaged leg. I placed the cat gently on the passenger seat and prayed it wouldn't try to escape, but it seemed to know that I wasn't a threat.

I buckled my seat belt, put the 'Vette in DRIVE, and headed for the veterinary clinic where my roommate, Nikki, took her cat, Simon. Fortunately, the clinic was only a five-minute drive, because the injured tabby's plaintive meows were breaking my heart. How could I have been so careless? Why hadn't I noticed the animal in the road?

I approached the reception counter, babbling wildly, holding the cat in my arms; the receptionist looked up in surprise, then jumped off her chair and ran to get an aide.

Within five minutes, Dr. Christine Kelly had the cat on a stainless-steel table and was administering a painkiller so she could perform an exam, while I sat on an orange plastic chair in the corner enveloped in remorse.

"Is this an outdoor cat?" she asked.

"I don't know. I'd never seen the animal before I . . . hit it."

She glanced at me from under nicely arched brows, then continued her examination.

"I can feel a break in the hind foreleg," she said. "I'll need to get an X-ray before I set the bone to know how bad the damage is."

"That's fine. Whatever you need to do, Doctor, I'll take care of it. No problem."

"How did it happen?" she asked.

"Right after I turned off of Concord Avenue, I caught a glimpse of the cat in the street in front of my car. It must have been hiding under a parked vehicle or maybe in a hedge, but whatever. I didn't see it in time or I would have stopped. I just felt this *thump* — and I knew I'd hit it. Luckily, I wasn't going fast. Well, not so lucky for the cat, of course . . ."

Babbling again.

"You didn't run her over," Dr. Kelly said.

"What?" My brain cells were moving a little slow, no doubt due to shock.

"She would have suffered a lot more than a broken hind leg, trust me. This cat must have already been injured."

"Then what caused the *thump?*"

"You'd have to go back and look. All I know is that you didn't run her over or she probably wouldn't be alive."

I felt more tears welling up and quickly brushed them away. "I'm so relieved."

"No collar, I notice," the vet said, as her fingers gently probed, "but it looks like she might have had one once."

"Could she have been dumped?"

"Quite possibly. Or she got out and roamed, couldn't find her way back, and got so thin she slipped out of her collar. She's a female, around five years old is my best guess. I'll check for a computer chip. Smart people have chips implanted. If that's the case, I'll contact the owner. *Uh-oh.* I see fleas. So what would you like to do with her if we can't determine who the cat belongs to?"

Wait. What would *I* like to do? "I don't know, Doctor. What do you usually do in these kinds of situations?"

"Turn the animal over to the shelter."

With a broken leg? To crouch in a wire cage, alone and frightened, until someone adopted her? What if no one wanted her? What then? Could I live with that?

"You're good at solving mysteries," Dr. Kelly said. "Maybe you can find out where she came from."

I blinked in surprise. The doctor knew about me?

"I read the newspaper," Dr. Kelly said, seeing the question on my face, "and Nikki talks about you a lot. I have to say, you're amazingly brave the way you go after killers. That one murderer who tried to burn you alive? Wow. Solving the cat mystery should be a walk in the park after that. So what's your decision?"

After such praise, how could I tell her no? I glanced at the shabby tabby with the shattered leg that had suddenly become my responsibility. "If there's no chip," I said with a sigh, "I'll take her."

Dr. Kelly smiled for the first time. "I was hoping you'd say that. Why don't you have a seat in the waiting room while we fix her up? It'll be about an hour."

An hour? It was already eight thirty and Bloomers opened at nine o'clock. My assistants were undoubtedly wondering where I was. Plus it was Monday, which meant Lottie's delicious egg and toast breakfast was waiting for me. But perhaps missing breakfast was part of my punishment for careless driving.

I exited the clinic to make my phone call just as an elderly couple with a yapping schnauzer was entering. The gray dog strained at its leash, teeth bared, trying to reach me, but the woman dragged it away, talking in a soothing voice. "Now, haven't we discussed your behavior before? About being nice to strangers? Haven't we?"

That was a discussion I would have loved to witness.

Grace answered the phone, her delightful accent a reassuring sound to my frazzled nerves. "Good morning. Bloomers Flower Shop. How may I help you?"

"Grace, it's me. I hit a cat —" I paused as a woman carrying a feline into the clinic gave me the evil eye.

"You hit a cat with what?" Grace asked.

16

"My car."

"Well, that's a relief, isn't it? I didn't like to think you'd gone off your rocker, running about whacking animals with your purse."

Sometimes there was just no way to understand the workings of Grace's mind. "The cat's hind leg is broken," I said quietly, as more people walked past with their pets, "but that may not have been my fault. I'm at the veterinary clinic now. I should be back in about an hour."

I heard Grace whisper, "It's Abby. She hit a cat. She's at the vet." Then I heard Lottie say, "Lordy, what will that girl get into next?"

Grace said to me, "Well, that's a bang-up way to start the week, isn't it? And you freshly engaged."

"You know about my engagement?"

"It would be a rather odd statement to make otherwise, wouldn't it?"

Damn! I'd wanted to make the announcement at breakfast. We'd only revealed the news to our family two and a half days ago. "Who told you? My mom?"

"Would you like the whole list?"

I heard paper rattling.

"First off, your mum rang up at eight o'clock on the nose."

17

"That figures."

"And five times thereafter."

Still figured.

"Then your cousin Jillian phoned —"

The mouth that roared.

"— but said she was going back to bed so she would call you at lunchtime. The next call was from Marco's mum."

"She must have wanted to let me know she made it back to Ohio safely. She was supposed to get in late last night."

"I believe she's still here, love. She said she'd see you later today."

What? No! That wasn't the plan. The plan was for Francesca Salvare to go back home so she wouldn't be here to pester us for wedding details. Because there weren't any yet.

"Then Marco called," Grace said, "but he didn't say a word about the engagement."

He'd probably phoned to enlighten me as to why his mother was still here. I couldn't wait for that explanation. "Okay, Grace. Thank you. I'll be there as soon as I can."

"I hope so, dear. A large shipment of flowers just arrived, and Lottie said many of them are damaged. She's trying to sort through them now, but we'll be opening soon, and you know the rush we always have in the coffee shop on Monday mornings.

And don't forget today is the meeting of the Monday Afternoon Ladies' Poetry Society."

Twelve senior citizens waxing poetic about the benefits of fiber. "Can't wait. Listen, Grace, this cat appears to be a stray. If the vet can't determine the owner, I'm going to have to bring her home with me unless . . . you or Lottie want to take her?"

I heard Grace whispering, and heard Lottie whisper back. Then Grace said, "Shall I keep your breakfast in the fridge, then?"

No takers. Damn. "Yes, please."

Cold scrambled eggs and hard toast.

"Just a minute, dear," Grace said. "Lottie would like a word."

"Abby," Lottie said a moment later, "how did you happen to hit the cat?"

"I don't know, Lottie. The cat must have darted out just as I turned off Concord."

"Why did you turn off Concord?"

"Traffic jam."

"Oh, good," she said with relief in her voice. "I'll see you back at Bloomers."

"Wait, Lottie, what's up? Why all the questions?"

"I just wanted to make sure you weren't trying to shake a tail."

"A tail?"

"Well, a stalker."

At once I felt someone's eyes upon me. Goose bumps dotted my arms as I glanced around. Then I saw the receptionist standing at the glass door, motioning me over.

"Okay, that's all," Lottie said.

*That's all?* "Lottie, don't leave me hanging like this —"

The line went dead.

The receptionist was motioning frantically now, so I ended the call and hurried toward the door. "Sorry," I said, following her inside. "It was a business call."

"That's okay. Dr. Kelly just wanted you to know that there's no microchip." She smiled. "Looks like you have yourself a cat."

# CHAPTER TWO

Okay. So. I had a cat. And possibly a stalker. To think I'd always loved Mondays, with their wide-open vistas and unexplored opportunities, blank canvases just waiting for my bold strokes of color. Not feeling so bold now, was I? More like petrified of what would be thrown into my path next.

Needing a sympathetic ear, I phoned Marco but got his voice mail. Since I couldn't fit all I had to say in a message, I merely said, "Can we elope? Tonight?"

There was no point in returning my mom's calls yet. She'd be teaching class, and Jillian was almost assuredly still asleep. Ditto with my roommate, Nikki, who worked the afternoon shift in County Hospital's x-ray department. I glanced through the veterinary clinic's plate-glass window and saw that the waiting room had filled up, and the yapping dog was trying to scale the reception counter. So I sat in my Corvette instead and turned on the CD that had me singing so joyfully before. Unfortunately, the bliss was gone.

After another half hour, I went back inside and took a seat on a yellow plastic chair opposite a huge aquarium filled with brightly colored fish. The people with the schnauzer were sitting across from me, the dog now standing on the woman's lap, barking at the fish. I could tell the woman was trying to catch my eye, so I kept my gaze on the floor.

"This is Stinker," the woman said loudly, petting the dog.

Seeing that she had directed her comment to me, I gave her a quick smile then checked my watch, willing the vet to hurry. I still had to take the cat home, and I had no idea whether Nikki's cat, Simon, would welcome a strange feline into our cramped quarters — or what I'd do if he didn't.

"Want to know why his name is Stinker?" the woman persisted. The dog had gone from her lap to the man's and back to hers, and was now slobbering on the aquarium glass, apparently trying to lick his way through to the fish.

"Because he's disobedient?" I asked.

The man and woman stared at me, aghast. Clearly it was the wrong answer. Did I want to know the right one? No.

The dog grabbed a magazine on the end table and started shaking it. The woman sniffed indignantly as she took the magazine away.

"Is your dog getting his worm medicine?" the old man asked, seeing as how his wife was now ignoring me.

"I don't have a dog." I checked my watch again. I could have wrapped my own leg in plaster in the time it was taking.

"Do you have a cat?" he asked.

"Um, I brought one in."

"She's one of those cat people," his wife whispered loudly, nudging him. She lifted her nose in the air and glanced away.

"What's the cat's name?" the man asked. His wife was pretending not to listen.

I blinked at him. The cat's name? Was I responsible for naming her now, too? "Exterminator."

They both gaped at me. "You named your cat Exterminator?" the woman asked.

"It's kind of a nickname," I said. "It comes from how she deals with noisy, ill-behaved dogs." I shrugged as though to say it was out of my hands.

The receptionist called their name, and they both hurried to follow her, casting vile glances at me over their shoulders.

Finally, I was taken into an examination

room, where the groggy cat was waiting in a cardboard cat carrier. I peered through the opening on top and saw a plaster cast on one of her hind legs. The little feline managed to lift her head to look at me. She opened her mouth in a silent meow as though she recognized me. I put my fingers through the opening to rub her fur, and she closed her eyes again.

Dr. Kelly gave me a starter kit of special food, a bottle of vitamin drops, an antibiotic, and probiotic capsules to counter the medicine's side effects. I was relieved to hear that she'd bathed the cat in baby shampoo to get rid of the fleas, a nontoxic alternative to oily flea sprays. Her holistic approach to pet care was the biggest reason Nikki brought Simon to her.

"Underneath all that grime, she's a nice cat," Dr. Kelly said. "What are you going to name her?"

Why was everyone so concerned about names? "I'll let whoever adopts her name her."

I made arrangements to pay the bill in three monthly installments, then carried the cat in her container to my car. As the engine roared to life, I glanced at the ragged little thing, visible through the cardboard bars. Fortunately, the tabby seemed content to sleep off the effects of the sedative.

At the apartment, I set the carrier in the hall outside the door, then let myself in and waited for Simon. As soon as he heard the door, the white fur ball came galloping around the corner, delighted to have a human playmate home so early in the day. But then he caught the scent of a foreign feline and immediately went into ferocious defender mode, arching his back and puffing his tail to twice its size, his ears flattened against his skull. He hissed, then pawed at the doorframe as though to say, *Let me at the intruder.* There was no way I could leave Simon and the injured cat together.

"Why can't you defend us like this when Jillian comes to visit?" I asked him.

Simon hissed at me as I scooped him up and carried him to Nikki's room, quietly opening the door and shoving him inside. Then I returned for the dozing cat and brought her into the living room. But I should have known Simon wouldn't be content for long. He began to meow and scratch at the bedroom door, until I heard the mattress springs creak and knew Nikki was stumbling from her bed to let him out.

I ran up the hallway in time to grab her doorknob from the outside and hang on. "Nik, wait! You can't let Simon out. I have another cat out here."

She stopped tugging. "You adopted a cat?"

"No. Well, sort of. It's a long story. Wouldn't you rather go back to bed and hear about it later?" I knew how testy Nikki got when she didn't get her full eight hours.

"No."

Muttering something to Simon, Nikki slipped out and shut the door. She had on her purple-and-pink-print pajamas, with her spiky blond hair in disarray, looking like a tall, thin, sleepy child. She padded to the living room and plopped down on the sofa, her elbows on her knees, hands propping up her head. "I'm awake. Tell me."

I sat on the sofa beside her and explained everything, concluding with, "So rather than drop her off at the animal shelter, I felt obligated to take care of her until she recovers."

"And then what?"

"If I'm not able to track down her owner, I'll find her a new home."

Nikki said nothing for a moment, absorbing the information. "What are we going to do with Simon? You know he hates other animals in his territory."

"How about if Simon stays in your room?"

"Are you crazy? Keep him in your room if you think it's such a good idea."

"I didn't say it was a good idea. Fine. I'll take Simon to Bloomers with me."

"Why can't you take the stray to Bloomers?"

"She's injured, Nikki. She's been traumatized. I can't expose her to all the germy people coming and going, and I wouldn't leave her there alone at night, either."

"But you'd leave Simon alone there?"

I hadn't thought of that. I hadn't thought of anything beyond why on earth I hadn't spotted the cat in the road in the first place. My mind was replaying that moment on a continuous, guilt-ridden loop.

Nikki leaned over to look at the stray through the top of the carrier. "She's scrawny, poor little thing. I'll bet she could use a good meal." She opened the top of the carrier, lifted the cat gently and held her like a baby, stroking her yellow head. The cat stirred, opened her blurry eyes, focused on Nikki, and gave a faint mew. I felt my heart breaking again.

Nikki let out a long, resigned sigh. "You'd better take Simon with you. He'll probably love being at Bloomers. He'll be fine at night as long as you leave food and water for him."

"Thanks, Nikki. You're the best. You know what this reminds me of? When we were in

27

fifth grade and found that stray dog that had mange. Remember that? I used to slip bologna out of the house to feed him."

"And I hid him in our garage at night." Nikki stroked the cat until it fell asleep again. "Didn't we talk the neighbor down the street into adopting that dog? The neighbor with the crazy wife? I think that ugly dog kept the man from going insane along with her."

"Yeah, those were good times." I stood up. "I'll call the newspaper right now to place a found ad, and when I get back to Bloomers I'll put a posting on Craig's List. I'll put the tabby's food and medicine in the kitchen. The doctor said she doesn't need anything until suppertime."

"Don't worry about the ads," she said, as I unpacked the supplies. "I'm awake. I can take care of them. And I'll watch the cat until I have to leave for work. Don't forget to set up a disposable litter box for her in your room. Oh, and take Simon's food and a portable litter box with you."

*Eww.* I hadn't thought about that. What would Grace and Lottie say?

Keeping my eye out for potential stalkers, I hunted for a spot for my car that was close to Bloomers without taking up valuable customer parking. The flower shop is on Franklin, one of the four streets that surround the courthouse square. It occupies the first floor of a three-story redbrick building, and has two bay windows on either side of a yellow-frame door. The left side of the building is the shop, while the right side is our Victorian-inspired coffee and tea parlor, where customers like to sit at white wrought-iron tables and sip from china tea cups while watching the happenings outside.

Two doors north is Down the Hatch Bar and Grill, Marco's place, and around the square are quaint gift shops, boutiques, a deli, a jewelry store, two banks, three restaurants, several law offices, including that of Dave Hammond, my former boss, and much more, all housed in two- and three-story brick buildings from around 1900.

When I got to Bloomers, my assistants were busy serving java, tea, and scones to a room jammed with customers, so I brought Simon and his necessities inside from the alley entrance, through our narrow galley kitchen, and into my workroom. Simon had howled in protest during the ten-minute ride from home and now darted out of his plastic prison and underneath the worktable, where he shook off his travel jitters, then began washing his face.

I uncovered his litter box and slid it under the table. Simon stopped his ablutions to sniff it, then resumed his facial. When he saw me head into the kitchen, he scampered after me and watched as I filled his bowl with water. It went under the worktable, too. Fortunately, the big table in the middle of the room was spacious.

The workroom was my happy place, my little piece of paradise, overflowing with the colors, shapes, textures, and scents of my profession. Lottie had designed it well. Two huge walk-in coolers sat side by side along one wall, dried and silk flowers filled tall containers on shelves on the back wall, vases and pots of all sizes and materials lined the top shelf, and slate counters ran along the opposite wall, ending at my desk. On the desktop sat my keyboard, computer monitor, a cordless telephone, an assortment of accessories, and a photograph of Marco and me taken in Key West last winter.

As Simon explored, I checked the orders on the spindle, overjoyed to see a thick stack of them. I inhaled and blew out, feeling much more positive. The day was finally getting better.

Lottie came through the purple curtain holding a stack of orders. As usual she was wearing lots of pink, from her pink plaid shirt to her bright pink sneakers, not to mention the pink barrettes in her brassy red curls. For a plus-sized woman, she wasn't afraid to wear strong colors. Then again, as the mother of seventeen-year-old quadruplet sons, there wasn't much that frightened her.

"Did you get the kitty home?" she asked.

"Yep. She's all settled in. How much of our flower order was damaged?"

"Not that much, luckily. I called the supplier and more are on their way. Now, let me see that ring." She took my hand to examine my engagement ring up close. It was a half-carat marquise-cut diamond set in a gold band etched with tiny chevrons on either side.

"It's bee-*you*-tiful, sweetie. How exciting. I couldn't be happier for you." She gave me a big hug, beamed at me, then showed me an order written in Grace's neat handwriting. "We need to discuss this."

No segue there.

I read it silently: One calla, any color, surrounded by sweet basil leaves, to be delivered this afternoon to the address below. I handed it back to her. "What's wrong with it?"

"It's from the stalker."

I shuddered. "Why am I the last one to know I have a stalker?"

"He's not *your* stalker, sweetie. At least I didn't think he was, but I figured I'd better check with you anyway, just to make sure."

*Wow.* The day just got a whole lot brighter. "Then whose stalker is he?"

"A nice-looking lady renting the Donnelly home on County Line Road. What you're looking at is his latest order. Here are the earlier ones." She pulled the paper clip off the stack in her hand and read them aloud: "A single tiger lily in baby's breath. One red hibiscus with thyme leaves. I had to substitute a red amaryllis for the hibiscus. One iris in statice. An amaryllis with palm leaves. And one primrose — but not an evening primrose — with oleander." She slipped the paper clip back on. "That's it."

I was missing something. "And that says *stalker* how?"

"Here's how it works. About twice a week, when we open up in the morning, we find an envelope filled with cash stuffed through the mail slot in the door. Within ten minutes a man calls in an order but won't leave a name. If we tell him we have to have a name, he threatens to take his business elsewhere. He's very specific about what he wants, the money always covers the cost, and he sends the flowers to the same house each time. Doesn't that sound like stalking behavior to you?"

"How long have these orders been coming in?"

"Several weeks."

"Why am I just now learning about them?"

"Come on, sweetie. Think back to what you've been through for the past month. You just got off crutches for your sprained ankle; Marco got called back to active duty with the Army Rangers; we had that vampire scare; your cousin was ill and hiding in our basement. . . . Seems like you had enough to deal with."

I saw her point. "Is the recipient of all these bouquets alarmed about the gifts?"

Lottie contemplated the question. "Now that you mention it, she doesn't appear to be. She just takes them, thanks me, and shuts the door."

"This really doesn't sound like a stalking situation, Lottie. I'll bet the man sending her flowers is married and doesn't want his wife to find out."

"Well, then he's a philanderer," Lottie said, folding her arms over her ample bosom.

"But he's a paying philanderer," I reminded her.

"I still don't like it," she said. "It doesn't pass the sniff test."

I took the stack from her hand. "Tell you what. I'll deliver the new order so I can check out the situation."

Simon jumped up on the table to see what was happening, nearly scaring Lottie pinkless.

"Lordy, where did he come from?"

Simon rubbed up against her hand, then sat directly between us, Zen-like, with his eyes half closed, soaking up our energy.

"This is Simon, Nikki's cat. I had to bring him with me because the injured kitty is recuperating at the apartment, and Simon doesn't play well with other felines."

"Well, hello, Simon," Lottie said, patting his head as though he were a dog. Simon ducked after the third pat and jumped off the table.

"Did I hear correctly that Simon will be our shop cat?" Grace asked, slipping through the curtain. She was an inveterate eavesdropper.

"I hope neither of you mind Simon being here," I said. "I really had no choice — unless one of you wants to keep him for a while."

"Sadly, my landlord doesn't allow pets,"

Grace said, without looking terribly aggrieved.

"I'd let Simon stay with me, sweetie, but our Labrador doesn't play well with felines either. Now, show Gracie your gorgeous engagement ring."

I held out my hand for Grace to admire. "Oh, Abby, it's lovely, isn't it? Not too small and certainly none too large, either."

Was that supposed to be a compliment?

At once, the phone rang and the bell over the door jingled. "I'll go see to the customers," Lottie said. "You get the phone, Abby."

I dashed across the workroom and picked up the receiver on my desk. "Bloomers Flower Shop. How may I help you?"

"Abigail, where were you this morning?" my mom asked. Obviously it was recess time at school. "I've tried to reach you several times."

"I just got in, Mom. I found an injured cat and took her to the vet."

"That was kind of you, honey. You always had a soft spot for animals. Over the years, how many did you bring home with you that we had to find homes for?"

A lightbulb went on over my head. My parents had been without a pet for years. I knew Dad would enjoy having company during the day. He had been forced to retire from the police department after a drug dealer's bullet put him in the hospital and surgery to repair his leg put him in a wheelchair. He'd learned to use crutches to get up and down stairs to a limited degree, but otherwise he stayed close to home. A sweet little cat would be perfect for him.

"Too many to count. Listen, Mom, this poor little tabby has a broken leg and no home. I don't want to turn her over to the animal shelter, so do you think you could adopt her? I'd take her myself, but Simon won't share his turf. She's a real cutie, Mom, and Dad might enjoy the comp—"

"Abigail, recess is only fifteen minutes long. I just called to say I'll be there right after school to drop off my latest art. We'll talk then."

The tone of her voice wasn't reassuring. "Okay, Mom. Bye."

"Hey there, beautiful," a deep male voice said near my ear as a pair of strong arms surrounded me. My heart skipped a beat as I turned and smiled into the face of my beloved.

"Hey, yourself, Salvare," I said, winding my arms around Marco's neck. "You're a welcome sight. After the morning I've had, I sure could use a kiss."

"Happy to oblige." He tilted his head to

meet my lips. There was nothing wimpy about anything Marco did, and that applied to his kisses, too. He pulled me against him, and I melted into his arms, feeling all my stress flow right out of my body. But right in the middle of our smoking-hot kiss, Simon launched himself onto the desk, and from there leaped onto Marco's shoulders.

"Simon!" Before he could dig his claws into Marco's flesh, I grabbed the cat and placed him on the floor. "Bad boy!"

"What's Simon doing here?" Marco asked, reaching down to scratch him behind the ears.

I told him the tale of my morning misadventure with the tabby cat as I gathered my tools and stems and started to work on the next order. "And if all that wasn't traumatic enough, my mom is bringing over a new piece of art after school today, Lottie is convinced one of our customers is a stalker, and your mom is still in town. By the way, I can't wait for you to explain that one. So all in all, I've had a very trying time, and it's not even noon."

Marco pulled out one of the wooden stools at the worktable and perched on it. He was wearing a long-sleeved black T-shirt with a white stripe down one arm and a Down the Hatch logo on the back, a pair of slim-fitting blue jeans, and black boots. I loved how the black T-emphasized his dark, wavy hair and chocolate-colored eyes. "Tell me about the stalker."

"Sure thing, right after you tell me why your mom is still in town."

"Sunshine, given the morning you've had, let's save it for when you're in a better mood."

I ruffled his hair. "How sweet that you want to protect me from further trauma, Marco. But now that you've made it clear my mood will have to improve before I can handle the information, after which my mood will undoubtedly go downhill again, could you just get this over with?"

Marco sighed. "My mom and my sister, Gina, want to throw you a wedding shower."

"Is that so bad? But let's not refer to it as *my* shower. I'm not going through this alone, remember? Did you remind your mom that our wedding isn't until September?"

"As I recall, she was in the room when we made the announcement."

"That doesn't mean she was listening. I love your mom, Marco, but she does like to talk. So you'd better explain to her again that there's no need for her to stick around town now since any prewedding activities won't take place for months."

Marco took my hand, palm-side up, and kissed the tender flesh in the middle, knowing full well it was one of my erotic zones and, as such, tended to melt my resistance. "Here's a better idea. She wants to have dinner with us at the bar, so come down right after you close up and we can tell her together." He kissed my palm again, then glanced up with a guileless smile.

When was this day going to get better?

# CHAPTER THREE

"Okay, I'll be there after I close the shop," I said with a sigh.

"Great. *Now* tell me about the stalker," Marco said, folding his arms over his chest.

"Hold on a minute while I get more flowers. I can work while I talk." I was the Rachael Ray of the flower industry.

I opened the cooler and stepped inside to survey my stock of flora. I emerged a few moments later with a beautiful peach calla and two handfuls of fragrant basil leaves. I liked using herbs, such as dill, parsley, rosemary, and basil, whenever possible and always kept them on hand.

"Lottie believes one of our customers is a stalker," I said as I trimmed the stems with my floral knife, "because he's been sending anonymous bouquets to a woman renting the Donnelly place. But she doesn't seem to mind getting them, so my guess is that this so-called stalker is sending the arrangements behind his wife's back."

"Is he someone from around here?"

"We don't know. He drops money through the mail slot, calls in his order, and won't leave a name. He seems to know how much to pay, too, so he's either looking up floral arrangements on the Internet, or he's a florist, too, and doesn't want the flowers traced back to his own shop."

Marco scratched his chin. "He doesn't sound like a threat, but I'd feel better if we could get his name. Do you have his phone number so I can trace it?"

"No."

"Then see if you can get him to tell you his name and number the next time he calls."

"I don't think this guy wants to be found out, Marco."

"Sunshine, I have every confidence in you. You're a pro when it comes to being . . . inquisitive."

"You paused before you said inquisitive."

"Nope."

"Yes, you did. You were going to say nosy, weren't you?"

His mouth curved up at one corner as he pulled me into his arms for another kiss. "Keep me apprised of the situation, okay? I've got to get down to the bar to let the electrician in."

The curtain parted and Grace entered the workroom, only to stop short when she saw us entwined. "So sorry. I wasn't aware you had company. Hello, Marco."

"Hi, Grace," Marco said with a nod. "You're looking well today."

She patted her hair. "Well, it's a wonder, isn't it, as busy as we've been. But I do thank you for saying so."

The sixtysomething Brit had on a tailored khaki dress, belted at the waist to show off her slender figure, and sensible brown pumps. Her short silver hair, cut in layers, showed off the elegant lines of her face. Grace had been a legal secretary at Dave Hammond's law office, where I'd clerked during my only year in law school. She had retired just before I bought Bloomers and was so bored at home that it hadn't taken much to coax her into work for me.

Putting her in charge of the newly opened coffee-and-tea parlor had been a stroke of genius. Grace was not only a pro when it came to brewing gourmet coffee and tea, she was also a skilled baker, turning out the most delicious scones in town, with a different flavor every day of the week. From the heavenly aroma in the shop, I was betting today's flavor was cinnamon.

"Abby, if you don't mind, I'd like to take the one o'clock hour for my lunch. I promised my friend Connie I'd meet with her today, and since I'll be busy this evening, lunch it must be."

"Got a hot date with Richard tonight?" I asked.

"Just our bowling league night," she said.

Richard Davis was a tough, old-time Texas businessman who favored string ties, cowboy boots, and ten-gallon hats and didn't take guff from anyone. His favorite mode of transportation was a 1971 big-finned, fire engine–red Cadillac Eldorado that made most of the men in town drool.

A recent widower, Richard had moved to New Chapel after his only son had settled here. Deciding it was time to retire, he'd sold his successful Texas roadhouse and land holdings; then, like Grace, he had found himself with too much time on his hands. He'd purchased an old bowling alley and miniature golf course and built a modern recreation center around them. Now he had a small sporting empire that employed more than one hundred people.

Grace had met Richard last summer while bowling with her league, and they'd been constant companions ever since. I suspected Richard wanted to marry her, but she seemed to value her independence too much.

"One o'clock is fine with me, Grace," I said. "I'm going to get this order finished and take it out to the Donnelly —" I heard a scratching sound and paused.

Marco and Grace heard it, too. They turned toward the coolers to listen.

"Where's Simon?" Marco asked.

"He must have slipped inside the cooler when I had the door open." I pulled open the thick, insulated door, and Simon raced out and gave himself a shake. Bits of greenery were stuck to his whiskers.

I glanced inside the cooler and saw shreds of feathery fern fronds all over the floor. "Bad boy!" I said sharply, closing the door. "You're not supposed to chew my inventory!"

He stopped grooming his hind leg to give me a look that said, *Serves you right for locking me in an igloo.*

"Stay out of the cooler, Simon," I scolded.

He spotted a glass bead on the floor and pounced on it, batting it under the worktable.

"Save your voice, love. He's simply being a cat," Grace said. "As Stephen Baker once said, 'Cats' hearing apparatus is built to allow the human voice to easily go in one ear

44

and out the other.' "

"Who's Stephen Baker?" Lottie asked, sticking her head through the curtain. "And why am I working both rooms alone?"

"There are actually three possible answers to your first question," Grace said, following her through the curtain, "and one answer to your second. First, there was Stephen Baker, the U.S. representative in the eighteen hundreds —"

"Grace is a human Wikipedia," I said to Marco.

He gave me another kiss. "I'll see you after work."

Simon saw Marco head for the curtain and galloped after him. I caught him before he could escape. "You can't go with Marco. How about some food?"

After spooning canned tuna into Simon's bowl, I finished the flower arrangement, wrapped it, and let my assistants know I was off to make the delivery.

"I hope you have better luck getting the woman to chat than I did," Lottie said, as she rang up a purchase.

"No problem," I told her. "I'm a pro when it comes to being inquisitive."

"Inquisitive," Lottie said with a chuckle. "I thought you were going to say nosy."

■ ■ ■ ■

I don't usually drive my Corvette to make deliveries, mostly because of its tiny trunk. But size was no deterrent today, and with the sun shining and the air smelling of spring, I put down the ragtop, turned on my CD player, and took off.

The Donnelly house sat by itself on a long country road, wedged in between a cornfield and a big tract of cleared land that was about to become a new subdivision. The two-story gray-frame house was old and badly in need of repair. The shingles on the steep roof were curled. The paint was peeling, or in some places, worn away completely. The wooden porch listed to one side. The garage, set some distance behind the house at the end of a gravel driveway, had boarded up windows.

The Donnellys had moved out years before, but because no one wanted to buy the old homestead, they had used it as rental property instead. I'd heard the inside was in better shape than the outside, but had yet to verify the claim. Regardless, the ghost aspect would give me something to chat about with the renters.

I pulled into the gravel driveway, turned

off the engine, scooped up the bouquet, and walked across the weed-infested lawn to the covered porch across the front of the narrow house. As I climbed the five steps, holding on to the weathered rail in case any of the boards gave out, I noticed heavy drapes on the pair of double-hung windows to the right of the door. It seemed odd to have them closed on such a beautiful sunny day.

I pushed the doorbell and heard a sudden pounding of heavy footsteps that got fainter instead of louder, as though someone was hurrying away. Then the door opened and there stood an attractive older woman with white hair cut in a blunt bob.

She had on a turquoise blouse, white slacks, and shiny silver flats — not the kind of shoe that would make much noise. She wore thick silver hoops in her ears, heavy, cuffed silver bracelets on both arms, and big turquoise rings on her fingers. She was taller than me, but at my height of five feet two inches, most people were. Her makeup had been put on with a light hand, her lips tinted a pretty peach color, and her eyelids a smoky gray. She had the attractive good looks of an aging movie star. Not the kind of person I'd expected to see renting a dilapidated house.

She smiled at me. "Yes?"

I didn't want to hand over the bouquet until I'd engaged her in conversation, hoping to keep her from closing the door in my face. So I said, "Have you heard that Johnny Appleseed stayed in this house when he was passing through town?"

"Really? Any truth to it?"

"According to the farmers around here, it's true."

"How interesting." She wasn't listening. Her gaze was on the wrapped flowers.

"Oh, I'm sorry. These are for you. I'm Abby Knight. I own Bloomers Flower Shop. I wanted to meet the woman who qualifies for getting the most floral deliveries in one month."

"Another bouquet," she said excitedly, peeling away the paper to see what it looked like. "Oh, it's so pretty! A calla. My favorite flower. And these greens are?"

"Basil."

"Calla and basil. How thoughtful my son is. He knows I adore them both. He spoils me terribly, I'm afraid. I used to tell him that one day I'd be so rich that I'd have fresh flowers delivered once a week. Well," she said with a light laugh, "as you can see, that never happened. But my son never forgot." She sighed wistfully. "Being a widow isn't easy. It's small pleasures like these that make life bearable."

The door had gradually swung open behind her, giving me a glimpse up a hallway to what appeared to be a kitchen. There I saw a tall, bulky man pass by the doorway.

The woman glanced back to see what I was looking at. "That's my youngest son. I have three boys, all single unfortunately. Two of them live here with me so I won't be all alone." She shielded one side of her mouth and whispered, "My oldest boy is the only successful one, sad to say. I don't know what happened to the gene pool after he was born."

"Genes can be tricky. I'm sorry, but I didn't catch your name."

"Dorothy," she said, "but please call me Dot."

"Hey, Ma," one of her sons called from the kitchen. "The oven's smoking. Want me to take out the bird?"

"I'd better go," Dot said with an exasperated sigh. "You'd think it took a mental giant to operate an oven. Thank you so much for taking the time to drive out here. It was a pleasure to meet you, Abby."

"You're welcome, Dot. Enjoy the flowers."

I hummed as I headed to the car. Lottie sure had called this situation wrong. There was nothing fishy about Dot or the thoughtful bouquets she was getting. I was satisfied that whoever was sending them, whether son or lover, wasn't a stalker. I couldn't wait to tease Lottie about it.

As I backed the Corvette out of the driveway, I caught sight of a man walking from the house to the old garage.

Interesting. At least one of Dot's sons was black. And had gray hair.

I was a block away from the Donnelly place when I glanced in my rearview mirror and spotted a faded black minivan with darkly tinted windows pulling out of her driveway. It turned in the opposite direction and headed away. A black van with tinted windows. Hmm.

Maybe I wouldn't tease Lottie just yet.

I parked in the public lot, dashed the block and a half back to Bloomers, and stepped inside the shop, the familiar jingle of the bell over the door such a happy sound. It still gave me tingles to know that the lovely little flower shop was mine, and sometimes I had to stand there for a moment taking it all in.

With its high, tin ceiling, mellow wood floors, exposed brick walls, charming Victorian-inspired tea parlor, big bay windows on either side of the door — one in the parlor and one in the main shop — the entire space abounded with the colors and scents of fresh blossoms, freshly baked scones, and invigorating coffee. It didn't get any better than that.

I heard a meow and glanced up see Simon watching me from the top of the open armoire that we used for displaying silk arrangements and other gift items. "Hey, Simon. How are you?"

He meowed again, then began to wash his ears. He'd found the perfect perch.

I filled my assistants in on Dot and her *sons,* then grabbed a quick sandwich in the kitchen so I could work the shop while Lottie took the noon lunch break. Simon decided to help with the entertainment and became an instant hit with the customers. When he wasn't supervising from his lofty perch, he was racing around after a stray leaf, leaping into the air, rubbing against people's legs, and generally showing off. He ate up the attention.

Speaking of someone who ate up attention, I thought briefly of calling Jillian to find out what she'd wanted. But then I came to my senses, concluding that whatever had prompted my cousin's call had resolved itself. Please?

At just past two o'clock in the afternoon,

members of the Monday Afternoon Ladies' Poetry Society arrived and made straight for the parlor, where Grace was supposed to be waiting to serve up scones and tea. The only problem was that Grace hadn't returned from her one o'clock lunch date, so Lottie had to work the parlor while I stayed up front in the shop.

By two thirty, Grace still hadn't returned, and we were getting concerned. It wasn't like her to be gone so long without calling. I tried to reach her on her cell phone, but it rang six times, then went to voice mail. After I tried calling her home phone repeatedly, Lottie urged me to contact the police, but I phoned Marco instead and asked him what to do.

"I'll call Sean," he said of his buddy Sergeant Sean Reilly of the New Chapel PD. "He'll know if there've been any reports of accidents. But I'll bet Grace just got busy helping her friend and forgot to check the time."

"Grace is too conscientious to forget about her responsibilities, Marco. I wish I knew where her friend Connie lives."

"Don't fret, Sunshine. Who is more level-headed than Grace? If she were in trouble, you'd know about it. I'll call you after I hear from Sean."

The other line began to blink, so I ended the conversation with Marco and switched over to find Nikki waiting to update me.

"I'm about to head for the hospital," she said, "but I wanted to let you know that your little tabby has been dozing for most of the day and seems to be doing very well. So, how's my Simey-wimey?"

"Loving the attention from the customers. He's quite a ham."

"I'm glad he isn't causing trouble."

I decided to save the fern story for later and instead tell her about my missing employee.

"Oh, wow," Nikki said. "That's weird for Grace not to at least call. As soon as I get to the hospital, I'll check to make sure she hasn't been brought in."

"Thanks, Nikki. I'm really starting to worry."

I went back to work, dividing my time between waiting on customers and slipping into the workroom to fill orders. Nikki phoned later to let me know Grace was not at the hospital; then Marco phoned to say that he'd left a voice mail for Reilly. Lottie tried again to reach Grace on her mobile and at home, but no luck there, either.

Where was Grace?

# CHAPTER FOUR

When my mom arrived at three thirty with a big cardboard box in her arms, the poetesses were gone, and the shop was quiet. Normally, the sight of my mother carrying in a box was enough to send all of us running for cover, because most of her projects were unmitigated disasters. For instance, she'd once made beaded jackets using one-inch wooden beads. Not only were the jackets uncomfortable, but they also rolled right off the shoulders onto the floor.

Then there were her humongous feathered hats made with neon-colored feathers, the dyes of which ran down the wearer's face when the weather turned muggy or wet. And there was the hideous footstool, modeled after an actual human foot, down to the hairs on the toes.

Today, however, Mom and her carton of unknown horrors were a welcome distraction.

"I can't wait to show you what I made," she said, her cheeks flushed with excitement.

"Let me help you with that box, Mom," I said, taking it from her arms. "You must be exhausted after teaching all day. Why don't you sit here and rest?" I placed the container on the wicker settee next to the umbrella plant and patted the cushion.

"Are you being solicitous because of the injured tabby you mentioned this morning?" she asked.

"No!" Not my only reason, anyway.

"Because if you are, let me clarify this right now. I don't want any more animals to care for. A llama is more than enough for your dad and me to handle."

"I know that. I just want you to be comfortable."

Eyeing me skeptically, Mom took off her tan-colored spring coat and sat down. She was wearing one of her standard teacher outfits — a powder blue pullover sweater with brown slacks and brown flats. She kept her light brown hair chin length, framing her soft features and peaches-and-cream complexion, which, unlike mine, had not one freckle on it. I was my dad's daughter all the way: red hair, freckled skin, and a short temper.

"Technically, however," I said, "the llama lives outside the house in his heated barn. Pets live inside."

"He's still a pet, Abigail. And don't forget, we had cats for years while you kids were growing up. I'm done with litter boxes now and into a new phase of my life. Please respect it."

Well, fine. I'd find someone else to love little Tabitha.

Oh, no! Had I just named her?

"Before I show you what I brought," she said, "remember the trip your dad and I took to Florida last winter? Remember me telling you that collecting seashells was passé and the big thing was sea glass?"

"What's sea glass?" Lottie asked, bringing in an armful of red roses to restock the display case.

"They're shards of old colored bottles that were tossed out to sea and have been cooking in the ocean for decades," Mom said. "When they wash ashore, they're smooth and beautiful, in colors like aqua, foam green, orange, yellow, and even some rare cobalt and red ones. Sea glass has become very valuable."

"Valuable broken bottles," Lottie mused. "Can you beat that?" Shaking her head, she shut the cooler and headed for the work-room.

"Anyway," Mom said, "I brought back a big jar full of sea glass shards, but I didn't know what to do with them. Yesterday, as I reached for my reading glasses, I happened to spot the jar sitting on my bookshelf, and it came to me."

She opened the box and removed a bald manikin's head onto which she'd painted a woman's face in full makeup — bright red lips, pink spots on her cheeks, purple eye shadow that coated black-rimmed eyelids, and shell-shaped ears, into which she had stuck knobby white pins. As a finishing touch, she'd borrowed a nose from an old Mr. Potato Head set and jabbed that in the middle of the face. The only thing missing were eyebrows, and because of that, the manikin had a weird, space alien appearance.

I stepped back for a better look. It wasn't as tall as her giant bowling-pin hatstand, but it was just as scary. And where was the sea glass?

"So you made a painted wig stand?" I asked.

"Not even close." Mom rubbed her hands together. "Prepare yourself for the big reveal."

Was that possible?

She pulled out a pair of sunglasses whose entire frame, including the bridge of the nose, was covered in small, smooth pieces of blue-and-green-colored glass.

"Sea glasses!" Mom sang out, mounting them on the head. "So you can see by the sea."

"See by the sea," I said, nodding approvingly. "Clever."

She smiled. "Then you like them?"

"Yes! They're very pretty."

"Thank you, Abigail. I think they're my best work so far. I'm considering making a line of reading glasses, too, but we'll see how these sell first. I'll have my hands full if they catch on."

They had a better chance of catching on fire. "How much are you going to charge?"

"Considering that each pair is a one-of-a-kind fashion statement, I think fifty dollars is a fair price."

Fair for whom? I glanced inside the box and saw a dozen more pairs.

"Now we have to figure out where to display them," Mom said.

As she reached for the manikin, the Mr. Potato Head nose popped off, unable to withstand the pressure from the heavy frames. The sunglasses slid down over the face and lay against the chin, hanging on by the two white push pins. The orange plastic nose skittered across the floor, attracting Simon's attention. He leaped from the top of the armoire to the settee, startling Mom, and from there to the floor, where he batted the nose through the purple curtain into the workroom.

Mom shrugged. "My model isn't quite right yet."

"Why don't you take the glasses and the manikin home with you so you can refine your design?"

"There's nothing wrong with the glasses' design, Abigail." She handed me a pair. "Try them on and see for yourself."

I donned them and checked my reflection in a brass pot. *Yeesh.* Thank goodness there were no customers in the shop. My temples started to pound so I handed them back and massaged the bridge of my nose.

"Well?" she asked hopefully.

"They're a little tight, Mom. And heavy. Maybe you should cut down on the glass pieces."

"Really? Your sisters-in-law said the glasses fit fine. You must have inherited your father's wide head."

I did not have a wide head, and my sisters-in-law were big fat liars.

The phone was ringing, so I excused myself and dashed to the front counter to answer it.

"Abby," I heard Grace whisper, "something dreadful has happened. My friend Connie has met with an untimely death."

I glanced around to see my mother disappear through the purple curtain, probably on a hunt for the missing nose. "I'm sorry, Grace," I said quietly. "What happened to her?"

"She took a fatal fall down the cellar steps. I was the one who found her."

"Oh, Grace, that must have been terrible."

"Tragic, Abby. Simply tragic. The police are here now. I'm afraid I won't be able to leave until they finish their investigation."

"Don't worry about it, Grace. Do you want someone there with you?"

"Thank you, dear, but I'll be fine. Please don't let this get around — other than to Lottie, of course."

"Not a problem. How far away are you, Grace?"

"I'm at the Newport mansion."

"Really?" The Newport mansion was the biggest, costliest piece of real estate in the county. I'd heard the home had ten bedrooms and fourteen bathrooms, plus a ballroom and a ten-car garage. "Is your friend the housekeeper?"

"No, dear, and I forgive you for thinking that my friend would be merely the house-keeper. She's Constance Newport."

For a full ten seconds my brain froze. Constance Newport, the wealthiest woman in New Chapel, was Grace's friend? Why hadn't Grace ever mentioned that?

"Grace, I didn't mean to imply —"

"Never mind that now." She cupped her hand around the mouthpiece to whisper, "I'm alone for the moment, so listen care-fully. Connie was murde—"

She stopped speaking.

"Grace? Are you there? Did you say your friend was murdered?"

"I can't talk now," she whispered.

And I'd thought the day was on the up-swing.

My mom came back into the room hold-ing up the missing nose. "Found it."

I said into the phone, "Grace, would you hold for two seconds?"

"Yes, but hurry, dear. My mobile isn't get-ting a signal here, so I'm using their house phone."

The second line flashed to indicate an incoming call, but I ignored it, knowing Lottie would pick it up in the other room. I put Grace on hold, then turned to my mom.

"I've got to get back to my desk to take down some information. I know you have to get to school, so just leave everything here with me and I'll take care of it."

"Thank you, Abigail. And here's a thought: The manikin display would be smashing in your bay window."

More likely the people walking *past* the manikin would be smashing in my bay window.

I blew her a kiss good-bye, then darted through the curtain to my desk and sat down. Lottie handed me a sticky note that said, *Marco — line 2.* I whispered to her, "Make sure my mom leaves. I don't want her to hear this conversation."

Lottie nodded and headed out.

"Grace?" I said quietly. "Are you sure Constance Newport was murdered?"

"Absolutely, but I can't discuss it now," she whispered. In a normal voice she said, "The crime scene chaps are downstairs taking photographs and collecting evidence, so perhaps I'll know more by the time I get back to the shop. I hope to be there within the hour."

"Take as much time as you need, Grace. And I'm very sorry about your friend."

"I have to go, love. One of the detectives would like to interview me again."

"Again?"

"Well, dear, I *did* discover the body. And no one else was around at the time, so I imagine they consider me a suspect."

She was unbelievably calm, as though reporting a flat tire. "I'm going to call Dave Hammond. Don't say anything more to the detectives until you get some direction from him. You probably shouldn't have talked to them the first time without Dave there."

"It's all right, love. All I told them was how I happened to find Connie. The police could hardly proceed with their investigation otherwise."

For a woman who'd once worked as Dave's legal secretary, Grace was startlingly naive. "Do you remember what happened when I found one of the law professors dead? I became the number one suspect. So please do not say anything more about anything."

"Duly noted. Henceforth, my lips are sealed."

"Okay. Sit tight until you hear from Dave."

Before I could dial out, Lottie came through the curtain. "I found a place for the manikin head on the second shelf of the armoire, in the corner, so all that's left to do is to price the glasses. But first tell me what happened to Grace."

"She found her friend dead at the bottom of the basement steps. Now the cops are there and they won't let anyone leave until they finish investigating."

"Oh, Lordy," Lottie said, holding her hand against her heart. "Poor Grace. How awful for her. Which friend was it?"

"Constance Newport."

Lottie's eyes grew wide. "Constance Newport, the heiress?"

"That's her. Did you know she and Grace were friends?"

"I'd heard her mention her friend Connie, but I hadn't made the connection. The woman had to be about ninety years old. I'm not surprised she kicked the bucket."

"According to Grace, Connie didn't kick the bucket. Someone pushed her. Grace believes she was murdered."

I didn't think Lottie's eyes could have opened any wider, but she proved me wrong. "Not another murder! I don't know what's happening to our town, Abby."

"It's becoming a city, Lottie," I said, "with all the bad stuff that goes along with it."

Hearing the bell over the door, Lottie headed up front, muttering, "Lordy, Lordy, Lordy. Save us from ourselves."

I connected with line two. "Marco?"

"Abby, I just got a call from Reilly that

Constance Newport is dead."

"I know. Grace just phoned, too. She found the body."

"Is she all right?"

"She sounds fine, but, Marco, she said no one else was around when she made the discovery and she thinks Constance was murdered. You know what that means. The cops will treat her as a suspect."

I could hear the shift in Marco's voice as he went into PI mode. "Why does Grace suspect murder?"

"She wouldn't say over the phone. I've got to call Dave and have him talk to Grace before she says something that might incriminate her, if she hasn't already."

"Got it. Call if you need me. Otherwise, I'll see you down here for dinner."

I connected with Dave ten minutes later, and after explaining Grace's predicament, ended the conversation knowing she was in good hands. With that worry off my plate, I returned to the workroom and immersed myself in floribunda, which always soothes my frazzled nerves. My state of oblivion lasted until three thirty, when the bell over the door jingled, and my mother called jauntily, "Yoo-hoo! I'm here." This was followed by a terse, "Lottie, why did Abigail put my manikin in the armoire?"

Because the alternative was stashing it in the basement.

I hurried through the purple curtain to find Mom pushing aside the arrangements in the bay window to make room for the head. Lottie stood off to the side, watching with a pained expression as the display she'd worked on for two hours ceased to exist, while Simon occupied himself with throwing up undigested greens in the corner.

"I'm not surprised you haven't sold a single pair of glasses," Mom said to me, stepping back to admire her handiwork. "No one could see them tucked back in that shelf."

Lottie muttered something and left the room.

As I tore off a paper towel from the roll under the cashier's counter to clean up Simon's mess, Mom sighed contentedly. "Isn't that much better?"

"Well," I said, drawing out the word while I thought of a response that wouldn't be a lie. I ran out of breath before anything came to mind.

She turned toward me, a worried look on her face. "Well what? I thought you liked my sea glasses."

"I *do* like them." In the same way I liked a paper cut on the second day. "I thought they displayed better in the armoire, that's all. Tell you what. Let's just leave the manikin there and see what happens." Which would be nothing if I didn't find some way to make that bald head more appealing.

"I don't see any price tags," Mom said. "I have some time before I have to take your dad to the dentist if you want me to —"

"We'll take care of it, Mom," I said, ushering her to the door. "You go get Dad — you know how he hates to wait — and give him a big hug from me. Bye!"

I closed the door and glanced over at her display. Maybe the sun would melt the head and solve one problem.

At fifteen minutes before five, Grace returned to Bloomers looking shaken and exhausted. We had no customers, so we closed the shop early and sat her in the parlor with a cup of tea so she could tell us about her tragic discovery. Not wanting to be left out, Simon jumped onto my knees and sniffed the table to see if there was anything to eat. Finding nothing, he curled up in my lap.

"Gracie," Lottie said, "take your time. Tell us whatever you feel like talking about."

"I suppose I should start from the beginning," Grace said, wiping her eyes with her lace handkerchief. She took a deep breath, then straightened her shoulders. "I sensed something was up when I couldn't get anyone to answer the front door. As I'd phoned Connie earlier to tell her what time I'd be there, I knew she wouldn't have left the house, so after ringing the bell several times, I decided to go 'round to the back entrance. Let me tell you, that was quite a hike. There are some fifteen thousand square feet under that roof."

"Is it true they have twenty toilets?" Lottie asked, propping her chin on her hand. At my astonished glance, her cheeks flamed scarlet. "Forget I asked that. Go ahead, Gracie."

Grace took a swallow of tea and then continued. "I rang the bell, then rapped quite forcefully, but once again no one answered. I tried to use my mobile to ring the house, but I couldn't get a signal. I tried the door and found it unlocked, so I opened it and called inside to see if I could rouse someone. Still receiving no response, I stepped into the kitchen for a look around.

"Well, there was simply no one there, so I continued to call out, 'Connie? Halloo?' I circled 'round the kitchen — it's very large,

68

you see — and then I noticed a light coming from behind a door that was left ajar, and I thought perhaps I'd discovered someone at last. Well, indeed, I had.

"I opened the door and found myself at the top of a staircase looking down into the cellar at a suit of armor that had fallen over. Sticking out from underneath the armor were two spindly legs, two thin arms, and a head. I knew at once that it was Connie."

Grace's chin began to tremble. She stopped to press the handkerchief into the corners of her eyes. After taking a deep breath, she said, "I ran downstairs to help her, but after pushing aside the armor, I couldn't find a pulse, so I hurried upstairs again and used the house phone to ring for assistance. As I explained the situation to the dispatch operator, Connie's housekeeper, Mrs. Dunbar, came into the kitchen with her arms full of radishes.

"As you can imagine, the poor woman was shocked at what she overheard. She dropped the radishes and would have run downstairs had I not stopped her. I sat her at the kitchen table, where she sobbed until the paramedics arrived. They were followed in short order by the police, who took our statements and had us sit for an hour before we could make any calls."

"Poor Gracie," Lottie said, and leaned over to give Grace a hug. "It must've been a terrible fright seeing your friend under all that metal."

"Did the police say anything about her death being suspicious?" I asked.

Grace shook her head. So hopefully the cops, being more experienced than Grace, had seen clear indications that the fall was an accident rather than a homicide. "Tell me again why you suspect murder," I said, running my hand down Simon's soft fur.

Grace closed her eyes for a moment, as though reimagining the scene. "Have you ever slipped on a step? Then you know that your foot slides forward, your other leg folds beneath you, then you either tumble forward or slide down footfirst, unless you're lucky enough to grab onto a railing.

"When Connie landed, however, she was faceup. Her head was the farthest part of her body from the steps, and her heels were resting on the bottom stair, as though she'd been standing at the top facing someone and was given a hard shove backward. It appeared as though she had tried to grab on to whatever she could to stop her fall and pulled the suit of armor down on top of her."

"Her position alone wouldn't necessarily

mean she was pushed," I said. "There are many ways to fall. Maybe she took a step backward and didn't know she was so close to the edge."

Lottie nodded. "Abby's right. I remember one of my boys tumbling down the steps and landing faceup . . . Never mind. I just remembered. One of his brothers pushed him."

"That's what I mean," Grace said, her eyes filling with fresh tears. "Connie didn't die accidentally. Someone in her own house murdered her! Abby, we must do something about it."

"What is it you're always saying about putting the cart before the horse?" I asked. "You might *suspect* she was pushed, but until the detectives find evidence of foul play, you can't know that for sure."

"Yes, I can," she stated.

Grace could be exasperating at times. "Okay, how?"

When Grace didn't reply, Lottie said in a coaxing voice, "That's okay, Gracie. You don't have to prove anything to us. If you're afraid to say how you know, then just tell us to leave you alone."

"I'm not afraid. I simply know how you'll react," she said, lifting her chin. "You'll think I'm off my nut."

71

Lottie held up her hand. "I swear we won't. Right, Abby?"

I nodded.

"Very well." Grace folded her hands on the table. "Connie told me."

"What do you mean?" I asked. "Did she have a premonition before she died?"

Grace shook her head.

"Well, Lordy, woman," Lottie said. "She couldn't have told you *after* she died."

Grace took another sip of tea. The clock in the other room ticked loudly.

"Grace?" I said.

Without glancing at us she said, "I told you that you'd think I've gone bonkers."

# CHAPTER FIVE

I glanced at Lottie, but her mouth was hanging open.

Seeing our startled expressions, Grace said, "She told me in a dream. What did you think I meant?"

"Maybe I should write down exactly what happened so we can sort it out." I held Simon against me as I dashed to the cashier's counter, grabbed a pen and pad, and hurried back. Simon huffed as he settled himself again.

"Okay," I said, uncapping the pen, "let's start from when you discovered the body. You said that Connie had no pulse, and this was after you pushed aside the armor."

"Correct."

"Did any family members show up while you were there?" I asked.

"Connie's grandson did," Grace said. "His name is Griffin Newport. He's Burnett Newport Jr.'s son. Also Connie's daughter-in-law, Juanita, came in while I was there."

I wrote down *Griffin Newport, grandson; Juanita Newport, daughter-in-law.* "Is Juanita Griffin's mother?" I asked.

"No. Juanita is Burnett's fourth wife. His first wife was Griffin's mother."

I wrote it down. "What were their reactions to the news?"

"Griffin was overcome with anguish. He and his grandmother were very close. He lives in an apartment over the garage, you see, and kept going on about how he was only yards away and should have been there to help her in her hour of need."

"So Griffin believed his grandmother had had an accident?" I asked.

"It appeared that way." Grace paused to drink more tea. "As for Juanita, Connie's daughter-in-law, she seemed more interested in my reason for being there, questioning me as though she suspected *me* of pushing Connie down the steps."

"She had her nerve," Lottie said, slapping the table. "I hope you gave her a piece of your mind."

"No," Grace said, "but I did fix her with a chilly glare."

"Who else lives in the mansion?" I asked.

"Connie's son, Burnett," Grace said, "and her daughter, Virginia, who, as it turned out, was in the house at the time of Connie's death but was in her third-floor studio. She's an artist and paints up there."

"Did Virginia hear anything?" I asked. "An argument, a scream . . ."

"I don't know," Grace said. "The detectives questioned Virginia privately. I did overhear Juanita tell the detectives that her husband, Burnett — Connie's son — was at the horse races."

She waited for me to finish writing, then said, "I should mention that there's also a young man who lives on the property. He maintains the autos and was Connie's chauffeur. She called him Luce and spoke highly of him. The detectives located Luce in the garage working on a motorcycle and brought him into the house. He seemed completely stunned to hear of the tragedy. I'm afraid that's all I can tell you about him."

"Why were you meeting Connie today?" I asked.

"She wanted to give me a book, so we arranged a time for me to pick it up. Connie has quite a collection of first editions. We became friends through our mutual love of literature."

Grace sighed and smiled wistfully. "We spent many happy hours discussing plots, characters, and symbolism over countless cups of tea. It seems impossible to believe that we shall never be able to have those discussions again." At that, Grace put her handkerchief to her face and wept silently.

Lottie got up to refill the teapot and I petted Simon, giving Grace a few minutes to compose herself.

"I'm sorry," she said tearfully. "I don't know why I'm blubbering so. Connie wasn't the most likable person you'd ever want to meet. She could be quite vindictive, or so I've been told. Still, she always treated me with respect and kindness."

Lottie started to refill her cup, but Grace held her hand over it. "No, thank you, love. I'd like to go home now."

"I'll call Richard and have him come get you," Lottie offered.

I glanced at the clock. "Yikes. I've got to take off. I was supposed to meet Marco and his mom fifteen minutes ago."

"You go on, sweetie," Lottie said. "I'll wait with Grace until Richard comes, and then lock up the shop."

"I'm sorry for your loss, Grace," I said, giving her a hug, while Lottie ran to use the phone at the cashier's counter. "If there's anything I can do, please tell me."

"Then, if it wouldn't be too much bother,"

Grace said, "would you and Marco find Connie's killer?"

I'd left myself wide open for that one. "You want us to investigate?"

"We know how the system works, don't we? The last person to be with the victim is the first one the police suspect."

"We won't let that happen, Grace."

"I trust that's a yes?"

I put fresh water and food out for Simon, lined a large straw basket with thick towels, and moved it under my desk. "Here, Simon. Here's your bed."

He sniffed all around the basket, deemed it safe, and stepped inside, kneading the towels with his front feet until he'd softened them to his liking. He curled up in the basket, licked his paws, and began to wash his ears.

"Be a good boy," I said, and turned out the overhead lights, leaving only the security light on in the workroom.

The day had turned breezy and cool, so I slipped my denim jacket over my white shirt, slung my purse over my shoulder, and headed up the street to Down the Hatch. I was not looking forward to having dinner with my future mother-in-law, Francesca Salvare, because I wasn't sure how to talk her out of sticking around for the next five months. The only positive thing about the forthcoming conversation was that it gave me something to think about other than that Grace could be the prime suspect in a murder investigation.

Down the Hatch Bar and Grill was housed in a narrow, high-ceilinged building that stretched from Franklin Street to the alley in back, just like Bloomers. It had two rows of tables running parallel to the big plate-glass window up front, a polished walnut bar running long and deep, and a row of booths directly opposite it. Marco had purchased Down the Hatch a year ago, just before I'd emptied out my bank account to take over Bloomers. We'd met shortly afterward, when my freshly repainted 1960 Corvette suffered damage in a hit-and-run accident that ended up kicking off our first murder investigation.

Marco's bar was the local watering hole, and one of the hot spots in town, despite decor that hadn't changed in almost forty years. I'd been urging Marco to remodel, but most of the patrons believed the interior should be left untouched because it was a piece of local history.

I disagreed. If a town's history could be represented by wall art consisting of a fake carp mounted on wood, a bright blue plastic anchor, 1970s-style orange padded benches, dark wood paneling, and an old fisherman's net hanging from the ceiling, then the town needed an image makeover.

I caught sight of Marco in the last booth, holding up his hand in greeting. His mother turned and waved, too. As I approached, she slid out of the booth and opened her arms.

"Bella Abby," she said in her Italian-accented, full-throated voice. She gave me a fierce hug, then held me at arm's length. "Here you are at last. We were beginning to worry."

Francesca was a tall, beautiful, energetic woman who'd been blessed with an hour-glass figure, high, prominent cheekbones, the same big brown eyes Marco had, and a generous mouth. She had a wide, warm smile, and hair a rich brown color high-lighted naturally with silver strands. To complement her red silk blouse and black trousers, she wore large, silver hoops in her ears and oversized, tortoiseshell-framed glasses that would have swallowed up my face, but made her look like a younger Sophia Loren. And no matter what time of day it was, Francesca always looked classy and elegant; unlike me, whose best moments were when I first walked out of the apartment. It went downhill from there.

Marco let me slide into the booth first, then took a seat beside me so we were facing his mom. "I ordered a bottle of red wine," he said to me.

"Just one?" I joked, slipping off my jacket. "After the day I've had, I could handle one all by myself."

Francesca's smile stiffened. Marco lifted his eyebrows to signal that I'd made a gaff.

"Just kidding," I said. "One glass will be enough. Actually, not even one. Maybe half. A small half — more like a third."

"Tell me about your terrible day," Francesca said, reaching across the table to put her hand over mine, probably to make me stop babbling.

I ran through the list in my head and came up with only one item I felt comfortable telling her. So I recounted my tale of the tabby cat and left it at that. She seemed disappointed.

"A minor problem," she said, sitting back.

"You wouldn't want to take the cat back to Ohio with you, would you?" I asked hopefully.

She gave me a classic Italian shrug. "I can't make any decisions until I know for certain whether I'm staying in Indiana."

A horrible feeling rocked the pit of my stomach. "Staying? Here?"

"I keep asking myself why I should remain in Ohio," she said, gesturing with her hands. "My other children are scattered all over the country. But here" — she reached across to pinch Marco's cheek, but he dodged her — "I have Marco, Raphael, Gina, and my grandbabies. And you, bella. Then there are your wedding events to plan. That will take a lot of work. And soon after your wedding, maybe more grandbabies for me, eh?"

I locked my jaw so my mouth wouldn't fall open.

"Ma," Marco said firmly, "we're not here to discuss babies."

I knew he was irritated with her because he hadn't called her *Mama,* as he usually did.

Gert, the waitress who'd been at Down the Hatch since it had opened, put a bottle of Cabernet in front of us and got out her corkscrew. I took the opportunity to whisper to Marco, "I really think we're going to need more than one bottle."

"A toast to your future." Francesca raised her wineglass, and we clinked rims. Then she got up, went over to the bar area, and came back with two plates of manicotti with sides of garlic bread, both of which Fran-

81

cesca had made especially for us.

"Now you can nourish your bodies while we discuss business." This time she managed to pinch Marco's cheek. "Only the freshest ingredients for my bambinos. Bella, do you have the magazines I sent you?"

The ten bridal magazines she'd mailed me last winter that had piled up in my closet until I threw them out? I scratched my forehead. "Um."

"Don't worry. I have backups."

While I tasted her manicotti, which had to be the most delicious I'd ever eaten, Francesca pulled a large file folder from her oversized purse and opened it up. Inside was a stack of pages she'd clipped from bridal magazines. She slid them toward me.

"These are the wedding gowns that would work best with your figure. I phoned the bridal salon and all of the gowns can be ordered in plenty of time to make any necessary alterations. We can make an appointment to have a look at the ones they have in stock, eh?"

As she pulled out a spiral-bound notebook, I gave Marco a pleading look. This was exactly what I didn't want to happen. We'd agreed to keep our wedding simple and sweet, and that included my dress, flowers, bridal shower, honeymoon, and all the other elements associated with getting married.

Marco gave me a look that said, *Humor her.*

I gave him a look back that said, *Okay, as long as we're on the same page about this.*

He gave me a nod.

Francesca opened the notebook to a page marked *Shower #1,* and uncapped her pen. "First we work on the Italian shower."

I glanced at Marco in bewilderment. "What?"

"I think she means a shower for my relatives," he said.

"Don't worry," she said, "we'll have an Irish-English shower, too."

That sounded like trouble. "I really think one shower would be better," I said.

"The guests wouldn't all fit in one room," she said, chuckling as she wrote in her notebook. I couldn't read her handwriting upside down, but it probably said something about me being a dunderhead, or whatever that translated to in Italian.

"Exactly how many guests are you talking about?" I asked, glancing from her to Marco, who merely shrugged just like his mom had.

"I haven't finished making my list," she said, still writing.

"Mrs. Salvare," I said in a pleasant voice, "I know you're excited about our wedding, but, with all due respect, we want to keep it simple, and that means one shower, one small shower, with just close relatives and friends in attendance. Anyway, we're not getting married until September. Why do we need to plan the shower now?"

Francesca laughed merrily. "Bella, when you've thrown as many showers as I have, then you will understand. It takes time to do all the necessary work. There are the invitations to select, the menu to decide, food to prepare, cakes to bake —"

"That sounds like a wedding," I said with a light laugh that had a desperate note in it.

"We'll get to the wedding later," she said. "Tomorrow during your lunch hour, we can go to the stationery store and pick out your invitations."

I was losing control fast. "Actually," I said, "Marco and I can do that. You don't need to bother with it."

"It's no bother," she said, clearly amused.

"But Marco and I *want* to do it," I stated.

Francesca turned her liquid brown eyes on her son, as though to say, *Is this true?*

"This is more of a woman thing," Marco said. "I don't really need to be invol—"

I squeezed his knee hard. "The wedding

shower is for *us,* Marco. *We* need to decide. Together."

Francesca smiled at me. "Good. We'll all go look for invitations tomorrow. Now for the food. Lasagna is always good for a crowd. Let me think." She tapped the pen against her nose. "We have my side and the Salvare side . . . Twelve baking pans should do it."

Gert stopped by our table to ask, "Anything I can get you folks?"

An escape hatch?

# CHAPTER SIX

I gave Marco a look that said, *Speak now, buster, or forever hold your peace — and know that I will be out of here if you don't.* He gave me a nod.

"Mama," Marco said, "put down your pen and listen to me. Abby and I don't want a big wedding or big showers. We want to keep it simple." He gazed at me. "One combined shower, right, Sunshine?"

"Right." I smiled at him. We were a team. "With no more than fifty guests, twenty-five per family."

"Impossible," Francesca said, throwing down her pen. "Do you know how many cousins you have, Marco?"

He turned to give me a helpless look. "Cousins, Abby."

"Okay, then, one hundred guests," I said, wavering. How could we cut out his cousins? I picked up my burger and took a bite.

"It cannot be done," his mom said, sitting

back and crossing her arms. "Four hundred, and then it's possible."

The food stuck in my throat. I grabbed my napkin to cover my mouth as I coughed.

"The alternative, Mama, is no shower," Marco said. "Now let's eat before our meals get cold."

My hero! I smiled at him and he winked back. Team Knight-Salvare was a force to be reckoned with.

We finished our meals in record time, mostly because Francesca didn't talk after that. She was miffed. But we both got hugs before she left, so I held out hope that once she thought about it, she'd see our side.

After she left, we took our wine and went to Marco's office to talk about Grace's situation.

In sharp contrast to the 1970s bar decor, Marco's office was sleek and modern, with dove gray walls, silver miniblinds, black leather furniture, a black-and-chrome desk, and a TV mounted in a corner opposite the desk. While I made myself comfortable in one of the black leather chairs, he sat down at his desk, turned the television on, and tuned in to WNCN, the local cable news station, hoping to catch a report on Constance Newport's death.

"Okay, fill me in," he said, lowering the

volume.

I repeated Grace's account of finding the body without disclosing her startling revelation. Then I filled him in on the other people living on the property. Marco listened without interruption, rubbing his jaw as he absorbed the information, which is what he did when he was piecing things together.

I ended with Grace's request that we find Connie's killer.

"The woman's death hasn't been ruled a homicide," Marco reminded me.

I didn't want to broach the subject of Grace's communication with her friend because I knew Marco wouldn't believe it. I didn't believe it myself. So I tried logic instead. "Think about how Grace described the body lying on the basement floor. What's your gut telling you? Because mine is saying to trust Grace's assessment."

"I understand that you have a lot of faith in Grace, Sunshine, but she doesn't have any experience in homicide investigations. Seeing a body sprawled at the bottom of the steps is shocking, to be sure, but it would take a skilled investigator to decide whether it was murder."

I couldn't argue with that. "The problem is that Grace asked that we find her friend's killer, and I volunteered to help in any way I could."

Marco rubbed his jaw. "Then why don't you tell her that *if* Constance Newport's death is ruled a homicide, we'll investigate."

"You get a kiss for that."

Marco's attention suddenly shifted to the TV, so I swiveled for a look. He picked up the remote to turn up the volume as a photo of a distinguished older woman was displayed on the flat screen.

"Tragedy has felled a local hero," the anchor woman reported. "Constance Newport, philanthropist, patron of the arts, and humanitarian, died today at the age of eighty-seven from unknown causes."

"Nothing about police suspecting foul play," Marco said.

The news anchor continued. "Newport was instrumental in the creation of an art museum and gallery within New Chapel University, in the funding of the hospice center and the new wing on the public library. She was married to Burnett K. Newport, a prominent businessman, entrepreneur, and collector of Victorian art, for over forty years. Newport is survived by a son, daughter, and grandson. No decision has been made about funeral services, but Newport's attorney said an announcement would be forthcoming."

As the reporter launched into a retrospective of Constance's life, Marco lowered the volume. "Did I tell you how hot you look in that outfit?"

I glanced down at my white blouse and dark jeans. "No, but go ahead."

He crooked his finger at me. "Come over here."

I loved it when he got that primordial glimmer in his eye.

He turned his desk chair so I could crawl onto his lap; then he gathered me in his arms for a smoldering kiss. With his lips against my ear, he murmured, "What do you say we go back to your place, open that bottle of champagne we saved from our engagement dinner, and then . . ."

He whispered the *then* part in my ear. "Does that sound like a plan?"

I gazed into his deep brown eyes. "I like the way you think, Salvare."

I tilted my head to meet his lips again just as the TV anchor said, "In breaking news, New Chapel Police are now calling Constance Newport's death a homicide. A police spokesman declined to comment on reasons for the ruling but said only that an official investigation has been opened."

Those pesky goose bumps came back with

a vengeance. Grace had been right after all.

The anchor continued. "A reporter caught up with Newport's son, Burnett Newport Jr., minutes ago. He had this to say."

The next image showed a frowning, doughy, bald man in Ray-Ban sunglasses and a dark suit. He was sitting inside his silver BMW convertible with the top down, waiting for the wrought-iron gates outside Newport mansion to open. With a microphone thrust in his face, he snarled, "I haven't heard anything about an investigation. As far as I know, my mother slipped and fell."

"How do you feel about her death being called a homicide?" the reporter asked.

His scowl deepened. "How do I *feel?* What kind of idiotic question is that? How would you feel if someone stuck a mic in your face and told you your mother might have been murdered?"

The reporter's mouth opened and shut again.

The gates had finished opening, so Burnett pulled forward, calling, "If you have any other asinine questions, talk to my attorney."

When the news went to a commercial break, Marco shut off the TV. For a moment, he said nothing; then he sighed. "Go ahead. Tell me your gut was right."

*Nah.* No need to rub it in. "We need a plan, Marco."

"We have a plan."

I gave him a kiss. "Not a plan for tonight. That's been firmed up."

"You're telling me." He started nibbling along my jawline.

I ignored the innuendo and tried to ignore the nibbling. "How about we have a meeting at noon tomorrow to see if there's been any more news on the homicide investigation, then take it from there? Does that sound like a plan?"

"Yes," he said, "but remind me in the morning to cancel the shopping trip with my mom."

All part of the plan.

When we got back to my apartment, the little tabby cat was curled up in a comforter Nikki had folded and placed on the living room floor. The kitty raised her head, her eyes alert, and tried to get up on three legs, but wobbled unsteadily.

"Poor little lost Tabitha," I said, crouching down to pet her.

"You named her Tabitha?" Marco asked, hunkering down beside me to scratch the cat behind her ears.

"I didn't name her, per se. Tabby is too masculine for such a petite thing. Tabitha sounds more feminine."

*Way to kid yourself, Abby. You named her.*

I got up and glanced around for a dish. "I wonder if Nikki fed her."

I trotted to our tiny galley kitchen just off the front entranceway and discovered a note from Nikki: *Kitty wouldn't eat Simon's tuna, so I bought some different brands to try. She finally settled on the fancy (read: pricey) kind. That was at 2 p.m. Try to get her to eat more. No calls or e-mails from the ad I posted.*

While Marco opened the champagne and filled two flutes, I put some of the gourmet poached salmon into a bowl and hand-fed Tabitha. Poor thing practically gobbled it down. I brought her water, which she lapped thirstily; then I carried her to the litter box and placed her inside.

She kept trying to balance on her broken hind leg and didn't know what to make of the cast. But finally she figured out how to crouch in the litter on her three good legs to do her business. When she was finished, I carried her back to the living room. She snuggled against my neck, purring, reinforcing my belief that she'd been someone's pet.

Tabitha was a puzzle I was determined to solve. But not with Mr. Tall, Dark, and

Handsome waiting for me. Tonight I was all Marco's.

*Tuesday*

The Newport Heiress Murder, as the press had labeled it, was all over the news the next morning. When I got to Bloomers, I could tell by the dark circles under Grace's eyes that she had not had a restful night, so I knew she'd heard the reports.

I fed Simon and cuddled him awhile; then Lottie and I sat down with Grace in the parlor for our morning meeting. But after only a few minutes it was obvious that Grace's mind was elsewhere.

"Okay," Lottie said, holding a small cardboard box on her lap, "we've got to decide how to price these sea glasses so we can get them sold. Are we going to leave them in the window?"

"Anyone know a friendly optician who would take them off our hands?" I asked.

"The glasses aren't prescription, sweetie," Lottie said. "Opticians wouldn't touch them."

"I shouldn't have touched anything either," Grace said, twisting her fingers together.

"What was that?" Lottie asked.

"I shouldn't have touched anything. I

94

shouldn't even have entered Connie's house. I should have come back here and phoned the police."

"*Should haves* aren't fair, Gracie," Lottie said. "Don't go down that road. You don't know where it will lead, and what are you always telling us about anticipating trouble?"

Despite Grace's apprehension, she couldn't resist sharing from her enormous repertoire of quotations. " 'What we anticipate seldom occurs; what we least expect generally happens.' Benjamin Disraeli, Earl of Beaconsfield."

"See there?" Lottie said, as if that settled the matter once and for all, while I was still working on the fact that Grace knew Disraeli was an earl of something.

"Grace," I said, as Simon jumped up onto my lap to survey the table, "I made a promise to you yesterday, remember? Marco and I will investigate."

"Thank you, love," she said tearfully. "I simply cannot fathom anyone purposefully ending Connie's life. It's horrible, just horrible, to think about."

"Then don't think about it," Lottie said. "Get your mind on something else, like what price to put on these sea glasses. I'll bet any money that Maureen will stop by after school to see if any of them have sold."

"I wish I could set my mind to work on something else," Grace said.

The phone rang, and Grace rose to answer it at the cashier counter. As soon as she was gone, Lottie said in a hushed voice, "Poor Gracie. She's usually so upbeat. It isn't like her to be so bleak."

"She had quite a shock finding that body, Lottie, not to mention that she lost her friend."

"I know, sweetie. It's just hard seeing Gracie like this. Oh, before I forget, Jillian called here looking for you this morning."

"That's two days in a row she's made it up before midmorning," I said. "I wonder why she didn't use my cell phone number."

"I don't know, but she said not to call her because she was going back to bed. She'll phone you later."

"That's what Jillian said yesterday and then never called," I said.

"You're not complaining, are you?" Lottie asked.

Grace returned with a puzzled look on her face. "That was Thurmon Duval, the Newport family attorney. He'd like me to be present for the reading of Connie's will at four o'clock."

"Today?" I asked. "So soon?"

"It was Connie's request," Grace said. "Thurmon allowed that it was highly unusual. He wouldn't say more than that. Perhaps he'll explain the reason for the rush. He also mentioned that a police officer is to be present, as well. Isn't that odd?"

"Did Mr. Duval say why?" I asked.

"Only that he wanted to prepare me so I wouldn't be alarmed by it," Grace said.

"The attorney must be expecting trouble among the relatives," Lottie said. "You know what this means, don't you? Your friend Connie left you something!"

"Let's not put the cart before the horse," Grace said. "As Shakespeare so aptly wrote in the *Merchant of Venice,* 'Let none presume to wear an undeserved dignity.' "

"Gracie," Lottie said, "if all Connie left you was dignity, I doubt the lawyer would call you in for it. Now, it's almost time to open, so let's get these sea glasses stickered. Did your mom say how much we should charge, Abby?"

"Fifty dollars," I said, then cringed at the look both women gave me. "It *is* art," I reminded them.

But after we had trooped out to the shop to take another look at the display, Grace said, "Shall we say ten dollars?"

"Done," I said.

"I'll get them tagged now," Lottie said, "but I have to tell you, that bald head reminds me of the Star Wars robot. Remember the gold butler with the British accent?"

"You're thinking of C-Three PO," I said.

"I think we should name the head," Grace said. "It would make her less of a fright."

"How about *Sea* Three PO?" I asked, spelling out the word *sea.*

Grace placed her hand on the manikin head. "I hereby christen thee Miss Sea Three PO."

"What should I tell my mom about the price change?" I called, as Grace headed into the parlor to get the coffee machine and tea kettles ready.

She turned with a serene smile. "You'll think of something."

The phone rang, so I answered at the cashier counter. At the sound of Marco's voice on the other end, my pulse did its usual trick of shifting into overdrive. Was it crazy to still feel that way about a guy I'd known for almost a year? Would it bother me either way? No.

"Hey, Fireball, how's the world's sexiest florist this morning?"

"Missing you, Salvare. How's the world's hunkiest PI?"

"When I see him, I'll ask."

"Great. Also ask him if he called his mom to cancel our noon shopping trip. He and I have a meeting planned, remember? Plus we have to discuss recent developments."

"Why cancel? I've got time for that meeting right now."

"We scheduled that meeting at noon for a reason, Marco. You didn't forget to call your mom, did you?"

"I didn't forget, and I will call her."

Translation: He *did* forget, and he will make sure to call her when she can't answer so he can leave her a voice mail. In his place, I'd do the same.

"So what are the latest developments," Marco asked, "or are you going to make me wait until our meeting?"

"I'll give you the condensed version. Grace got a call from Constance Newport's attorney asking her to be at his office at four o'clock for the reading of the will."

"So soon?"

"Those were Constance's instructions. And get this, Marco: A policeman will be present."

"Sounds like the attorney is expecting trouble."

"That's what Lottie said. Poor Grace will be in the thick of it."

"I'm sure she'll be fine. Now, then," he

said, his voice turning husky, "about that payback?"

"What payback?"

"The one you'll owe me for canceling your shopping trip with my mom."

"It's *our* shopping trip, and why would I owe you for dealing with *your* mom? All you have to do is make a simple call."

"If it's so simple, why don't you do it? She'll be your mother-in-law."

So either I had to call and cancel, or I owed Marco a payback. That was a no-brainer. "I'm all ears, Salvare. How about we discuss your payback at our meeting?"

"Want to clarify what you mean by *discuss?*"

"I'd rather leave it open for interpretation."

"Your interpreter will be waiting, baby."

*Fantastico.*

When Grace returned from her meeting with Constance Newport's attorney, she came straight into the workroom where I was putting together a wedding bouquet of ivory callas and baby's breath, and sat on one of the wooden stools, staring straight ahead. When she didn't say anything, I said, "Grace, are you all right?"

"I'm flummoxed." She paused to shake

her head in disbelief. "Completely flum-moxed."

Lottie came in behind her. "How did it go?"

When Grace merely shook her head, I said, "She's flummoxed."

"Why?" Lottie asked, pulling up a stool to sit beside her.

"I don't know what Connie could have been thinking," Grace said.

As we waited for her to finish her thought, Simon leaped onto the work surface and came over to sniff the callas. Finding them uninteresting, he began pushing stray leaves off the side of the table and watching them float to the floor.

Grace sighed loudly. "It was simply ap-palling. I still can't believe it."

"If you're going to tell us," Lottie said, "could you make it sometime today? The suspense is killing me."

Grace looked up, surprised to see us both watching her. "Sorry. I suppose you'll be wanting to know what happened, won't you?"

"Ya think?" Lottie asked.

"She cut her family out, Connie did. Or nearly so. They will receive only token amounts of money. She was obviously ter-ribly angry with them."

"Who's getting the rest?" Lottie asked, ever practical.

As though Grace didn't hear her, she went on. "And yet Connie was quite generous with her housekeeper and chauffeur. Thinking back to our last meeting, however, I do remember her complaining about her family's laziness, bemoaning that the only thing they were good for was spending her money. Connie's hope had been that they would carry on her charitable work, but it seemed that day she had given up."

"So the housekeeper and driver got all her money?" Lottie asked.

"No, her housekeeper, Mrs. Dunbar, is to receive all of Connie's silver," Grace said. "Twenty-four antique silver place settings, a complete tea set, and a candelabra. Her chauffeur, Mr. Luce, will receive her Bentley. Can you imagine? Her *Bentley*. And her liquid assets, some five million dollars' worth, will be divided among her pet charities."

"That's terrific. Now, get to the good part," Lottie said, her knees bouncing in anticipation. "What did Connie leave you?"

"A first-edition book," Grace said, pulling a tissue from her sleeve as her eyes welled up with tears. "Apparently, it was the one I was to collect on Monday, which makes me think Connie wanted to explain the circumstances of her will. But now we'll never know, will we?"

I watched Lottie's expression go from excited to disappointed as she absorbed the news. "Are you telling me that her housekeeper gets the family silver, her driver gets a go-to-heck car, and you got a *book?*"

Grace nodded, sniffling. "Mr. Duval said it is worth approximately ten thousand dollars."

Lottie shook her head in disbelief. "A ten-grand book? I don't know what to say to that."

"That's a drop in the bucket for the Newports," I said, shooing Simon away from the greenery on the table.

"Who gets the house?" Lottie asked.

Grace shook her head. "It's unbelievable. Simply incomprehensible."

"Gracie, I'm gonna get an ulcer waiting for you to finish this story," Lottie said.

"I'm sorry, Lottie, dear. The fact of the matter is that Connie has directed that the mansion and its entire contents, including her husband's priceless Victorian art and antiques collection, go to Charity."

"Constance Newport was enormously generous to the town, but I never knew she had such a giving heart," Lottie said.

"You have no idea," Grace said. "From what I gathered, the oil paintings alone are worth millions of dollars. A guard is to be posted at the house tonight and an art appraiser is to arrive tomorrow to assess the collection's value."

"What's the rush?" Lottie asked.

"Perhaps Connie was afraid the collection would be spirited out of the house once the family was informed," Grace said. "Whatever her reason, I can't begin to describe the mood in that office. Connie's daughter threatened to contest the will."

"Sounds to me like Connie felt she'd given them enough already," Lottie said.

"Leaving her entire fortune and all her belongings to charitable organizations is very altruistic," I said. "But that seems to be in character with Connie's philanthropy."

"I'm sorry, love," Grace said. "I should have clarified that last part. Charity, you see, is her cat."

I was beginning to understand Grace's shock.

"That's gotta be one pampered pet," Lottie said. "I'm surprised her name isn't Duchess."

"Connie adored the chubby little beast," Grace said, "but from what I gathered, everyone else found her a nuisance."

"How much of a nuisance could one little kitty be?" Lottie asked.

All three of us jumped as a glass vase fell to the floor and shattered. Simon crouched on the shelf, staring in fascination at the destruction below.

"Simon!" I snapped. He jumped off the counter and scooted under the worktable.

"Let me ask you this, Gracie," Lottie said, as I went for the broom and dustpan. "If the cat inherited the house and everything in it, who gets the cat?"

"Well, that's the thing, you see," Grace said, twisting her fingers together. "I did. Connie named me Charity's guardian."

# CHAPTER SEVEN

I paused my sweeping to let Grace's news register, while Lottie just stared open-mouthed.

"Dreadful business, isn't it?" Grace asked, wiping her eyes.

Simon jumped onto the worktable, padded over to her, and rubbed his nose against her chin, as though trying to cheer her up.

"What does being the cat's guardian mean?" I asked, emptying chunks of glass into the trash can.

"I'm to make sure that Charity is being properly attended to, that her house is maintained, and that her food and veterinary needs are seen to, even down to hiring a caretaker."

"A cat nanny," Lottie said with a laugh. "Can you beat that?"

"Will you have any authority over how Connie's money is spent on the cat?" I asked.

"Not just any, love," Grace said. "I'll have complete authority. Can you understand why I'm all at sea?"

"Can you take the cat to your house to live?" Lottie asked.

"Connie's wish was for Charity to live out her life in the house. She has her own bedroom there, you see. But ultimately it is to be my decision."

Lottie was right. That was one pampered pet. "Will you be paid a salary?" I asked.

Grace nodded. "An annual stipend of fifty thousand dollars."

No wonder the attorney had asked for a cop.

Lottie let out a low whistle. "With that kind of money in your bank account, Gracie, you won't need to work here anymore."

Yikes! I hadn't thought of that. What would I do without Grace?

"I work here for the enjoyment, dear," Grace said, "not for the money. But there's a rather significant stumbling block to carrying out the terms of the will. The cat is missing."

"The duchess abdicated?" Lottie asked.

Simon tried to stick his nose into Grace's cup, so I put him on the floor. "Simon, behave! Grace, maybe the cat I found is the missing heiress."

"I doubt that's possible," Grace said, plucking a cat hair from the hot liquid. "The family is of a mind that the cat slipped out when the paramedics arrived. In fact, Juanita believes the poor thing was run over by a car. She told the attorney that she heard the most awful screech of tires some time after the coroner got there. I didn't hear anything myself, but I was in quite a state of distress. Everyone agreed that Charity wouldn't stay away unless something dreadful had happened to her."

"Did anyone actually check the street to see if that's what happened?" Lottie asked.

Grace scoffed. "I doubt they cared enough to check. They were probably hoping it was true. All I know is that Charity didn't escape when I let myself in because I would have noticed a fat cat darting past me."

"That answers my question," I said. "The cat I found is skinny and raggedy."

"What happens if Charity doesn't come back?" Lottie asked.

"After a certain amount of time," Grace said, "she'd be declared dead. The attorney didn't really go into it, but basically Connie's assets would be liquidated and the money distributed among the charities she'd named in the will. I would serve no further function and my stipend would stop."

"Did you have any clue that Connie was going to appoint you?" Lottie asked.

"None," Grace said. "However, once again, as I think back to our last meeting, I should have suspected something. Before I left, she quizzed me about my love of animals, whether I'd ever kept pets, and why I didn't have any now. I told her I'd owned cats and dogs, but that after my old cat passed on years back, I didn't want the heartbreak of losing another. Connie told me I was flat-out wrong, that having another cat would be just the remedy for me."

"Were any family members present when you had this talk?" I asked.

Grace sipped her tea, thinking. "It's possible. We had our book discussions in the dining room, over tea and petit fours. I know there were occasions when Connie's daughter and daughter-in-law were around, but they were never in the room with us for longer than it took to say hello. That's not to say they weren't listening in from the other side of the door."

Said the master eavesdropper.

Grace checked her watch. "Oh, good heavens, it's almost five thirty. Richard must be waiting outside for me."

Yikes. And Marco would be wondering where I was.

"I've got to get home and start supper," Lottie said. "Four hungry teenaged boys can wipe out the contents of a refrigerator in an hour flat if they're not fed on time." She gave Grace a hug. "I know this has been a tough day for you, Gracie. If you need me, I'm as close as a phone call."

As Grace rose to take her cup to the kitchen, her cell phone began to chime. "That's probably Richard now."

While Grace answered her call, I did a quick cleanup of the worktable and fed Simon, then put my purse over my shoulder, grabbed my jacket, and walked through the shop.

"Was it Richard?" I asked, as Grace slid her phone into her purse.

"Dave Hammond, actually. He said the detectives want to talk to me in the morning. After being informed about the provisions in the will, the police have more questions. I'm so glad I retained Dave this morning. I hope you don't mind, but I took the liberty of telling Dave that you and Marco will be investigating. He asked that one of you contact him tomorrow."

"When are you supposed to meet with the detectives?" I asked.

"Dave said he'll let me know," Grace said, a deep worry line forming between her eyebrows. I knew she was doing her best to put on a brave front.

"How would you and Richard like to walk over to Down the Hatch and have a bite to eat with us?" I asked. "I know Marco will want to talk to you before he sees Dave."

"I'm sure Richard will be in favor of it, but I should do him the courtesy of asking. I spotted his car parked across the street. I'll meet you outside."

Ten minutes later, we were seated in the last booth at Down the Hatch, Grace and Richard on one side of the table, Marco and I on the other, with a bottle of wine in the middle, courtesy of Richard. The handsome Texan had on a blue denim shirt and string tie, jeans and snakeskin boots. With his tanned, leathery face and thick white hair with long sideburns, he looked just like he'd ridden out of a Western movie.

We avoided the topic of the murder while we ate, but as soon as we finished, Marco brought a legal pad to the table so I could take notes.

"I put in a call to Sean Reilly," Marco told us, "asking him to find out if the police saw any evidence of theft at the Newport residence. It would help to know that before we start investigating. He said he'd contact me as soon as he had any news."

"Sergeant Reilly was among the police at Connie's house yesterday," Grace said, "but I wasn't able to talk to him. Please pass along my thanks for his help."

"Abby told me a little of what you said about Connie's children's laziness," Marco said. "Did she mention anything specific as it related to their inheritance?"

"Only at our last meeting," Grace said, "when Connie said she feared there would be terrible fighting among them. She wanted them to remain close to one another, but because of their greedy natures, was afraid that was something of a pipe dream."

"Would you give me a list of everyone living on the Newport estate?" Marco asked.

As Grace went through the names, I wrote fast, trying to get it all down.

Mrs. Dunbar lived in an en-suite bedroom at the back of the mansion on the main floor, giving her a private bathroom plus easy access to the kitchen. Constance's son, Burnett Jr., and his wife, Juanita, lived on the second floor in the east wing. Constance's divorced daughter, Virginia, had a suite across the hall from her third-floor studio, accessible from the back or front staircase.

Luce the chauffeur's quarters were in one of two apartments on the second floor of the garage, which had ten car bays. Constance's grandson, Griffin, occupied the other apartment. And last but not least was Charity the cat, who occupied the former nursery, connected by an inner door to Constance's master suite and accessible from a separate door off the second-floor hallway.

Marco looked over my shoulder as I wrote, asking questions as he thought of them.

"What do you know about Burnett Junior?" he asked.

"Only the bits I've picked up from Connie," Grace said. "Burnsy, as she called him, took over the management of their rental properties after his father died. Then he retired at the ripe old age of fifty so he could spend his time as he saw fit, which was primarily to lose money at the racetrack."

"Whose money?" I asked. "His mother's?"

"It came down to that, yes," Grace said, "but in the form of a salary paid to him by the Newport estate. Connie complained that Burnsy was not a chip off the old block. She said her husband hadn't amassed his fortune by gambling away either his time or

113

his assets.

"She was also displeased with the way Burnsy ran through wives. Connie seemed to be quite fond of Burnsy's first wife — that would be Griffin's mother. Unfortunately, she moved to Florida after the divorce. Connie also liked Burnsy's second wife, and I can't remember what she said about wife number three, but she barely tolerated Juanita, who is a great deal younger than Burnsy. I believe she's thirty-two. Connie referred to Juanita as *the shopaholic.*"

"How long have Burnsy and Juanita been married?" Marco asked, as I scribbled to keep up.

"I can't say exactly," Grace said, "but Connie did remark that she doubted the marriage would last to its third anniversary, so my guess is around two years."

"Just out of curiosity," I asked, "how old is Burnsy?"

"Sixty-two," Grace said.

Sixty-two and people still called him Burnsy?

"As Connie was wont to point out," Grace continued, "with thirty years between them, Juanita could be his daughter."

"How old was Constance?" Marco asked.

"She had just turned eighty-seven," Grace

114

said. "A remarkable woman for her age, too. She swam daily in the indoor lap pool and attended yoga classes three times a week. The grass certainly didn't grow under her feet." Grace's lower lip began to tremble. "She was such a vital woman."

Richard put his arm around her shoulders. "If this is too much for you, honeypot, say the word and I'll whisk you right home in my carriage."

Grace smiled into his eyes. "Thank you, dear Richard, but if there's anything we Brits do well, it's soldier on. Continue, Marco."

"Let's go back to Juanita," Marco said. "Did you notice friction between her and Constance?"

"No," Grace said. "Connie was polite to a fault with her."

"Does Juanita work?" I asked.

"She teaches a yoga class several times a week, I believe," Grace said.

"How did she meet Burnsy?" I asked.

"Juanita was a renter in one of the family-owned apartment buildings," Grace said. "One day she went to the management office to complain about a broken dishwasher, and Burnsy happened to be there. Being the eternal skirt-chaser, he volunteered to fix it. Well, the silly man knew nothing about repairing machines, but he couldn't resist trying to impress a beautiful young woman, and, according to Connie, Juanita couldn't resist a wealthy man."

*Burnsy likes sexy babes,* I wrote. *Juanita likes money.*

"What do you know about Constance's daughter?" Marco asked.

"Virginia Newport-Lynch," Grace said, then spelled it out for me. "Virginia is middle-aged, divorced, has no children, and fancies herself a painter. However, from what Connie said, she's never sold anything of note. She studied art in college, then moved to Taos, New Mexico, married an artist living on a commune, and painted pictures of vases and pueblos. Later, she moved to Chicago and worked at the Art Institute. She's a plain woman with an odd taste in clothing and with features that are rather ratlike, if truth be known, although her whiskers are on her chin rather than below her nose."

Grace stated that as a fact rather than as a joke, but I couldn't hold back a snicker as I wrote it down.

"How did she get along with her mother?" Marco asked.

"The air fairly crackled with animosity when Virginia and her mum were in the same room," Grace said. "Connie called her daughter a contrarian. If she said black, Virginia said white. Connie once said they couldn't even agree on the time."

"Been there," I said.

Marco's cell phone rang, so he left the booth to take the call. When he returned he said, "That was Sean Reilly. The police found no evidence of theft or of a break-in, and no one had reported anything other than the cat missing. He also mentioned that according to the coroner's preliminary findings, there are bruises on Constance's shoulders consistent with being pushed."

"Poor dear," Grace muttered, shaking her head sadly.

"Is that all Reilly told you, Marco?" I asked.

"He wanted me to pass along a message for Grace," Marco said, prompting Richard to put his arm around her shoulders in a reassuring way.

"Yes, Marco, please proceed," Grace said.

"Reilly said to prepare yourself, Grace. They're calling you their top suspect."

# CHAPTER EIGHT

Seeing the anguish in Grace's eyes, Richard said, "Whatever it takes, Grace, I'm here for you. I don't want you worrying about legal expenses, hear? That includes paying for these two young people to investigate. The police may be starting with you, but they sure as heck aren't going to end there. Marco, how soon can you and Abby get to work?"

"We've already started," Marco said.

"Richard, love," Grace said, her eyes filling with tears, "I appreciate your offer, but this is not your responsibility. I'm perfectly able to pay for my own defense."

"Grace, my little English dove, I don't want to step on your toes, but please let me help you. This money you're due to receive may be frozen. So indulge me a little, honeypot. I like taking care of you."

"Thank you, dear, but it's a matter of pride, you see."

"Pride, is it?" he asked. "And what's that little ditty you're always telling me about pride?"

Grace sighed resignedly. "It's not a ditty. It's a verse from Proverbs. 'Pride goeth before destruction, and a haughty spirit before a fall.' That's all well and fine, Richard, but —"

He put his fingers over her lips. "Hush, now. I want to take care of this for you. Will you please let me do that?"

The sweet, loving look that passed between them nearly made my own eyes well up. I glanced at Marco to see if he'd caught it, and the corner of his mouth turned up in that quirky, endearing way of his as he gazed at me. He squeezed my hand beneath the table.

This was definitely the man I wanted to share my life with.

"Shall we get on with it, then?" Grace asked.

"You were telling us about Connie's daughter," I reminded her.

"That's really about all I know of Virginia's personal life," Grace said, "other than that she has a disorder called syncope, which causes her to faint under stress. For a woman who likes to be in control at all times, it infuriates her."

"Does she work outside the home?" Marco asked.

"Not for several years," Grace said. "Sadly, neither one of Grace's children feels the need to be industrious, hence Connie's disgust. She worked very hard raising funds for her favorite philanthropic organizations and had always encouraged Virginia and Burnsy to do the same, but they weren't interested."

"What about Griffin?" I asked.

"Ah, yes, Connie's grandson," Grace said. "Griffin is a scholar. He studied history at Oxford and now writes papers on the Victorian era. It's too small a niche to make any sort of living from, but Griffin has never had to worry about money.

"He's forty years old, good-looking, and always well turned out. Connie had seemed to dote on him, but at our last meeting, I sensed a strain of some kind between them that was unrelated to her worries about the inheritance money."

I put a star beside Griffin's name. Grace's observation was something to explore in greater depth. As Marco had taught me, sometimes the tiniest detail could prove to be the most important

"What about Griffin's relationships?" Marco asked. "Was he seeing anyone?"

"He had been seeing a young woman but broke it off several months back and wouldn't tell his grandmother why. That didn't sit well with her."

"Which?" Marco asked. "That he broke off his relationship or that he wouldn't tell her why?"

"Connie wanted him to marry and have children. However, she also hated being denied her way. So perhaps both."

"Tell me about the housekeeper," Marco said.

"I would guess Mrs. Dunbar's age to be about seventy," Grace said, "and she's worked for the Newports for many years. Other than that, I'm afraid I can't be of much help. Connie didn't have any complaints about her. In fact, she hardly mentioned the woman at all. I believe she rather viewed her staff as invisible."

"What about the chauffeur?" Marco asked.

"Mr. Luce functions as both chauffeur and mechanic," Grace said. "He's very young, perhaps your age, Abby, quite good-looking, and has a passion for automobiles and motorbikes. I got the distinct impression that Connie viewed him as a pet. Interesting, isn't it, that he came out the best of all?"

I finished writing and moved the list to where Marco could see it better.

"Grace, remind me where everyone was when you found the body," Marco said.

Grace took a sip of wine and thought about it. "I only know what I heard, which is to say, it hasn't been proven. Supposedly, Virginia was in her attic studio, Mrs. Dunbar was in the garden, Griffin was in his apartment, Luce was working on a motorbike in the garage, Burnsy was off gambling, and Juanita was shopping with a friend."

"Make a note to find out the name of her friend," Marco said to me. "Grace, was the back door unlocked when you arrived?"

"That's right. I knocked twice and called out, then tried the door, found it unlocked, and stepped inside for a look around. I noticed a door ajar on the other side of the kitchen, with a light coming from behind it. When I opened it, I found myself looking down a flight of stairs to their lower level, and there lay Connie at the bottom beneath a suit of armor. It was horrible."

"I know this is hard for you," Marco said, "but could you describe the position of her body?"

Grace drew a deep breath, as if steeling herself. "She was faceup, with her arms flung awkwardly to the sides and her heels still on the bottom step. The fingers of her right hand were curled, too. As I told Abby, I suspected at once that it was more than an accident because all the signs indicated that she'd been pushed."

"Did you take her pulse?" Marco asked.

"I did," Grace said. "There was none, yet her forehead was still warm, so she couldn't have been dead long. I ran upstairs to call for help and was talking to the police when Mrs. Dunbar came through the back door. She heard my end of the conversation, dropped the bundle of radishes in her apron, ran to the basement door, and would have charged straight down the steps had I not caught her in time.

"Heaven knows what evidence she might have destroyed in addition to what I may have done. The poor old dear was so distraught that I immediately sat her down at the table and attempted to distract her by asking her questions until the police arrived, but she kept going on about how she might lose her position now that Connie's gone, and she was barely able to manage a complete sentence."

"Was she able to furnish any information?" Marco asked.

"About the only thing she said was that when she left to go out to the garden, Connie was searching for Charity. The police arrived at last and they were followed by Juanita. The three of us were separated not long afterward and put in various rooms to be interviewed."

Marco waited until I'd finished writing, then said, "Anything you want to ask, Abby?"

"Grace, you've met Connie's family, haven't you?"

"Yes, superficially."

"If you had to pick one person from this list to be our prime suspect, who would it be?"

"Oh, dear," Grace said, rubbing her forehead. "I hate to point the finger of guilt at anyone. If you were to phrase it differently, perhaps?"

"Try this," I said. "Who should we investigate first?"

"Juanita and Virginia, without a doubt," Grace said. "Connie wasn't on good terms with either one."

"Was she on good terms with her son?" Marco asked.

"Not particularly, but it was the two women whom she complained about the most."

I put stars beside the two names. Marco read over the notes, then said, "That should do it, Grace. Go home and relax, and we'll take it from here. Thanks for your patience, Richard."

"Anything to help this sweet little lady," Richard said. "Now, before we go, how about a toast to a speedy resolution of this matter?"

"Hear, hear," I said, and we clinked glasses.

As soon as Grace and Richard left, Marco said, "I'll meet with Dave Hammond first thing in the morning; then we can head over to the Newport mansion during your lunch hour and see who'll talk to us."

"I'll bring a bouquet of flowers to get us in the door. But why wait until tomorrow when we can get started now? More people are home during the evening hours than at lunchtime."

"Sorry, babe. I've got plans for this evening."

I couldn't keep the disappointment out of my voice. "A new PI case?"

"No." Marco picked up my hand and began to draw lazy circles in my palm, where the nerve endings seemed particularly sensitive. He knew it drove me wild. "I believe there's a small matter of a payback?"

Ah, the payback. Disappointment gone. "Check, please."

As Marco helped me into my jacket, I asked, "Was your mom okay with canceling the shopping trip?"

"I didn't cancel it," he said, ushering me out of the booth. "I postponed it."

"Marco, that won't work. I don't want to pick out shower invitations with her. They'll be what she wants, not what we want."

"Sunshine, I've never seen you do anything you didn't really want to do, and that would include agreeing to buy invitations you don't like."

"You make it sound so easy, but I couldn't do anything that might hurt her feelings."

"You worry too much. Now, wait right here."

He slipped through the crowd to talk to his head bartender, then came back to take my arm and escort me out the door.

"Instead of putting her off," I said, as Marco walked me to my car, "just tell her we'll choose our own invitations."

*"Mmm,"* he said, hurrying me across the street.

"It's not fair to your mom to keep putting her off if we have no intention of going shopping with her in the first place, wouldn't you agree?"

"Yep."

We stopped at my car, parked on the

diagonal facing the courthouse, across the street from Bloomers. "So will you tell her, please?" I asked, gazing up at him.

"Sure." Marco put his hands on either side of me, so that my back was against the driver's door, and leaned in for a kiss, his body pressed against mine.

Clearly, his thoughts were on the forthcoming payback, not the situation with his mother. It just showed how single-minded a male could be. Even now, while in the midst of one of his hot kisses, a fraction of my brain was working on other things. For instance, by opening one eye, I could peer over Marco's shoulder and see Bloomer's bay windows across the street. And in the bay window was that ugly bald head . . . with a white fur cap?

Wait. Was that Simon draped over the head? Chewing on Mom's sea glasses?

"Marco," I said, between kisses, "Simon is destroying Mom's head."

*"Mm-hmm,"* he murmured.

I broke the kiss, ducked beneath his arm, and started running across the street. "I've got to stop him!"

Marco jogged after me. "Did you just say he was destroying your mom's head?"

I stopped in front of the bay window and knocked on the glass. "Simon! Bad boy!"

Simon's mouth opened in a meow of recognition. Then he slid backward off the head and disappeared over the back of the wide ledge. I pulled out my keys, opened the door, disarmed the burglar alarm, and ran to the front window.

The head, made of dense plastic foam, had deep puncture marks in it where Simon had hung on to keep his balance. The pair of sea glasses dangled by one ear pin. The nose was missing, and half the paint was gone from one eye. Miss Sea 3PO looked like she'd been zapped by a Storm Trooper's laser gun.

"Look at this!" I said, shaking the head at Simon, who had returned to his perch on top of the armoire. "How am I supposed to fix it? You are a bad boy!"

Simon gave me a bored look, then began to wash his ear.

Oblivious to the annihilation I held in my hands, Marco slid his arms around my waist and nuzzled my ear. "Did someone call for a bad boy?"

Yep, single-minded.

*Wednesday*
Tabitha woke me up Wednesday morning by dragging her cast over the kitchen floor to get to her litter box. I was delighted to

see that the little tabby was doing so well. She was even starting to look less gaunt, no doubt from Nikki plying her with tempting morsels all day.

I gave her fresh food and water, then showered and got ready for work. When I came out to make breakfast, Tabitha was sitting on the desk in front of our picture window, calmly watching the birds in the trees, whereas Simon would have been hurtling himself at the glass trying to get to them. How the injured cat had managed to jump up there was a wonder.

Lottie was already at Bloomers when I arrived and had not only fed Simon and played with him for a while, but had also made a pot of coffee for us, a task Grace tried to discourage either of us from doing. She was quite territorial when it came to her coffee machines. But since Grace had an early meeting with Dave and Marco before her face-to-face with the detective, the two of us muddled along without her. I wished I could have attended the meeting, too, but Lottie couldn't handle the shop alone.

"Guess who called again this morning," Lottie said.

"Jillian?"

"Yep. Same message as before."

"I'd better call her. Something is up."

Lottie held up her hands. "Proceed at your own risk, sweetie."

I called Jillian's cell and it went to voice mail, so I left a message. Then I dialed her house phone and the answering machine picked up with Jillian saying: *Jillian and Claymore's residence. If you're calling for Claymore, press one. If you're calling for an expert wardrobe consultation, press two. If you're calling for Jillian before ten a.m., shame on you. Hang up now.*

Nothing I could do about Jillian's crazy head, but there had to be a way to salvage the manikin's. I took Miss Sea 3PO to the workroom and placed it on the table, trying to decide on a course of action. The nose had to be in the shop somewhere. The eye . . . well, maybe I could fashion a patch and make her a space pirate. The puncture marks would just have to stay. Battle scars, perhaps.

Simon jumped up on the table to see what I was doing. "See what you did?" I asked.

He sniffed the head, then, apparently having bonded with Miss Sea 3PO, rubbed his nose against the remains of her face.

"Simon, where's Mr. Potato Head's nose? What did you do with it?"

He was biting the push pin in the ear, trying to pull it out. I set him on the floor, took a clear glass marble out of a container, and sent it rolling. Simon pounced and batted it with his paw. It went under the curtain and so did the feline, so I followed him into the shop, hoping that wherever the marble ended up, the missing nose would be there, too.

Simon disappeared behind the big umbrella plant in the back corner, so I got on my hands and knees to look for the nose there. At a rapping on the door, I turned and saw my cousin Jillian motioning for me to open up.

A visit from Sleeping Beauty first thing in the morning? That never bode well.

# CHAPTER NINE

"I need a bouquet of roses," she announced, sweeping into the shop as I shut the door behind her. "Stat." And then she headed for the workroom. Simon skittered in the opposite direction. Maniacs made him nervous.

Jillian Knight Osborne is my first cousin not removed even once. She's a year younger, a head taller, and unlike me, will step in front of a mirror without flinching. Her hair is a copper-hued silken waterfall. Mine is a bed of rusty roses with thorns. Her mother had maids to clean their house. My mom had kids.

Despite those differences, Jillian and I grew up practically sisters, which was great considering we each had only brothers. Our families spent every holiday together, many vacations, and plenty of birthday parties. Because Jillian had a severe case of scoliosis as a child, I was always protective of her.

132

She had surgery and was in a body cast when she was twelve, and from that moment on, she believed the world owed her.

Apparently, this morning it was my turn to repay the debt.

"Why haven't you called me back for the past two days?" I asked my cousin, following her into the workroom. "And why do you need roses stat?"

"Answer to question one, I got busy. Answer to question two, I have to drive to Chicago to meet my client at Nordstrom to pick out her summer vacation wardrobe —" Jillian stopped when she saw Miss Sea 3PO, then stood with one hand on her hip. "What on earth is this pathetic wig head for and why is it mangled?"

"Answer to question one," I said, "it's part of a display for my mom's sea glasses. Answer to question two, Simon got hold of it last night."

A normal person would have inquired as to what sea glasses were and why Simon was at Bloomers, but Jillian did neither. She was too busy checking her reflection in the shiny surface of one of the walk-in coolers.

"I need to fix this head before my mom sees it, Jill. Any ideas on how to do that?"

Being a wardrobe consultant, Jillian has an eye for design. With an expressive pout and a narrowing of her pretty green eyes, she turned the head to examine it from all angles. "Cover it in flowers."

I stared at her in amazement. "That's a great idea!"

"*Duh.* Now let's get moving on those roses, 'kay? Do a mix of white and yellow. Chop-chop, Abs." She made shooing motions with her hands.

Had I not been so pleased about her manikin idea, I would have *chop-chop*ped her out the door.

"That's a great idea about the head, Jill." And how I wished I'd thought of it. I opened the walk-in cooler to pull rose stems and stepped out again to find her studying the photo of Marco and me in Key West.

She tapped the photo. "Is this where you're honeymooning?"

"We haven't discussed a honeymoon."

Jillian's mouth fell open. "Well, you'd better discuss it. Do you know Key West is one of *the* hot wedding destinations in this country, ranking number two behind Las Vegas? And do you know how quickly honeymoon spots fill up? Years in advance!"

"Years, Jillian? I don't think so." I dethorned and trimmed the first stem and set it aside.

"What about a hall for your reception?"

she asked, returning the photo to the desk.

"Nope."

"Abby, I'm serious. If you want to get married in September, you have to take action now."

"Let me get these wrapped for you and then you can go."

She clamped her hands on my shoulders and turned me to face her, then leaned down so she could look me in the eye. "You do want to marry Marco, don't you?"

"Of course I do. Marco is the man of my dreams. The only one I want to marry. I love him with my whole heart."

"Or so you say."

It was my turn to clamp her shoulders. "Never, never say that to me again."

"Then why are you dragging your feet?"

"I'm not."

"Are, too. It's become such a habit, you don't even realize you're doing it." Jillian brushed a lock of hair away from my eyes, then decided it looked better the first way. "You have to dig way down inside yourself to learn why you're making these excuses, Abs."

That was pretty deep for Jillian. "Okay, sure. Right after I finish making your bouquet."

"I'm serious."

"I'm certain you are."

She huffed impatiently, then began to pace as I wrapped her flowers. "It appears that I'll have to take matters into my own hands."

"No, Jillian, no! Marco and I will take care of *matters* ourselves."

Ignoring me, she muttered something about checking with wedding planners and caterers, then pulled a BlackBerry from her oversized gold tote bag and began to type a note. I tried to read it, but she held the device above my head. It was one of the many disadvantages of being short. "Okay, then," she said, dropping her phone into the bag, "time to get moving."

She reached for the bouquet, but I put it behind my back. "You're not getting this until you promise to leave the wedding planning to us."

It was a standoff, just like when we were kids. "Tell me why you're stalling," she countered.

"I'm not stalling. I'm just trying to keep control of my wedding. I mean our wedding. It's bad enough that Marco's mom wants to run things. Now you're trying to take over. So if you want your flowers, swear you'll stay out of my business."

She folded her arms. "You're not fooling me, Abs. This isn't about control. It's about fear. You're afraid of something. Tell me what and then I'll go."

I held out the flowers. "Take them. Go."

"Nope. Not until you spill your guts."

"You're going to be late. Chop-chop, remember?"

"My client will wait. I'm worth it." Jillian pulled out a stool and sat down. "You know I can outlast you. Remember our staring contests? Or our lemonade-drinking matches?"

My cousin had the bladder of an elephant. "Fine. You want to know the truth? I'm afraid I'll jinx the marriage. Happy?"

Jillian nodded knowingly. "I thought so. It was about this time in your engagement to Pryce that you ordered your gown and reserved the hall. And we know how that ended. Pryce jilted you two months before your wedding day and humiliated you in front of the whole town."

"Thanks for that special trip down memory lane, Jill."

She hopped off the stool and enfolded me in a hug that squished my nose against her jacket zipper. "I know you have abandonment issues" — she was speaking into the top of my head — "but he isn't Pryce. Marco's not going to abandon you. He's madly in love with you."

"I realize that, Jill. That doesn't mean the fear isn't still there." Why in heaven's name was I confessing to the town crier? "Look, Jill, please don't say anything about this to anyone, especially not to Marco. It might hurt his feelings. I'll work through it, I promise."

"And I'll be here to help you every step of the way," she said, leaning back to smile at me. "Every. Step. Of. The. Way. Let's do lunch this week to work out the details. Now I've got to get going." She held out her hands, and I put the flowers into them.

"You didn't say why you needed the roses," I said, following her through the shop.

"I'm using your method of getting inside a place when someone doesn't trust you."

"Your client doesn't trust you?"

She stopped at the door to put on her tortoiseshell sunglasses. "Nordstrom."

"Someone at Nordstrom doesn't trust you?"

"Let's just leave it at Nordstrom."

With Jillian, it was always better to quit while you were ahead. Speaking of which, I had to cover that bald head in flowers and get it back in the window in case Mom decided to stop by after school. I even had a floral scheme in mind, so I set quickly to work.

For the hair, I used *Amaranthus caudatus,* or green tails, and *Myosotis alpestris,* or alpine forget-me-nots. For the eyes, a dainty blue flower with a yellow center. For the nose, a bleeding heart blossom, and for the mouth, a lip-shaped petal of Cattleya Chocolate Drop. When her makeover was finished, I turned Miss Sea 3PO around to view her from all sides. "You, Missy, are a real *eye*-catcher. Let's hope Mom approves."

The flower shop was busy when Grace returned, so we had time for only a brief conference at the cashier counter, where she summarized the meeting with the detective as intense and unsettling. Detective Al Corbison had tried every trick in the detective handbook to get Grace to say she knew ahead of time about Constance's plan to make her guardian, but under Dave Hammond's steady counsel, Grace maintained her innocence and her composure.

"Are they done with you now?" Lottie asked.

"They told me to stay in town," Grace said with a sigh, "and we know what that means. I'm exceedingly relieved that you and Marco will be conducting your own investigation, Abby."

"I am, too, Grace. Make sure you let me know the minute you hear anything, okay?"

"Absolutely, love. And on a cheery note, you've completely transformed Miss Sea 3PO. She looks lovely now. I could see her in the window as I crossed the street. How are you managing to keep Simon away from her?"

"I don't think he cares for the taste of *Amaranthus caudatus.*"

"Where *is* Simon?" Grace asked.

I glanced around but didn't see him. So while my assistants waited on customers, I set off on a cat hunt, checking first the parlor, then obvious hiding spots in the shop, and finally the workroom. As I walked around the far side of the large worktable, I stepped on a pile of dirt. Crouching down, I found Simon sitting in the middle of a bag of potting soil that he had split open with his sharp little claws. He meowed innocently when he saw me, then got up, stretched, and shook his fur, sending dirt flying in all directions, including into my face.

Exploring further, I discovered that not only had he ripped open a bag of soil, but he'd also gotten into my green foam, which was sticking to the ends of his fur.

"Simon, what am I going to do with you?"

He rubbed his forehead against mine, purring loudly. With an exasperated sigh, I went for the broom and dustpan, and as soon as I'd cleaned up the mess, I texted Nikki: *Please find a home for the cat soon.*

She texted back: *No replies to my ads yet. Sorry. You did mean Tabitha, right?*

I decided not to reply until I was in a better mood.

At noon, Marco and I left for the Newport estate located outside the town limits across the northernmost border of New Chapel. I brought along a bouquet of yellow daisies, purple anemone, and white spider mums in case we needed to coax a reluctant witness to talk.

The magnificent black and gold wrought-iron gates were open, to my surprise, so we drove up the tree-lined brick driveway until it split. The right fork led to a drive that circled in front of the enormous residence; the left fork led along the side of the house to the ten-car garage in back. I gaped at the mansion as Marco passed it, heading toward the garage.

Looking like something out of a movie set, the brown-brick three-story mansion, with wings on either side, had a high slate roof with eight dormers across the front, ten chimney stacks, a stone facade on the entrance, and a wide portico to shade the shiny black front door. The garage was a slightly smaller version of the house, with the same brick and stone construction, same slate roof with dormers, but only two stories high.

Marco pulled up behind a rental truck that was backed up to the first bay, where an attractive guy in a white T-shirt, tight-fitting jeans, and blue athletic shoes was carrying a large cardboard box up a ramp.

"Let's get to it," Marco said, shutting off the engine. I left the bouquet on the floor and followed him around to the back of the truck.

"Afternoon," Marco said to the guy, as he came striding down the ramp.

"Hey," he replied with a nod. "If you're looking for the appraiser, he's already at work. You'll find him in the art gallery."

Marco opened his wallet to show his ID. "We're private investigators. I'm Marco Salvare. This is Abby Knight."

"Guy Luce. What are you investigating?"

Did that really need explaining? "Your employer's death," I said.

Guy scratched his ear. "Aren't the cops

doing that?"

"We were hired privately," Marco said. "Got a minute to help us with some details?"

"I don't know, man. I'm kinda in a hurry."

"We won't keep you long," Marco said.

Guy eyed him skeptically. "You look familiar."

"Maybe you've seen me at Down the Hatch. It's my place."

"Sure. That's it. Hey. Nice to meet you." Guy shook his hand, suddenly at ease. "Come on inside."

We followed him into the first bay, where I saw stacks of cardboard boxes waiting to be loaded. I glanced down the long building and saw several expensive autos sitting in bays, including a black Mercedes-Benz, a highly polished green Bentley, and a black Rolls-Royce. At the far end were two more cars, but they were so far away I could only guess at their make.

Guy stepped inside a storage closet at the back of the bay and removed three folding chairs. He handed Marco one and set up the other two so we could sit. Then he went back to a small refrigerator beside the closet and called, "Beer or soft drink?"

"Neither, thanks," we said in unison. While Guy took a beer for himself, Marco motioned for me to take notes, so I pulled out a small black notebook and pen.

"I've been packing all day," Guy said, sitting down with a weary sigh. He placed the cold beer can against his forehead, under a lock of dark brown hair, then opened the can, tilted his head back, and took a long drink.

Grace had pegged him as twenty-seven, though he seemed much younger than that. But he certainly fit his nickname of Gorgeous Guy. He had lots of thick brown hair, nicely shaped brown eyebrows, big blue eyes, and features that were almost too perfect. I didn't get any bad vibes from him, but I reserved my final judgment for later.

"Are you moving out?" Marco asked.

He shrugged. "No reason for me to stay now."

"You were Constance Newport's chauffeur, right?" Marco asked.

"And mechanic. I've even got a motto. 'Guy the Driver Guy. Luce-limbed but not loose-tongued.' Luce is my last name. Get it? *Luce*-limbed?"

"That's clever," I said, writing *lame* after his motto.

Guy beamed. "Thanks."

"I understand the Bentley is yours now," Marco said.

He smiled with delight. "Can you believe it? A Bentley Continental GTZ. Want to have a look?" He jumped up and motioned for us to follow. "She's awesome."

He strode to the deluxe vehicle and lifted the hood so we could see inside, talking about it with something akin to reverence. "It's got dual KKK Turbochargers, with four valves for each cylinder. Six hundred bhp, a six-speed automatic transmission, cast-alloy twenty-inch wheels with carbon discs, and Pirelli P-Zero tires. Isn't she awesome?"

I gave up trying to get all that info in my notes, and just wrote *tricked-out Bentley.*

"How much does something like this cost?" Marco asked.

"Two hundred thousand plus change, brand-new," Guy announced proudly. "I still can't believe she's all mine. Mrs. Constance told me she was gonna leave it to me, but come on! Leaving a car like this to her driver? Who does that?"

"Then you didn't believe her?" Marco asked.

"I guess I should have. Mrs. Constance wasn't the kind to go back on her word."

"When did she tell you?" I asked.

"Maybe three weeks ago. She just walked out here one day and told me. Like, 'By the

way, Luce, I'm leaving you my Bentley.' "
He shook his head, as though he still hadn't
recovered from the shock.

Guy knew he was going to get the car. Was
that enough of a reason to kill her?

"Your employer was a generous woman,"
I said.

"She was awesome. You should see my
apartment. All the best appliances, flat-
screen TV . . . Man, I love my job."

At that, he seemed to sober. "I mean, I
*loved* my job. I'm not sure what I'll do now.
I had planned to work for Mrs. Constance
until I had enough saved to become a race-
car driver, but I've been asked to leave."

"You could sell the Bentley," I said.

He shut the hood, then used the hem of
his T-shirt to wipe off his fingerprints. "I
couldn't do that. Mrs. Constance gave it to
me. That means a lot. I guess I'll try to find
a mechanic's shop that needs an extra
hand."

Marco asked, "How do you feel about
your employer's death being ruled a homicide?"

"I can't understand why anyone would
want to, you know, do that to her. It ain't
right. Mrs. Constance could be really bossy,
but that was her right. She called all the
shots because she had the money."

I wrote: *No bad vibes. Seems genuinely sad about Constance's death.*

"Mind if we sit down again?" Marco asked.

After we'd resumed our seats, Marco asked, "What do you remember about your employer's movements Monday morning?"

Guy rocked back on his chair, thinking. "Mrs. Constance usually gets a manicure at nine o'clock every Monday morning, but this Monday she said she wouldn't need me."

"What time did she tell you?" Marco asked.

"Around eight thirty. I was already out here shining up the car for her, so I started working on my Harley instead."

"Is that your Harley?" Marco asked, pointing to a black motorcycle at the back of the second bay.

"That's it. I'm rebuilding it. Got it for a steal, man. I like to work on it in my spare time."

"You worked on your Harley all morning?" Marco asked.

"And straight through my lunch hour. Then right after that, two cops came out here and told me they needed to question me."

"Do you know why your employer canceled her manicure?" Marco asked.

Guy shrugged. "She didn't say."

"Was it unusual for her to cancel her appointment?" I asked.

"She was kind of particular about her fingernails," Guy said, "so yeah, it was unusual."

"What was her mood like? Did she seem happy? Anxious? Nervous?" Marco asked.

Guy smoothed his hair down over his forehead as he thought. "Not nervous. Not happy either. I guess you could say that she wasn't in the best of moods."

"How did she show her mood?" Marco asked.

"Well," he said, thinking, "she kind of made this thing with her mouth, kind of twisted her lips to one side as she talked. That meant she wasn't pleased."

"Because of something you did?" Marco asked.

"No," Guy said, "it wasn't me because she smiled at me. But then right away she made that mouth. I'd say she was in a bad mood when she came to tell me."

"Can you think of any reason why she might have been in a bad mood?" I asked.

Guy's gaze moved to the floor as he shook his head, as though he didn't want to look me in the eye. It was one of those signals

Marco had taught me to watch for, a red flag.

"Take your time," Marco said. "This could be important."

Again he said no, his gaze still on the floor. Guy Luce took his motto seriously, because loose-tongued he was not.

I could see by the way Marco studied Guy that he was trying to figure out a way to get the chauffeur to open up. To Marco, it was a chess game, so I leaned back to watch the match.

# CHAPTER TEN

"What family members were at home at eight thirty Monday morning?" Marco asked. He was obviously going after the information from a different angle.

"Wow, it's hard to say for sure," Guy said, scratching his ear again.

"Can you picture which cars were here?" Marco asked.

Guy turned to look down the bays. "Mr. Burnett's car was here. I remember that."

"What about Virginia's?" I asked.

"I think so."

"Griffin's?" Marco asked.

"Yeah, his was here."

"And Juanita's car?" Marco asked. Getting information from Guy was, as Lottie would say, like pulling hen's teeth.

The chauffeur suddenly found a speck of dust to flick off the side of his black sneakers, a reason not to look us in the eye. "Miss Juanita is always coming and going, so it's hard to keep track of her."

That was called a red flag.

"Are you saying that her car wasn't here," Marco asked, "or that you don't remember?"

"I, uh"— more ear scratching — "don't remember."

I wrote: *Does Guy know something about Juanita that he's afraid to tell?*

My cell phone rang, and my heart started to gallop, thinking it was Grace. Then I saw Jillian's name on the screen, so I got up and moved away. "Jillian, I'm busy now."

"I had a brilliant idea, Abs," she said, rock music playing in the background. She must have been in her car. "While I'm at Nordstrom, I'll be able find you the perfect shower ensemble. You wear a six-and-a-half shoe, right? Oops. Just ran another toll booth."

"You are not picking out an outfit for me, and what do you mean you ran another toll booth? How many have you run?"

"Today? Don't know. How many are between New Chapel and Chicago? Three?"

"You've done this before? Do you realize you'll be ticketed for each one of those?"

"I live in Indiana. What can they do to me? My exit ramp is coming up. Talk to you later."

Was that the sound of my first gray hair growing? I tucked away the phone and returned to my chair, where the interview continued.

"Was the housekeeper in the house?" Marco asked.

"Mrs. D is always here," Guy said.

"Did you witness your employer talking to any of those people?" Marco asked.

He took a swig of beer. "Nope."

"Had Mrs. Constance mentioned any problems she'd been having with any of her family members?" Marco asked.

"She never talked about family stuff with me," Guy said. "I was just her driver."

"Let's fast forward to when the cops came to get you," Marco said. "Which cars were in the garage then?"

"Ah, man, I have to think about that," Guy said. "I was kind of in shock, you know? But I know Mr. Burnett's car wouldn't have been here because I always had to bring it around front at ten o'clock in the morning so he could make it to the racetrack over in Illinois by noon. Ms. Virginia's car was probably here because she hardly ever leaves the house."

"How about Griffin's car?" Marco asked.

Guy swirled the contents of his beer can. "I think it was here."

Marco glanced around the garage. "Which one is his?"

The driver nodded toward a black Mercedes E Class in the next bay. "That one."

"Do I have it right that Griffin lives above the garage?" Marco asked.

"Yeah." Guy pointed up. "My apartment is right overhead. His is at the other end."

Marco nodded toward a door in the side wall. "Does that lead to both apartments?"

"Just mine. His door is at the opposite end." Guy pointed straight down the row. "You can see it from here."

"What about Juanita's car?" Marco asked.

Guy crushed the beer can in his hand. "Don't remember."

I wrote: *Eye avoidance again, and no hesitation at all in answering about Juanita. He knows something!*

A movement at the back of the garage caught my eye. I zeroed in on the baseboard and saw a brown mouse scurry along the wall. With a smothered yelp, I pulled my feet up and hugged my knees. Not that I feared a tiny, furry rodent with teeth that could chew through aluminum siding, but there was that one time I opened a drawer in Mom's kitchen and . . .

"You okay?" Marco asked.

When I realized he was talking to me, I

said without turning my head, "Just keeping my eyes on a mouse."

"We get a lot of them here," Guy said. "Happens when you live in a woodsy area."

"Didn't having a cat around help?" I asked, watching the mouse stop to nibble something on the floor. Brazen creature. Didn't he know he'd been spotted?

"You mean Charity?" Guy asked. "She wasn't allowed outside the house. I've got traps set back there, so if you hear a snap, he's dead."

"Pleasant." Noticing that Marco was now drumming his fingers on his knee, I held up my pen. "Ready." Mouse or no mouse, feet going numb or not.

"What does Juanita drive?" Marco asked.

"A red Porsche," Guy said.

I glanced down the long row of bays but didn't see the car.

"Man, it's lightning fast," Guy said, suddenly animated. "An awesome machine." He seemed most comfortable when the talk turned to vehicles.

"I'd think a red Porsche would be pretty easy to keep track of," Marco commented.

The chauffeur shrugged. "Sometimes I get so caught up in fixing my cycle that I don't pay attention."

I wrote: *Double-check Juanita's alibi.*

"Did you see anyone visit your employer on Monday morning?" Marco asked.

"Not in the morning," Guy said. "I did see the English lady's car outside around lunchtime when I stopped to eat."

"What kind of car would that be?" I asked.

"A red and white MINI Cooper."

Grace's new car was a white MINI Cooper with red trim.

"You know what everyone here is saying about the English lady, right?" Guy asked us. "That she murdered Mrs. Constance so she could get her hands on the money."

"That's untrue!" I said. It made me furious to hear my friend slandered. "First of all, the English lady has a name. It's Grace Bingham. And if you knew Grace as well as I do, you wouldn't believe that gossip for a minute."

"Doesn't matter what I believe," Guy said. "That's up to her judge."

"Her judge? Are you kidding me?" I asked. "She hasn't been charged with anything. Where are you getting this nonsense?"

"Hey, don't get angry with me," Guy said. "I'm just telling you what I heard Mr. Griffin say — that the cops have already decided that the English lady did it."

Marco must have sensed that I was on the verge of losing it, possibly by what I'd just

written in all caps: *GRACE DID NOT DO IT!!*
He put his arm around my shoulders and said quietly, "Sure you don't want to take Guy up on that beer?"

I drew in a calming breath and let it out. "No. I'm okay." Except for the tingling in my feet. I wondered if I would be able to stand.

Marco patted my shoulder, then withdrew his arm and returned to his questioning. "All right, Guy, when you saw the MINI Cooper in the driveway, where were the other family members?"

Guy tossed the beer can into a wastebasket. "You're asking too much of me, man. I see these cars coming and going all the time."

"If I were to tell you that it wasn't Grace Bingham who pushed Mrs. Constance, but was someone living on the estate," Marco said, "who would be the first person that came to mind?"

"No one," he said, suddenly angry. "You shouldn't ask me questions like that, man."

"Why?"

"It just ain't right, is all."

"Are you afraid of what might happen to you?" Marco asked.

"No," he said, rocking back in his chair, "that ain't it at all."

156

Marco leaned forward, turning up the intensity. "You can speak honestly, Guy. You don't need to worry about being fired anymore."

"Luce?" I heard a man call.

Guy jumped up, suddenly alert, as a man came around the corner into the bay. "Yes, Mr. Griffin?"

So this was Constance's beloved grandson. He certainly wasn't what I had expected. Griffin Newport had the dashing good looks of a college professor straight out of a Hollywood movie. He had thick, wavy brown hair that appeared finger-combed away from his face, a square jaw, broad forehead, and lively brown eyes magnified by stylish, wire-rimmed glasses. He was wearing a brown tweed jacket over an open-necked white shirt, blue jeans, and brown loafers.

Seeing us, he stopped short and said with a smile, "I'm sorry. I didn't know anyone was here."

I untucked my feet and realized I'd lost feeling in them.

"Did you need something, Mr. Griffin?" Guy asked, smoothing his hair down against his forehead. I wrote: *Griffin makes Guy Luce nervous. Is that how the chauffeur acts around the other family members?*

"It can wait," Griffin said, eyeing us curiously.

Marco got up and extended his hand. "Marco Salvare. This is my fiancée, Abby Knight."

"Griffin Newport," he said amiably.

I reached my hand as far as I could without standing, forcing Griffin to take three steps forward. "Nice to meet you," I said.

If he noticed anything unusual, he didn't show it. "Luce, enjoy your company. I'll talk to you later."

"Would you have a few minutes to speak with us?" Marco asked. "We're private investigators."

"Oh?" Griffin asked curiously. "Investigating what?"

Had everyone forgotten what had just happened? "Your grandmother's death," I said.

"For whom are you investigating?" Griffin asked, his eyes drifting to my breasts.

"Attorney David Hammond," Marco replied, crossing his arms over his chest and fixing him with a stare that said, *Eyes over here, dude.*

"Attorney David Hammond would be representing whom?" Griffin asked smoothly.

"Grace Bingham," Marco said. "Your grandmother's friend."

He arched his right eyebrow and said in a droll voice, "*That* remains to be seen."

There was no way I could let him get away with disparaging Grace. "Excuse me, but Grace is the one who *found* your grandmother and tried to get help for her."

Griffin gazed at me as though I were a small, delusional child who needed a pat on the head. "I'm sure you believe so, but would you mind explaining why you're conducting this private investigation? Has this Bingham woman been charged with a crime?"

"We're just trying to make sure that doesn't happen," Marco said evenly. "We'll keep our questions brief."

"I truly wish I could accommodate you," Griffin said, "but my lawyer insists neither I nor my employees discuss the matter with anyone. Anyway, so nice to have made your acquaintance." He shook hands with Marco, nodded at me, then gave Guy a pointed look and strode through the garage to his Benz. A minute later, he backed out and took off up the driveway.

"I guess I shouldn't have talked to you," the chauffeur said, looking distressed.

"Technically," Marco said, "you're not

Griffin's employee. It wouldn't apply to you."

"I'd better get back to my packing," Guy said, walking backward. "I've only got the truck for another two hours."

"Where are you moving to?" I asked.

"My parents' house in town," Guy said, "until I find a new job."

Marco handed him his business card. "Abby is right, Guy. You were employed by Mrs. Newport, not by Griffin. You can make up your own mind who to talk to. So if you remember anything more about Monday morning, will you let me know?"

Guy flipped the card over a few times, as though considering Marco's request, then tucked it in his shirt pocket. "I'll keep that in mind. See you over at your bar."

"Ready?" Marco asked me, seeing as how I hadn't moved from the chair.

"A hand, please?"

Once Marco pulled me up and the feeling had returned to my feet, we walked some distance from the open bay to talk. "Did you notice how edgy Guy got when you questioned him about Griffin?" I said.

"I caught that, but it could be that Guy's being cautious because he's angling to stay on here."

"Did you also catch Griffin referring to

Guy as his employee?" I asked.

"I have a feeling Griffin said that for our benefit. He doesn't want Guy talking to us."

"Doesn't that make you wonder why?"

"You bet it does. Let's see who's home."

Hearing footsteps, I turned to see a thick-waisted woman with short, steel-gray curls coming up a path from the back of the property. She was wearing a long-sleeved blue denim work shirt, khakis with dirt-stained knees, rubber-soled, brown slip-on shoes, and a no-nonsense expression. Over one arm, she carried a flat basket filled with greens and she had a blue-handled trowel in her hand. In the distance I could see a shrub hedge of some sort that appeared to function as a fence. I was guessing it enclosed their garden.

"Unless Constance Newport had a gardener, I'm guessing she's the housekeeper," Marco said.

The woman trudged along the flagstone path with a purpose, like a steam engine heading for the station. She crossed through a small courtyard filled with rosebushes and fenced in by a two-foot-tall brick wall, placed the trowel in a bucket by the wide, cement stoop, removed her shoes, and stepped inside the house through the back door.

"I'll bet that's the way Grace got into the house," I said.

"One way to find out," Marco said.

"Wait. I'll get my bouquet. She looks like the kind that needs a little softening up first."

I hurried to the car and retrieved my flowers; then we headed up the path that took us to the back door.

I was so tempted to stop along the way — the dozen or so rosebushes in the courtyard had budded out because of the warm spring days we'd had, and I was dying to see if I could identify them — but Marco was already rapping on the door.

The woman with the steel-gray curls answered the knock. She had heavy jowls and two chins, with dirt smudges on both of them. "Can I help you?"

"Are you Mrs. Dunbar?" I asked.

She glanced from me to the flowers to Marco, keeping one hand on the door as though ready to slam it in our faces should we prove to be a threat. "Yes."

"These are for you." I held out the bouquet. "I'm Abby Knight. I own Bloomers Flower Shop. This is my fiancé, Marco Salvare."

"Daisy Dunbar," she said, seeming bewildered as she finally accepted the gift.

"We know this is a sad time for you," I said. "We wanted to let you know how sorry we are for the tragic loss of your employer. We thought the flowers might brighten up your kitchen."

Clutching the bouquet against her, the housekeeper burst into tears and fled back inside the house, where I could hear her wailing at the top of her lungs.

Not the reaction I was expecting.

I motioned for Marco to follow me, and proceeded through a mudroom that was about the size of my apartment bathroom and into the kitchen. The distraught housekeeper was leaning against the kitchen counter in front of the sink, sobbing uncontrollably.

"There, there," I said, patting her back. "I know losing someone you care for is tough. Why don't you sit down at the table and I'll get you a glass of water?"

Sniffling hard, she managed to say, "I need to — wash up. I'm all — dirty from the garden and — dare not mess up the kitchen. Mrs. Connie — can't stand an untidy kitchen."

That set her off on another noisy crying jag, bending over at the waist as though in physical pain. I glanced at Marco and he raised his eyebrows as if to say, *You're a woman. Make her stop.*

Channeling my mom, I took the house-keeper's arm and guided her toward an old-fashioned round oak table in a sunny window bay. "Sit here," I said, pulling out one of the white chairs. "I'll get you a glass of water."

As she sank onto the chair, weeping wildly, I spotted a coffee mug upended in a dish drainer on the black granite counter-top and ran water into it. When I placed it in front of Mrs. Dunbar, she pulled a tissue from her pants pocket and wiped her eyes, smearing a big streak of dirt across her cheek.

"Thank you," she said in a raspy voice, then drank thirstily from the mug before digging for another tissue. "That was so kind of you to bring me flowers. It isn't often people remember the help. And just out of the goodness of your heart, too."

"We're glad to do it," I said, giving Marco a nod to take it from there.

Prince Charming went right into action. He leaned forward to give her one of his soulful gazes. "We need to ask you for a favor, Mrs. Dunbar."

Sniffling, she managed to give him a trembling smile. "You can call me Daisy."

Well, of course he could. He was Marco

the Magnificent.

"I'm a private investigator," he said. "Abby and I are here to gather some information for David Hammond, Grace Bingham's attorney."

Mrs. Dunbar paused, the new tissue halfway to her eyes. "Why?"

"It's part of Mr. Hammond's standard practice," Marco said in his usual calm, confident manner. "Nothing to be alarmed about. I just want to get the details right."

"So it's all legal-like?" she asked. "I won't get into trouble for talking to you?"

"I can assure you that it's perfectly legal for me to ask you questions," Marco said smoothly.

That seemed to put the housekeeper at ease, so I casually took out a notepad and pen and got ready to write.

"I'd like you to tell me what you remember about Monday morning," Marco said.

Mrs. Dunbar thought for a moment. "It started out like most mornings. I put on the coffee and made the batter for buckwheat pancakes, then went out to the mailbox to get the newspaper. Miss Connie always reads it at breakfast. I mean, she used to read it. . . ."

Mrs. Dunbar pressed the tissue into the corners of each eye to blot fresh tears.

"While she was eating, I went to the laundry room to sort clothing, and when I came back to the kitchen, I saw her through the kitchen window walking toward the garage."

"Was that a normal activity?" Marco asked.

"For Mondays it was," the housekeeper said. "That was her manicure day."

"When you saw her heading toward the garage, were you aware that she had canceled her manicure?" Marco asked.

"When she came back from the garage, I figured she'd changed her mind about going."

"Did that seem odd?" Marco asked.

"Miss Connie was always making spur-of-the-moment decisions."

"How long was she out in the garage?" Marco asked.

Mrs. Dunbar stopped sniffling to think. "Fifteen minutes or so."

"Are you sure it was that long?" Marco asked.

"Yes, sir. I was peeling carrots and potatoes for vegetable soup while she was out there and that takes about fifteen minutes."

"You've timed it?" I asked.

"I make that vegetable soup every day, miss. I know how long it takes."

That seemed like a long time to tell Guy

he wasn't needed. I put a star beside the note.

"What did Mrs. Connie do after she came back from the garage?" Marco asked.

"I couldn't say, sir. I was busy tending to my normal duties."

"When did you see her next?" Marco asked.

"When Mrs. Connie came down at noon for a meal in the dining room."

"Was that the last time you saw her?" Marco asked.

"No, sir. I saw her before I went out to the garden." The housekeeper's chin began to quiver. "She was going all around the house looking for her cat."

"Would that be Charity?" I asked.

Mrs. Dunbar nodded, then burst into tears once again. "She loved that cat so much!" she wailed, rocking back and forth in her chair, her work-roughened hands covering her face. I'd never heard anyone cry that loudly. Didn't her throat hurt?

I leaned over to say to Marco, "Didn't Grace tell us that the general consensus was that Charity got out when the paramedics arrived?"

Marco took my notepad and flipped through the pages, while I tried humming to myself to block out the sound. He handed the notepad back and pointed out what I'd written when we'd talked to Grace: *Family thinks cat got out when EMTs arrived. Juanita believes cat hit by car. Heard tires screech.*

"Maybe the family didn't know the cat had gotten out," Marco said.

"If Constance Newport loved that cat enough to leave her millions, she'd be asking everyone in the house to help find her. That's what I'd do."

"Mrs. Dunbar?" Marco said, but the woman was too distressed to hear him.

I spotted a box of tissues on top of the refrigerator and jumped up to get it. "Here you go," I said loudly, stuffing a tissue into her hand.

When at last she'd calmed down, Marco said, "Did Mrs. Connie find the cat?"

"I don't know," the housekeeper said through loud sniffles. "When I came back in from the garden, Mrs. Bingham . . . Mrs. Bingham —"

Back to wailing.

My head was starting to throb. I glanced at Marco and rubbed my temples. He nodded. "Mrs. Dunbar — Daisy — would it be better if we came back later?" he asked.

She was unable to speak because of the waterworks.

"May I get you more water?" I asked, then

mimed it in case she couldn't hear me.

She shook her head.

Okay then, a tranquilizer dart? Funny mushrooms?

Mental note: Carry earplugs.

My cell phone rang. I pulled it out of my purse, checked the screen, saw Jillian's name, and let it go to voice mail. Marco gave me a questioning glance, so I shook my head, letting him know it was nothing.

Finally, Mrs. Dunbar got up to throw away her used tissues and splash water on her face. When she returned she said, "I'm sorry. I just can't believe that Mrs. Connie is . . ."

"We understand," Marco said, as she plucked a fresh tissue from the box. "Take your time, and when you feel up to it, I'd like you to tell us what you remember when you returned to the house."

She wiped beneath her eyes. "The first thing I saw was Mrs. Bingham using the kitchen phone to call the police. That's when I heard her say" — Mrs. Dunbar's lip joined her chin in a quivering duet — "that Mrs. Connie . . ." At that, she burst into a new round of sobs.

"I'm sorry if this is painful, Mrs. Dunbar," Marco said at full volume. "We'll do our best to keep this short so you can get on with your day. Is that okay?"

My phone beeped and vibrated to let me know I had a text message. I checked the screen and saw it was from Jillian.

"Excuse me for a moment," I said. "I need to take this." There was a first — I was actually glad for my cousin's interruption. I hurried across the kitchen and stepped outside the back door.

Then I read her message: *Help! Emergency! Mayday!*

Really, Jillian? I dialed her phone number and when she answered, said, "I hope you know I'm right in the middle of —"

"Abby, shut up and listen. I'm being held captive. You've got to help me."

# CHAPTER ELEVEN

"You're a captive? Is it a hostage situation? Hold on, Jillian. I'll call the Chicago police."

"Abby! Shut up! I'm in Nordstrom's security office."

"Does Nordstrom's security know you're a captive? Are they aware of what's happening?"

She huffed with exasperation. "Would you listen, please? They're the ones holding me. Well, actually just the chief at this point. I need you to verify that I didn't steal the flowers."

"Wait. What?"

"Just verify that you own Bloomers and that you gave me the flowers. Oh, and he'll need your driver's license number and credit card information."

"Are you crazy? I'm not giving out that infor—"

"Okay, here's Bob."

"Jillian, wait!"

I heard her whispering to someone; then a male voice said, "Miss Knight? Abigail Knight?"

"Yes, sir."

"This is Robert Dooley, chief of security. Would you verify your identity?"

"If I have to. Will you tell me why I need to?"

"We caught your cousin with four pairs of shoes in her bag, along with a bouquet of flowers."

Dear God.

In the background I heard Jillian say, "If you'd put the shoe department with the designer clothing, I wouldn't have needed to carry four pairs to the third floor."

"Okay," I said with a sigh. "I own Bloomers Flower Shop in New Chapel, Indiana. I gave my cousin Jillian a bouquet of flowers to take with her today, and if you're going to charge her with anything, then Jillian needs to talk to an attorney now."

"Yeah, I know that," Bob said, "but she asked for you."

Lucky, lucky me. "Then let me assure you that what may seem like a shoplifting situation is actually a fluke. She probably has an ear infection or a tumor or something, because this isn't like my cousin at all. I can say honestly that Jillian Knight Osborne is trustworthy to a fault, not that being trustworthy is a fau— Well, never mind. But believe me, she's not a shoplifter."

"You don't need to convince me. We know Jillian." He let out a long sigh. "We know her very well."

"I'm confused. Why are you holding her?"

"She couldn't prove where she bought the flowers. The guard who saw her stuffing shoes in her bag thought she might have stolen the bouquet. The Flower Cart in the mall uses the same kind of clear plastic wrap."

"A lot of florists use clear plastic wrap," I said.

"Look, as long as you swear she got the flowers from you, I'll let her go, okay?"

"Then you don't need my driver's license number or credit card information?"

"*Nah.* I'm handing the phone back to your cousin now."

"Here, Bob," I heard Jillian say. "The bouquet was for you, anyway." Then to me she said quietly, "That wasn't so bad, was it? Okay, buh-bye now. Talk to you later. Oh, and Abs? I'll need some more flowers." The line went dead.

Was this karmic punishment for hitting the cat?

I returned to the kitchen and sat down beside Marco. He had made notes in my absence, so I read over them. He'd written that Mrs. Dunbar was seventy-one-years old, had worked for the Newports for thirty-one years, and had no family. She'd lost her husband twenty years ago and her only child, a son, died in a car crash after graduating from college.

"Are you planning to stay on as housekeeper?" Marco asked her.

"God willing," she said, making the sign of the cross. "I don't have much money tucked away and I can't afford to retire, so I hope the family will keep me on."

"I'm sure they'll want you," I said. "Someone has to run this big house, right?"

She pressed her hands together in prayer. "From your lips to God's ear. This job has been my salvation."

Seeing her eyes fill up with tears, I braced myself for more wails. My headache had just begun to subside, too.

"Were you aware that Grace Bingham was coming to visit Mrs. Connie on Monday?" Marco asked.

I gave him a grateful smile for changing the subject. He quirked one corner of his mouth to let me know he understood.

Mrs. Dunbar shook her head. "No, sir.

I'm not told of such things unless I'm needed for something."

"Have you seen Mrs. Bingham here before today?" Marco asked.

"Oh, yes. Mrs. Connie has entertained the English lady on many occasions."

"Would you say they're good friends?" I asked.

She shrugged. "I couldn't say, miss. I'm not privy to Mrs. Connie's thoughts."

"Did Mrs. Connie seem agitated about anything besides her missing cat?" Marco asked.

Mrs. Dunbar thought for a moment. "She did seem a bit on the snappish side after she talked to Mrs. Juanita."

That was new information. "When did she talk to Juanita?" I asked.

"During breakfast. I could hear them arguing all the way back in the laundry room." She paused, considering. "Come to think of it, they were at it again later, too, during lunch."

"What were they arguing about?" Marco asked.

"I never listen in on private conversations, sir," Mrs. Dunbar said, shaking her chins.

"So you have no idea what their argument was about?" I asked. Seriously, who could resist listening to an argument?

"No, miss, I don't." She began brushing invisible crumbs from the table into her palm. It seemed to give her somewhere to look other than at me. I made a note of her reaction and put a star beside it.

"Did the two women argue often?" Marco asked.

"I wouldn't say often. They seemed to go out of their way to be polite to each other."

"Are you sure you didn't hear any of their argument?" I asked. "It might be helpful."

Mrs. Dunbar shook her head but she didn't meet my eyes. I put another star beside my previous note.

"Is Mrs. Connie's daughter living here?" Marco asked.

"Yes, sir, that would be Ms. Virginia," the housekeeper said.

"Has she always lived here?" Marco asked.

"No, sir. She moved back home from Chicago after her divorce. That was about five years ago."

"How does Virginia get along with her sister-in-law?" Marco asked.

Mrs. Dunbar shook her head slowly. "Ms. Virginia and Mrs. Juanita don't get along at all. They avoid each other."

"Why don't they get along?" I asked.

"I couldn't say." She hesitated. "I can offer an opinion, though."

"That'll work," I said.

"There's a big difference in their ages," Mrs. Dunbar said, "and in their personalities."

"How would you describe Juanita's personality?" Marco asked.

"On the prickly side." Mrs. Dunbar smiled at some inner thought, shaking her head as though amused. "Mrs. Connie refers to Mrs. Juanita as the spoiled brat. That was one of the few things Ms. Virginia and her mother agreed upon."

Apparently, the housekeeper *did* listen in on conversations.

"Where was Juanita when you went out to the garden?" Marco asked.

"I don't know, sir. I expect she was still in the house." She was back to sweeping away more of those invisible crumbs.

"Who else was in the house when you went out to the garden?" Marco asked.

"As far as I know, it was just the three: Mrs. Juanita, Mrs. Connie, and Ms. Virginia."

"Was Virginia present during lunch?" Marco asked.

"Just for a bit, sir. Then she went up to her studio, as usual. We don't disturb her once she's there."

"You mentioned that Juanita was one of

the few subjects Virginia and her mother agreed upon. Did mother and daughter not get along, then?" Marco asked.

"Oh, my, not at all," Mrs. Dunbar said with a scowl. "Mrs. Connie was extremely unhappy when Ms. Virginia lived on a commune, and she sure didn't like it when Ms. Virginia took up with that professor, either."

"Why was that?" Marco asked.

"Mrs. Connie had her reasons, but I wouldn't know what they were, sir."

"Can you tell us anything about the professor?" I asked.

"Only a little," the housekeeper said. "His name is Francis Ta . . . Oh, phooey. It starts with a T. Taylor? No, Talbot. That was it. Francis Talbot. Ms. Virginia met him when she worked for the Art Institute in Chicago. He's some kind of art expert, from what I gathered. He came out to the house once to have dinner with the family and see Mrs. Connie's collection of Victorian art. That's how I got a look at him. I could tell by the way she acted that Mrs. Connie was impressed with him. But then later I heard her tell Ms. Virginia only a fool would fall in love with a man like that."

Nope. Never listened in on conversations.

"What was her objection to the professor?" I asked.

The housekeeper shrugged. "I wouldn't know, miss."

"Is Virginia still seeing Talbot?" Marco asked.

"You'd have to ask her that, sir. I'm not privy to Ms. Virginia's personal life."

"What can you tell us about Mrs. Connie's son?"

"I can tell you that Mr. Burnett has always been kind to me, but I hear he can be a bit forward with the ladies — a skirt-chaser, if you get my meaning."

I wrote *lecher* beside Burnsy's name.

Marco was on the verge of asking another question, but surprisingly, the housekeeper wasn't finished.

"I know Mrs. Connie wasn't happy at all when Mr. Burnett decided to retire, but why should he work when his mother was providing every creature comfort a body could want? It wasn't my place to say anything, but I have to tell you, sir, that I believe she did wrong by her children."

"It sounds like you've thought a lot about this," Marco said.

"I've watched those kids go from being young adults to middle-aged," Mrs. Dunbar said, "and I've seen their motivation fade right away. Mrs. Connie took away any desire to do for themselves; then, when she didn't like it anymore, she punished them for it."

"How did she punish them?" Marco asked.

"She changed her will," Mrs. Dunbar said.

"Were you present when the will was read?"

"Yes, sir." She shook her head. "Wasn't a pleasant time, no, sir."

"Did Mrs. Connie's children seem surprised by the will or did they seem to know what was coming?"

Mrs. Dunbar said carefully, "If they knew what she'd done ahead of time, they were mighty good actors, because they seemed shocked when the attorney read it."

"Were you surprised that Mrs. Connie left you all her silver?" I asked.

"No, miss," Mrs. Dunbar said, two spots of color darkening her cheeks. "Mrs. Connie told me what she was planning to do for me. She said it would help me in my old age."

"How long ago did this conversation take place?" Marco asked.

"Maybe a month ago."

"What prompted her to tell you about it?"

"I really couldn't tell you, sir," she responded.

"So out of the blue, she came up and said,

'Oh, by the way, I'm leaving you my silver?' " I asked.

Mrs. Dunbar began to sweep up those crumbs again. "I might have expressed some concern about my retirement. I expect telling me about the silver was her way of assuring me that I'd be provided for."

"It was a generous gift," I said.

"Yes, miss," she said, keeping her gaze lowered.

"Probably worth thousands of dollars," I added.

"I'm sure it is," she said, twisting around to see the clock on the wall behind her.

Why did she seem reticent to acknowledge the silver? Was she embarrassed — or afraid we'd think it was a good motive for murder?

"We're almost done," Marco said. "Just a few more questions. Do you know where Griffin was when you came back from the garden?"

Mrs. Dunbar smiled, as though Griffin held a warm spot in her heart. "He was in his apartment, working, as usual. He writes articles about the Victorian era, you know. He's quite an expert on the subject. Of course, he's been surrounded by all the collectibles since he was a boy, so it's no surprise, really."

"Where are the collectibles kept?" Marco asked.

"The most valuable paintings hang in the main hall and front parlor," she said. "There's also a temperature-controlled storage room where the paintings are kept that aren't on display. The art gets rotated every three months. The Victorian furniture is scattered all over the house, and the antiquities are displayed down in the lower level. Mr. Burnett Sr. set up quite a nice museum down there."

"What do you mean by antiquities?" Marco asked.

"Well, mostly they're a collection of ancient weaponry, suits of armor, that sort of thing."

An art gallery, a basement museum with suits of armor, ten bathrooms . . . I couldn't imagine living in such a house. I really wanted to take a tour, but didn't see how I could make that happen.

"Did I understand that there's an art appraiser here today?" Marco asked.

"Yes, sir," Mrs. Dunbar said. "That would be Mr. Ventury. Mrs. Connie's lawyer sent him over first thing this morning, just as Mrs. Connie wanted. He's in the storage room at present."

"Do you have any knowledge as to why

Connie wanted an appraiser to view her art collection immediately after her death?" Marco asked.

"No, sir. You'd have to ask the attorney."

"I'd like to talk to Mr. Ventury," Marco said. "Can you take me to him?"

A loud bang made me jump. It was followed by a bellow, and then rapid footsteps. Moments later, a portly man in a gray suit rushed into the kitchen, holding on to the fringe of gray hair above his ears as though he was about to tear it out. "Forgeries!" he cried. "They're forgeries!"

Without batting an eye, Mrs. Dunbar said, "Here's the appraiser now, sir."

# CHAPTER TWELVE

"Call the police!" the little man cried, flapping his arms as he circled the kitchen, as though unsure of which way to turn. "This is a disaster! A catastrophe of immense proportions!"

As Mrs. Dunbar jumped up to make the call, a tall, lean, middle-aged woman in a white artist's smock, long navy-and-orange plaid peasant skirt, and heavy Birkenstocks came striding into the kitchen. When she saw all of us, she stopped in surprise.

"What in heaven's name is going on here? Mrs. D., would you kindly tell me who these two strangers are?"

"Investigators, Ms. Virginia," the housekeeper whispered, still on the phone.

So this was Virginia Newport-Lynch, the attic artist. Someone should really have clued her in on that long gray braid. They'd gone out of fashion in the early seventies along with that voluminous peasant skirt.

"Marco Salvare," my intended said, showing her his ID. "And my fiancée, Abby Knight."

"Owner of Bloomers Flower Shop," I said, then remembered I had on the yellow T-shirt with the Bloomers logo on the back. I turned so she could see it.

"Why are you here?" she asked, looking down at me as though she'd scraped me off the bottom of her thick sandals. She talked through her nose, giving her voice the nasal quality of a honking goose. And Grace was right. Virginia did have a rat-shaped face. *Oops.* Right about those chin whiskers, too.

Hearing the appraiser wheeze, Virginia took hold of his arms. "Mr. Ventury, please calm down. You're hyperventilating. Whatever is the matter?"

"It's a cataclysm!" he cried. "A cataclysm, I tell you!"

"What's a cataclysm?" Virginia asked.

"Those priceless paintings," he cried. "They're . . . they're . . ." He shook his head, unable to finish.

"They're what?" Virginia demanded, her fingers tightening on his suit.

"They're *fakes!*" he squeaked.

Virginia's face drained of color; then she collapsed onto the floor in a dead faint.

As Marco and I jumped up to help, Ven-

185

tury backed away like a frightened puppy, his eyes as round as Frisbees, muttering, "Oh my, oh my, did I do that?"

Mrs. Dunbar was still on the phone, now describing the developing situation to the dispatch operator, and Marco was trying to find Virginia's pulse, so I ran to the sink to get a wet cloth and place it across her forehead.

"She's got a steady beat," Marco said, as the housekeeper hung up the phone.

"I'll fetch the smelling salts," Mrs. Dunbar said. "I always keep them on hand for her."

While she scurried out of the room, Marco left Virginia in my care so he could corner the panic-stricken appraiser, who was now circling the kitchen table. "Mr. Ventury, why don't you show me the art collection? I'm a private investigator. I'd like to help."

"Oh, thank you, sir," the man said, as though he was only too happy to have the burden of his discovery lifted off his shoulders. "Follow me."

Just as Virginia came around, Mrs. Dunbar ran into the kitchen and knelt at the woman's side. She abandoned the smelling salts and took the cold cloth from me to stroke across Virginia's forehead, crooning to her as though she were a baby. "Mrs. D. is here,

186

dearie. Mrs. D. is here."

With Virginia in capable hands, I jumped up and hurried through the nearest door in pursuit of my fiancé. It was one way to get a house tour.

Outside the kitchen, I found myself in a dining room of magnificent proportions. It reminded me of pictures I'd seen of castle dining halls, with a long, polished mahogany table running down the middle and — I stopped to count them — twenty chairs! In the center of the table, on a white lace runner, was an elaborate silver candelabra. I wondered if that was one of Mrs. Dunbar's pieces now.

A massive Victorian breakfront was set against one wall, and an eight-foot-long antique sidebar on the opposite wall. On the sidebar sat the most exquisite silver tea set I'd ever seen. I wondered if Grace had seen it on her visits here. A beautiful Oriental carpet in black, tan, beige, and rose covered the center of the black marble floor, with silk wallpaper in a deep rose color on the walls. But the dining room wasn't where I wanted to be. I'd chosen the wrong door.

I exited the dining room through a wide arched opening onto a center hallway that stretched up through the house to a huge foyer, where I could see a massive wooden door all the way at the far end. Along the walls of the hallway were large oil paintings, each lit by a spotlight above the frame. As I walked up the hallway admiring the paintings, I noticed that half of them were paintings of young Victorian women in virtuous poses — reading a book under a tree, in prayer beside a bed, knitting in a chair, penning a letter — and the other half of the paintings were of flower arrangements.

I heard Marco's voice and followed it around a corner into a grand hall that connected the east and west sides of the house. I saw an open door and peered into a large room filled with framed canvases leaning in stacks against three of the walls. Marco and the harried appraiser were standing in front of a painting where Ventury, a magnifying glass in his hand, was showing Marco something in the lower right corner.

"Do you see this?" Ventury asked. "To someone less experienced, it would go unnoticed, but I caught it immediately. Immediately!"

"What am I looking at?" Marco asked, as I peered around him for a peek.

"See the tail of the Y in the artist's signature? The curlicue is facing in the wrong direction. That tells me it's not authentic. Not authentic at all. Otherwise, it's a perfect reproduction. I've only seen three people in the course of my career who have the skills to produce a forgery this good, and one of them is elderly and quite ill. Quite ill! Besides, he always operated on the East Coast. Never in the Midwest."

"Who are the others?" Marco asked, as I dug the notebook out of my purse.

"Eamon MacShane and John J. Cole," Ventury said. "They've been in prison several times, but I believe both are out on parole now. They were big in the Chicago area at one time. Very big. Very big, indeed. Oh my." He clucked his tongue as he glanced around at all the artwork. "This is a calamity."

"Are all of the paintings in here forgeries?" I asked.

"So far, just two series," Ventury said. "I started with that stack behind the door. They're part of a Victorian art collection called the Love series."

"The Love series?" Marco glanced at me. "And I thought Victorians were prudes."

Ventury paused, as though thrown off track. "These are quite respectable, Mr. Salvare. Victorian women were always depicted in idealized form. Here, let me show you."

He pushed the door shut and picked up the first framed painting. "This one is entitled *Declaration of Love.* As you can see, this young woman appears quite virginal. Note the upswept hairdo and Romanesque profile, typical of this style of art."

He leaned the painting against his legs so we could see the one behind it. "This one is called *Eternal Love.* Notice the similarity in themes. Next we have *Young Love,* then *Everlasting Love,* and finally *Maternal Love.*"

The paintings of angelic-looking young women in Victorian dress were completely new to me, yet for some reason the titles rang a bell. Where had I heard of them? My experience with fine art was limited to one semester of art history in college.

"Now, this is the Beauty series," Ventury explained, moving down, "a collection based on another popular Victorian subject — nature, and in this case, flowers. First we have *Splendid Beauty,* portraying a single red amaryllis, then *Magnificent Beauty* portraying —"

"A white calla," I said. At Ventury's quizzical look I said, "I'm a florist."

"Yes," he said politely, then cleared his throat. "Next we have *Lasting Beauty.*" Ventury glanced at me, waiting. Marco's mouth quirked up at the corners. He was trying not to laugh.

"Statice," I said, "which fits perfectly with

the title *Lasting Beauty.* Statice lasts a long time. Callas are magnificent. So the names of the paintings match the flowers."

"This is odd," Ventury said, rummaging through the row of paintings. "*Delicate Beauty* is missing. I can't imagine that Mrs. Newport wouldn't have it in her collection. How very odd."

"Are all the paintings in here forgeries?" Marco asked again.

"So far just the oils in these two rows are. Heaven only knows to whom the thief sold the originals. It could be a buyer in Venezuela or an art museum in Switzerland. There's just no way of knowing what has happened to them. No way. Oh my, what a tragedy."

"They're just flower paintings," Marco pointed out astutely.

"Not *just,* Mr. Salvare," Ventury said, warming up to his subject. "These are very special flower paintings done in a style similar to Raphael's, who as I'm sure you know, was a famed artist of the Italian Renaissance. You've heard of John William Waterhouse, haven't you? One of the most prominent pre-Raphaelite artists?"

"Not too familiar with him," Marco said.

Ventury went on. "Do you see how colorful and detailed each blossom is? One could

191

say it's almost photographic. And typical of this style, the painter sought to transform Realism with typological symbolism."

Marco stood with one finger pressed against his lip, as though seriously contemplating Ventury's lecture. I was seriously contemplating a spot on my cuff until I realized Ventury had stopped. I inquired, "Are there more in the collection?"

"Just four paintings," he said. "Why do you ask?"

"There's a painting down the hallway that looks like *Splendid Beauty*," I said.

Ventury waved my words away with a flutter of his hand. "Impossible."

"Well, okay," I said, "but the red amaryllis in that painting looks just like this one."

"You must be mistaken," Ventury said, growing agitated. "It wouldn't happen. This is the forged copy, so an identical one would have to be the original, and a skilled art thief such as the one we're dealing with wouldn't leave the original behind."

"If you say so," I said with a shrug. "But isn't it strange that both red amaryllises are sitting in a tulip-shaped clear glass vase on a round table covered by a blue tablecloth?"

Ventury gazed at me for several moments, as though having trouble processing the information. "You'd better show me."

I led him back to the central hall and stopped before the canvas in question.

Ventury gasped. "I can't believe it. I simply can't! Yet here it is right in front of my eyes."

Shaking his head in disbelief, he examined the frame, then pulled out his magnifier and leaned close to study the canvas. Then he stepped back as though the flower had bit him. "How is it possible?"

"How is what possible?" Marco asked. I could tell he was growing weary of the man's mutterings.

"This one's a forgery, too!"

The appraiser took off up the hallway and rounded the corner, vanishing from our sight, so Marco and I started after him. Back inside the storage room, we found Ventury dragging *Splendid Beauty* closer to the light. He laid it on the floor, then got down on his hands and knees to examine it.

"I've never seen anything like it. Two forgeries of the same painting? Extremely unlikely. Forgers with this level of skill are usually so careful. But this! Oh my."

"Even if they weren't both forgeries," I said, "shouldn't Constance Newport have noticed she had two identical paintings?"

"That would depend on many factors," he said. "Did she know her inventory? Did she personally rotate the artwork? Did she know how to check for forgeries? Would she even suspect there were any?"

"The bigger question," Marco said to me quietly, letting the appraiser continue his work, "is how the thief got so many paintings out and the copies in without setting off the alarm and being discovered."

"Do they have an alarm system?"

"There's a keypad by the door in the kitchen," Marco replied.

How he managed to notice small details like that mystified me. All I'd noticed were the awesome granite countertops and pot of rosemary on the kitchen windowsill. "Someone would have had to give the thief the code."

"Or let him in. Either way it has to be an inside job. A thief, even an exceptionally clever one, wouldn't be able to move about the house carrying large framed canvases, bringing them in and out the back door time after time without ever being caught. And he couldn't have gotten them all out at once. It'll be tricky to find the inside man because I'm sure everyone in the house knows the alarm code, but we'll need to ask anyway. It's the logical place to start."

"*We'll* need to ask? We're going to investigate this, too?"

"We have to operate under the assumption that it ties in with the murder. It's too coincidental to think otherwise."

That was going to make our job a lot more complicated.

Hearing soft footsteps, I turned to see Virginia enter the room. Her face was the color of putty and she seemed drained of energy, but that didn't prevent her from giving us a disdainful glance as she walked over to the appraiser. "The police have arrived, Mr. Ventury. They'd like to talk to you."

He straightened with a groan, rubbing his lower back. "And I would like to talk to them, too. Indeed I would. This situation gets odder and odder."

"What do you mean?" she asked.

"Not only do you have forgeries of these valuable art pieces, Ms. Newport-Lynch," he replied, growing more agitated as he spoke, "but this particular thief had the effrontery to make identical copies of the *same* original. The very same one! I've never seen anything like it. Never, never, never."

"Do calm yourself, Mr. Ventury," Virginia said, putting her arm through his. She turned him so their backs were to us, then dropped her voice to a whisper so we couldn't hear. Lucky for us, Ventury didn't understand the need for discretion.

"Am I positive about the forgeries?" the little man exclaimed, puffing up his chest. "My dear lady, I would stake my reputation on it. Yes, indeed, I would. Now, lead the way, please. I still have much work to do here."

When Virginia turned, her face was no longer pale. Her cheeks now had spots of color in them, no doubt from embarrassment. That didn't prevent her from putting her nose in the air as she passed us.

"Ms. Lynch," Marco said, "excuse me, but would you mind telling me who sets the alarm system at night?"

"My mother always saw to it," she said. "And it's *Newport*-Lynch."

"Pardon me. Was the alarm set every night?" he asked.

Virginia heaved an annoyed sigh, as though Marco were taking up her valuable time. "I can't imagine why it wouldn't be."

"Who sets it now?" he asked.

"I would assume my brother does because he's usually the last one to get home in the evenings."

"Who else besides your brother knows the code?" Marco asked.

"All of us have it."

"Including the chauffeur and housekeeper?"

"Mrs. D. knows it, of course, but not Luce. Now, if you'll excuse me —"

Two cops strolled in, one of them Marco's buddy Sergeant Sean Reilly, a tall, brown-haired, brown-eyed, nice-looking forty-year-old who had trained under my dad. The other cop was a rookie, judging by the pimples on his forehead and the way he swaggered, trying to make himself look like a veteran.

Reilly gave Marco a friendly nod, but merely shook his head when he saw me.

"I'm not responsible for anything that happened here," I told him.

"Yeah, right," Reilly said.

"I was just bringing Mr. Ventury to you, Officer," Virginia said.

"No problem," Reilly said. "We can talk to him here. We wanted to get a look at the paintings anyway."

"I'll leave Mr. Ventury with you, then," Virginia said, and moved back as the cops stepped forward.

"Mr. Ventury is it?" Reilly asked, taking out his notepad. "Is that V-E-N-T-U-R-Y?"

"Yes, that's right," the rotund little man said.

"First name?" Reilly asked.

"Millard."

"Come again?" Reilly asked, cupping his

197

hand around his ear.

"*Mill*-ard," the appraiser said with a raised voice, clearly thinking Reilly was hard of hearing. "M-I-L-L-A-R-D."

I had to press my face into Marco's shoulder so I wouldn't giggle.

"Thank you. I can hear just fine," Reilly said. "Would you explain how you know these paintings are forgeries?"

"I'd be delighted." The appraiser cleared his throat, preparing to repeat his lecture.

Seeing that Virginia had managed to slip away, I tugged on Marco's sleeve, and he followed me into the hallway. "No sense sticking around for a rehash," I said. "Let's go pester Virginia."

"Why do you want to pester her?"

"I don't like her attitude."

"Come on, Abby, you know an investigator has to be objective."

"And you, my sexy Prince Charming, know I operate on gut feelings. And my gut is telling me that Virginia Newport-Lynch is hiding something, or is afraid of something, or is ashamed of something, and is using her snooty attitude to keep us at bay. We have questions in need of answers, Marco. Let's go get her."

I would have started up the hallway, but Marco caught my arm. "Virginia just came out of a dead faint, Abby. That's not some-one who'll appreciate being grilled. You're likely to get attitude but not much co-operation."

"Want to bet whether I can get her to co-operate?"

"It wouldn't be fair. I'd win. Let's come back to her later when she'll be more recep-tive."

"She might not be around later, Marco. Seize the day."

He gave me a kiss on the nose. "You're cute when you're feisty. If you're that determined, go for it, babe."

"Aren't you coming with me?"

"I want to stick around until Ventury is finished so I can talk to Sean. He might have an update on the murder investiga-tion."

"Okay, I'll be back. Oh, wait, Marco. What's the wager?"

"Whoever wins it calls it." He gave me a devilish smile. "And anything goes."

I felt the tingles start in my toes and work their way upward. "You've got a deal, Sal-vare." With a happy sigh, I turned to go, the repayment possibilities stretching out before me like the menu board at a day spa.

"Abby," Marco said, "if you do get Virginia to talk, see if she knows how much Constance was involved with the art collection."

"Take the *if* out of it. I'll be back with answers. Be prepared to lose the bet, bucko."

Marco stepped inside the storage room, so I took off in the direction I thought Virginia had gone. Once again I made a wrong turn, but this time I ended up outside what appeared to be a library. I walked around the walnut-paneled room, my head tilted back to see all the leather-bound tomes filling the floor-to-ceiling bookshelves.

The library had a rolling ladder to provide access to the top shelves, a fireplace on the outside wall, and a marble inlaid table in the middle surrounded by leather club chairs. It was the perfect room in which to curl up with a good book. But as tempting as that sounded, I had more important things to do.

As I continued up the hallway I heard murmuring in the next room. I tiptoed closer and paused outside the door to listen as a panicky voice said in a hushed tone, "We should have gotten rid of it right away."

Rid of what?

"I can't now," the same voice whispered. "It's too late."

I glanced behind me to be sure no one was watching, then inched closer to hear more, but all I heard was the soft rustle of fabric. Were two people in the room or was someone talking on the phone? I got down on my hands and knees but just as I was about to peer around the corner, the wooden floor creaked beneath me.

A jolt of fear shot through my body. I backed away from the doorway, then got to my feet and pretended to study a painting on the wall, while my heart pounded so hard, my chest hurt. When no one appeared after a few minutes, I guessed I'd over-reacted and sidled near the doorway again. But after waiting several long minutes and hearing only silence, I looked around the doorframe.

I was gazing into a formal sitting room, with an elegant pale green watered silk sofa and four striped club chairs framing a white marble fireplace. But whoever had been there was gone.

Spotting French doors on the opposite side of the room, I hurried around the grouping of furniture and opened one side of the double doors. I glanced up and down the brick walkway outside, and then stepped outside for a better look, but no one was in sight. Frustrated, I shut the door and returned to the hallway.

Hearing a rapid *tap-tap-tap* of high heels, I

turned to see a shapely young woman with long raven hair coming toward me from the direction of the front door. She had beautiful olive skin, glossy black hair, and more curves than I did. She wore a fitted hot-pink leather jacket, a black-and-red scarf around her neck, a black miniskirt, tight black leggings, and thigh-high black patent boots with spike heels. A glossy pink tote bag was slung over her shoulder, completing the fashionable ensemble. Lottie would be drooling over all that pink.

The woman's musky perfume reached me before she did, making my nose twitch with a building sneeze. "Can I help you?" she asked.

"I'm Abby Knight and I'm here with my fiancé, a private investigator. And you are?"

"I am," she said haughtily, "Juanita Maria Elena Garcia." Then, as though she suddenly remembered, she added, "Newport."

*Ah.* The daughter-in-law. I turned my head and sneezed hard. Not a fan of musk.

When I glanced back, Juanita was looking me up and down and wrinkling her nose, clearly finding my blue jeans, sneakers, and bright yellow T-shirt lacking panache. With a slight Hispanic accent she said, "What does your fiancé's business have to do with us?"

I didn't want Juanita to think she was intimidating me; at the same time, I couldn't make her too angry or I'd never get any information from her, so I tamped down my inclination to give her a flip remark and instead said in a friendly voice, "He's investigating Mrs. Newport's death. We just finished interviewing the art appraiser and now he's discussing the case with the police."

Putting a hand clad with diamond rings and long hot-pink fingernails on her hip, Juanita said, "Who put your fiancé in charge of the investigation? He's not a cop."

"Attorney David Hammond did."

That stumped her for a second. "Well, then, who put Mr. Hammond in charge?"

"Grace Bingham hired him."

I sneezed again just as Virginia came out of a door farther up the hallway, looking anything but in a mood to be cooperative. "Did I hear you say Grace Bingham hired you? The woman who murdered my mother?"

As the pair glared at me, waiting for an answer, I drew myself up — it doesn't make me taller; it only makes me bolder — and said, "Since there's not one shred of evidence that proves Grace murdered your mother, I'd be careful with those allegations."

"Or what?" Juanita asked, lifting her chin defiantly.

She would ask that. Well, two could play the intimidation game. I said casually, "Or I'll tell the cops that you're withholding information."

"What?" Juanita asked, then glanced at Virginia in wide-eyed disbelief — a little too wide-eyed to be sincere. "That's ridiculous."

"You have a lot of nerve barging into this house making wild accusations," Virginia snapped.

"I happen to know that neither one of you told the detectives everything you know about Monday morning." I gave each woman a meaningful glance. It helped that no one ever told everything at the first interview.

"Don't be ridiculous," Juanita said. "Why would you make such a ridiculous charge?"

"Want me to prove it?" I asked.

Juanita opened her mouth but quickly closed it again, as though she'd lost her nerve, while Virginia said with a smirk, "Please enlighten us."

I turned toward Juanita. "What did you and Constance argue about the morning she died?"

She stared at me wide-eyed, as if to say, *How did you know that?*

Seeing her response, or lack thereof, Virginia swung toward her sister-in-law. "Is that true? You had words with Mother on Monday morning?"

"I don't know what this crazy woman is talking about," Juanita said halfheartedly.

"The argument happened at breakfast," I said, "and another one before lunch. That makes two arguments that day."

Virginia stepped closer, causing Juanita to move back. "Is that why Mother was so upset when I came downstairs for lunch? What happened, Nita? Weren't you discreet enough that morning?"

*Discreet* was an interesting word choice. It suggested devious activities and sneaky schemes. I tucked that tidbit away for future use.

Juanita tossed her glossy black mane. "I will not waste my time defending something so ridiculous." With that, she turned and *tap-tap*ped away, muttering under her breath, "Totally ridiculous."

That must have been her word for the day. Interesting that she hadn't denied the accusation.

Virginia shifted her ferocious gaze to me. "How did you know about their arguments?"

"Investigators never reveal their sources."

She moved closer. "Was it from the English woman?"

"That has no bearing on the matter," I said, backing up a step.

"It was Bingham, wasn't it?" Virginia placed her hands on her hips. "How sad that you'd take the word of a murderer as the truth."

*Deep breath, Abby.* I filled my lungs and let out the air to the count of ten. "Whether you like it or not, Grace Bingham was your mother's friend and confidant. What Constance confided to her could help find the killer."

Virginia grew silent. Then she peered at me curiously. "What else did Grace tell you about Monday morning?"

If she wanted to know, she'd have to play nice. I had a bet riding on it.

# CHAPTER THIRTEEN

"Shall we sit down?" I indicated the green sofa in the sitting room behind me.

Virginia folded her arms. "I think not."

"Suit yourself." I walked into the room and took a seat on the sofa across from the white marble fireplace. It was important to establish who was in charge.

Virginia sighed loudly, then followed suit, folding her long skirt around her legs as she sat as far away from me as she could. She took a breath and let it out in a huff. "What else did Grace Bingham tell you about Juanita's argument with my mother?"

"I never said my source was Grace. And that's all I know about your sister-in-law, although her having two arguments with your mom on the day she died is quite a bit to know. It puts her in the category of strong suspect."

I watched how that news played out on Virginia's face. She was mulling it over, trying to decide if that would help her situation or not.

"What did your *source* tell you about me?" she asked.

"I'd be happy to share that with you if you'll tell me about the art collection."

"It would take an entire semester to enlighten you," she said snidely.

"How about this? Who was responsible for rotating the paintings in and out of storage?"

Virginia began picking at a thread on the sofa's rolled armrest, probably to show me how bored she was. "My mother saw to that."

"Is there a catalog of the paintings?"

"I believe so, but I can't say for sure."

I wasn't buying it. For a woman who claimed to be a painter, she had to have taken some interest in the collection. "Was your mom very hands-on with the collection?"

"If by hands-on you mean involved, then yes, out of respect for my father. Truth be told, she preferred books."

"Was your brother interested in the art collection?"

"Burnett," she said drily, "was interested in gambling and women, in that order."

"Women, plural?"

"You do know he's on his fourth wife, do you not?"

My cell phone chirped to signal an incoming text message. I hated to ignore it, but I felt that if I let up on Virginia, I'd never have this opportunity again. "What about your nephew?"

"What about my nephew?"

She was being difficult, and I was losing patience, but I wasn't going to let her know that. "Was Griffin interested in the art collection? Does he know anything about the inventory, storage, rotation —"

"Griffin is a scholar. He writes and studies all things Victorian. Period."

Another chirp of my phone distracted me momentarily. What were we talking about? Oh, right. Her nephew. "Does Griffin have a girlfriend at present?"

She huffed impatiently. "You really should speak with Griffin if you want to know about his private life."

"Is that a yes?" My cell phone chirped, throwing me off once again. "Okay, so that leaves Juanita. Did she take any interest in the artwork?"

"The only interest Nita had in the art was how much of the proceeds would have been hers and how many designer outfits she could buy with it."

Hearing another cell phone chirp, Virginia said, "Would you please either answer that damned thing or shut it off?"

I pulled out my phone and saw a text from Jillian that read, *Call me at once. Seriously!*

"I'll just take this out in the hallway," I said.

Virginia scowled.

I walked to the doorway and phoned Jillian. "What's the problem now?"

"Abs, is it true about the cat burglar stealing art from the Newports?"

"There is no way you could know that already," I whispered.

"You don't have a clue about the Internet, do you, Abs? Listen, I know exactly what to do to find the thief. First —"

"You are not a detective."

"Who needs to be a detective? I learned from the master cat burglar."

"Right. And that would be?"

"Cary Grant. He starred with Grace Kelly in *To Catch a Thief,* remember?"

"No. I'm not the Grace Kelly buff. You are."

Jillian had to be one of the world's foremost experts on Grace Kelly. Beginning at the age of fourteen, she had believed a prince would come along and sweep her away to a kingdom like Monaco. In preparation, she had watched every movie in which Grace had played a role, and even had outfits made that looked like Grace's.

"So after a big jewel heist where Cary becomes the prime suspect," she continued, "he —"

Virginia sighed loudly.

"Jillian, I don't have time for this. I'm in the middle of an interview."

"Okay, I'll text you instructions." The line went dead.

I shoved my phone into my pocket and hurried back to the sofa, trying to remember where I'd left off. "Sorry. Were you in the sitting room about ten minutes ago having a conversation with someone?"

"I'm not sure what business it would be of yours, but no. Perhaps you heard my sister-in-law. Why don't you go track her down and ask her?" Virginia glanced at her watch. "Would you be good enough to wrap this up? I really have much more important things to do."

"Do you know what happened to your mother's cat?"

"No, and I don't care, either. I detested the little pest."

I had a sudden vision of Grace replying with those exact words when asked one day about Simon's stay with us. "Did Charity get into a lot of trouble?"

"I wouldn't know. I rarely saw her. No, it was that my mother preferred Charity to her own flesh and blood. Now the silly animal is worth gads of money that should have been ours, and what does she do but scuttle off somewhere or get herself run over."

This woman was all sympathy. "I detect a hefty dose of jealousy."

"No, darling, not jealousy. Hatred."

"For the cat or your mother?"

She raised an eyebrow. "If you're insinuating that I pushed my mother because of my feelings about the cat, you will have to expand your suspect list to include everyone in this household. That's all I have to say. Now it's time for you to keep your part of the bargain."

I'd gotten a lot more information than I'd expected, and unfortunately for Virginia, she was about to get a lot less. "What I heard about you from my source was that you and your mother didn't see eye to eye on most things."

She gave me a look of incredulity. "You kept me here for that? Well, excuse me, but are there a mother and daughter anywhere who agree on everything?"

She had me there.

"I'd find a new source if I were you." She rose majestically and adjusted her braid to fall over one shoulder. Obviously she thought she had the upper hand.

"That's not all I heard, Virginia."

She folded her arms, tapping the toe of her shoe on the rug. I could tell she resented me calling her by her first name. "All right. What else?"

Having run out of things that Grace had told me, I started in on what I'd gleaned from Mrs. Dunbar. "I also heard that your mother wasn't happy that you got a divorce."

Virginia examined her fingernails. "Please. That's not news."

"And that she liked your professor boyfriend until he came out to the house for dinner; then she changed her mind."

"My mother was given to her whims."

This woman wasn't going to budge an inch. I'd have to resort to a method I'd used on Jillian, who was as gullible as they came. "Yes, but *why* your mother changed her mind is another story."

"What do you mean?" Virginia asked immediately, narrowing her eyes at me.

"You tell me." I gave her a pointed look, as though I really had something on her.

Virginia contemplated me for a moment,

then smiled, revealing teeth so white and even they had to be veneers. "You, my dear, are on a fishing expedition. Well, I hate to break it to you, but my mother didn't need a reason to change her mind."

"I'm not so sure about that."

She sat down on the sofa and rested one arm on the back. "Do tell."

"Your mother had a reason. Otherwise she wouldn't have warned you about getting more involved with the professor. You went against her advice and did so anyway."

She shrugged. "So?"

Okay, I had nowhere to go with that. I'd have to wing it. "So . . . you paid the price, didn't you?"

Virginia threw back her head and honked in what I guessed was supposed to be hysterical laughter. Having finished with the hilarity, she hardened her expression. "You," she said, leaning closer so she could point her index finger at me, "are a pathetic excuse for an investigator. So let me be absolutely clear on this once and for all. I did not push my mother for any reason. Do you understand? I did not cause her death in any way, shape, or form, so you'd best fish in other waters." Then she got up and marched out, her salt-and-pepper braid flapping against her back.

"I never said I was the investigator," I called. And Virginia was no Jillian.

Well, that was humiliating.

On the other hand, I'd won my bet with Marco.

I waited until I was sure she was gone; then I dashed out of the sitting room and up the hallway toward the back of the house, hoping I wouldn't get lost again. My head was spinning with so much new information that when I came to another hallway, I couldn't remember if I should take it or not. So I kept going and suddenly found myself at a dead end in a part of the house I'd never seen before.

I retraced my steps, then started off in a different direction, realized I was really lost, turned a corner, and plowed straight into Marco's arms. "Oh! Marco!" I said breathlessly, glancing around to be sure no one could hear me. "I'm so glad you found me."

"You took the words right out of my mouth. Where were you?"

"I'm not sure. But guess what? I won the bet! And just wait till you hear what I learned. First of all, I was walking up the hallway toward the front door when I overheard someone — I think it was a woman — in the sitting room —"

"Take a breath, Fireball," he said, placing

his hands on my shoulders. "There's no rush."

"Okay, hold on." I drew in a few lungfuls of air, then started again. "So I heard this unknown woman in the sitting room say in a whisper, 'We should have gotten rid of it right away. Now it's too late.' And by her tone of voice, I could tell she was in a panic.

"I tried to find out who was talking, but the floor creaked when I moved closer, and then the whispering stopped. So whoever was in the room must have been startled by the noise and slipped out. When I finally looked into the room, no one was there, but she could have left through French doors on the outside wall."

"Are you're sure you heard a female?"

"Ninety-one, ninety-two percent sure."

"Did anyone answer her?"

"Nope. No answer. She must have been using a phone."

Marco rubbed his jaw. " 'We should have gotten rid of it. Now it's too late.' " He thought for a moment. "She couldn't have been talking about the murder weapon because there wasn't one. What I'd like to do is get downstairs to take a look at the murder scene and see if anything clicks. Reilly said he was heading that way. Maybe he'll let us have a peek."

"Here's my theory, Marco. The woman was Virginia and she was in a panic because of the discovery of the duplicate paintings. What I heard was her chiding her accomplice."

"I'm following so far."

"Virginia is the only one in the family who was present when Mr. Ventury discussed the duplicate forgery. And remember how secretive she got, turning him away to question him so we couldn't hear? Then when the cops arrived, she took off like a woman on a mission. I think she ran off to call her partner in crime so they could decide their next move. Then she heard someone outside the room and slipped out the French doors."

"So how does this fit in with our investigation?"

"If Constance found out about the theft and threatened to call the police, exposing not only her accomplice, who's obviously the forger, but also Virginia, it's a classic motive for murder. We know Virginia was in the house at the time of the murder. She could have shoved her mother down the stairs and then hid in the attic waiting for someone to find the body."

"I'm impressed, Abby."

"Don't be yet. After I went in search of the voice on the phone, I came back to the main hallway and saw Juanita coming toward me from the direction of the front door. So it could have been her in the sitting room, too."

"How close is the sitting room to the front door?"

"I'm not sure. Maybe sixty feet or so. And it gets more interesting. As I was talking to Juanita, Virginia came out of the next room, which is even closer to the front door."

"Does it also have access to the outside?"

"I didn't check."

"Let's take a walk and find out."

"But there's a hitch," I said, trying to match his long stride. "Juanita wouldn't have known about the paintings, so she would have been referring to something else that should've been gotten rid of."

"Unless Virginia had just told her about the forgeries."

"True. And both of them gave me a hard time about investigating on Grace's behalf until I told them I knew that they had withheld important information from the police." I giggled. "You should have seen how fast they changed their attitudes."

"You told them they withheld information?"

At the shocked look on Marco's face, my jubilation dissolved. "Was that wrong?"

He held out his hand to give me a high five. "Awesome work, Sunshine."

"Thank you! And wait, there's more. Under my intense grilling, Juanita got very nervous and defensive about the arguments she and Constance had on Monday."

"Under your intense grilling."

"I can grill as intensely as the next florist, Salvare. Virginia apparently hadn't heard that Juanita and Constance had argued, so she turned on Juanita, insinuating that Juanita's indiscretion had caused the arguments."

"What indiscretion?"

"Virginia didn't offer an explanation and Juanita didn't ask for one, but I have a hunch I know. Here are Virginia's exact words. 'Is that why Mother was so upset when I came downstairs? What happened, Nita? Weren't you discreet enough that morning?' Now, what does that say to you?"

"That you have great recall."

I pointed to my head. "Mind always running, remember?" I stopped a few feet from the sitting room doorway. "Here's where I was standing when I heard the voice coming from inside this room. Now look over there. See the French doors? They lead out onto a brick walkway that runs alongside the house. Okay, let's move up to the next room."

We walked to the next doorway and looked inside. A glossy black grand piano filled at least a third of the room, with half a dozen upholstered chairs facing it.

"The music room," Marco said.

"This is the room I saw Virginia come out of when I was talking to Juanita." I pointed to a pair of French doors. "See? She could have left the sitting room and come back inside through those doors."

Marco walked over to the doors and tried one of the handles. The door opened without a sound. "Very possible," he said, returning to my side. "Now we need to know whether any of this is relevant to our investigation. I'm still waiting for your hunch."

"My hunch is that Juanita is having an affair with the art thief. Think about Virginia's words, Marco. What does, 'Weren't you being discreet' mean to you?"

"That she was rash, reckless, careless . . . let's see, blundering —"

"Okay, stop showing off your vocabulary. You're turning me on. You'll have to experience Juanita for yourself to understand."

"Are you sure that'll work? After all that intense grilling Juanita may be a shell of her former self."

"Make fun, Salvare. But just to remind you, I won our bet, so don't push your luck."

"I'll push whatever you want me to push," he said, putting his arms around me, stirring up all kinds of delicious sensations. There was nowhere in the world I'd rather be than in Marco's arms.

"Have I ever told you what an adorable investigator you make?" Marco murmured in my ear.

"Yeah, well, tell that to Virginia."

"Here's a better idea. Tell me how Juanita and her lover could be involved in the art theft and get away with it if Virginia knows about them."

"I haven't worked that part out yet, Marco, and with your arms around me, I probably won't. So here's an even better idea. Kiss me. Hard. Right here, right now."

He pulled me closer, his clean scent enveloping me in desire. "Are you calling this kiss your winnings?"

"It's only the beginning, Salvare."

With Marco's lips on mine, I totally forgot where we were. His taste and touch were so familiar, yet, at the same time, still had the power to send thrills throughout my body. If anything, I was more in love with him now than ever before.

We were on the verge of looking for a handy broom closet when I heard the telltale tap of high heels on marble and glanced around to see the rash, reckless, blundering Juanita stepping swiftly in our direction. Her pink fingernails were tapping the keypad of her cell phone as she texted, so she hadn't noticed us yet.

"Here comes your opportunity," I whispered to Marco.

Juanita's quickstep turned to a sashay when she glanced up and spotted Marco standing a mere few feet away. I had become invisible apparently because she seemed not to see me as she sidled up to my groom-to-be and said in a low purr, "Helloooo. Are you the private eye?"

"Marco Salvare," he said.

She held out a hand that glittered with diamonds. "I'm *HwanEEtaaaa.*" She let it roll off her tongue, her lips curving into a seductive smile.

He took her hand. "Nice to meet you. This is my fiancée, Abby Knight."

"We have already met," she said, refusing to glance my way. "Is there anything I can do for you, Marco?" She trilled the *r* in his name as she batted thick black eyelashes at him.

There was something Juanita could do for

*me* — back off. Now.

Never one to pass up an opportunity to question a suspect, Marco said, "Actually, there is. What's the easiest way to get outside? I want to see the grounds."

She tucked her arm in his and, slanting her eyes, said, "The easiest way is to come with me."

"Let's go, then. Abby, you might find Sergeant Reilly still in the basement. Be good while I'm gone."

"Ditto."

*Be good.* Huh. Too broad to be effective.

I watched them head across the music room toward the French doors, then considered my options. I could shadow Marco and *HwanEEtaaaa,* or go to the car and call the flower shop to see how things were going. Or I could take Marco's hint to do more snooping. Okay, no to the first option — no matter how tempting. Marco was a person to be trusted even if Juanita wasn't. No to the second, too. If there was trouble, I would have gotten a call.

That left option three, so I turned and went toward the back of the house, where the sound of voices led me to the kitchen. There I found Mrs. Dunbar chopping tomatoes at the kitchen counter, while Reilly and his partner sat at the table dunking cookies in dainty teacups filled with a dark brew of either coffee or tea, obviously having finished scoping out the crime scene. Drat.

Spotting me, Reilly said, "There you are. Marco thought you got lost." He glanced at his partner and rolled his eyes. "Surprise, surprise."

"Shows you how wrong Marco can be," I said, strolling over to the table. "He thought you were in the basement. Or wait. Maybe he said the doghouse."

At his partner's snickers, Reilly said with a smug smile, "I *was* in the basement."

"And I wasn't lost." Well, this time anyway.

"Mrs. Connie didn't like the word *basement,*" Mrs. Dunbar said, bringing a plate of fudgy brownies to the table. "She said it was the lower level."

"Thank you, Mrs. D.," Reilly said with a smile, reaching for a dark chocolate square. How could he be on a nickname basis with her already?

"So, Sarge," I said, "are you going back down to the lower level?"

"Nope." He licked chocolate off his fingertips. Classy.

"May I go down for a quick look around?" I asked him, taking a cookie off the plate. "I promise I'll be careful."

"Nope. Crime scene unit isn't finished."

*Damn.*

"Will that be all you need, Sergeant?" Mrs. Dunbar asked. "I should see to the laundry."

"Before you go," I said to her, then realized my mouth was filled with the most heavenly oatmeal-raisin cookie I'd ever tasted. "Oh, wow, that's good!" I mumbled.

Those cookies could go toe-to-toe with Grace's oatmeal-raisin scones any day, not that I would tell Grace that.

"Thank you," she said, giving me a nervous smile. She didn't appear to be used to smiling.

"What I started to say was, would you mind answering a few more questions?"

Both Reilly and his junior partner stopped chewing. "Abby, what are you doing?" Reilly asked.

"Okay, Reilly, did you miss the part where I asked if she minded answering questions?"

He put down his brownie. "Are you getting smart with me?"

Pressing my fist playfully against his shoulder, I said, "Come on, Sarge, you know me better than that. How many cases have we worked on together?"

"Then show some respect, all right?"

"Sure. Sorry." Wow. Someone was touchy

today. Reilly used to enjoy our back-and-forth bantering. It was part of our special relationship.

"Mrs. Dunbar, do you recall hearing any unusual activity or noises late at night or early in the morning?" I asked.

"I've already asked that," Reilly said.

"Great," I said. "We can share notes."

Reilly gave me a scowl, which I interpreted to mean, *Continue.*

"Thank you," I said. "Mrs. Dunbar?"

"As I told the officers here, I've always been one to hear creaks and bumps in the night."

"So, no unusual noises in the last month or so?"

As though she suddenly noticed a smudge on the tabletop, she lifted the hem of her apron and started to polish the surface. "That's right."

Reilly and his partner grinned at each other and went back to eating. But I wasn't satisfied with her answer. It sounded like one of those avoidance maneuvers Marco had trained me to watch for. Maybe I needed to refine my question.

"Just to clarify," I said, "you stated that you're used to hearing creaks and bumps. What about beeps?"

She stopped polishing for a split second.

"Beeps?"

"Like the beeps of an alarm system being shut off," I said.

"Are you asking if I've *ever* heard beeps?" she asked.

"Let's narrow it down to the past week," I said.

She polished the same spot over and over, as though not aware of what she was doing. Finally, she said, "I really shouldn't tell tales out of school."

Oh, great. She liked to bake cookies and brownies and sprinkle her conversation with old sayings. I was dealing with the American version of Grace. "What does that mean exactly? You don't like to gossip?"

"That's right," she said. "Idle gossip is the devil's workshop."

I took it back. Grace would never mangle a quote. I followed Mrs. Dunbar to the sink. "I understand your dilemma, Mrs. D., but your information could help us find Mrs. Newport's killer."

She pursed her lips as she washed and dried a paring knife and put it into a drawer. Finally she said, "I suppose I've heard some beeps."

I knew from experience that whenever a person used the word *suppose,* they were admitting to something without actually saying so. "When do you suppose you heard them?"

She waited a long time before answering. "Early . . . Before the sun was up."

"Did you hear this happen on more than one occasion?"

"I suppose."

"After you heard the beeps, did you hear someone come in or leave the house?" I asked.

"Well," she said slowly, "maybe both."

Reilly swiveled to stare at her. "What was that? You heard someone come into the house?"

"Do you think it was the thief moving paintings in and out?" I asked, ignoring him.

She shrugged. "That wasn't the thought that crossed my mind."

She was being very cagey all of a sudden. "What thought crossed your mind?"

She wrung out the dishcloth and draped it over the sink partition. "That something else was going on."

My inner antennae were up and waving at me. I had a strong feeling I was about to get confirmation on what my gut had been telling me. "Like what?"

The housekeeper shrugged again. "Lust."

# CHAPTER FOURTEEN

"Wait, what?" Reilly asked, scooting his chair back. "You didn't mention any of this earlier."

Seeing the alarm on Mrs. Dunbar's face as he strode toward us, I turned to squint my eyes at him, telling him silently, *Don't scare her!* "Mrs. Dunbar, by lust, are you saying someone in this house was sneaking out for a tryst?"

With Reilly and me gazing at her expectantly, Mrs. Dunbar turned red in the face and beads of sweat popped out on her upper lip. "I — I never should have said that. I don't like to say anything bad about the family. It's not my place. Can I please do the laundry now?"

"You need to answer the question first, Mrs. Dunbar," Reilly said, reverting to formalities. "Who did you hear leave the house?"

"I don't know who," she said, wringing

her apron. "All I know is that someone was using the back door early in the mornings."

"How do you know that?" Reilly asked, flipping open his little notepad.

"M-my room is right next to the kitchen. I c-could hear the beeps when the alarm was turned off and the latch click when the door was opened."

"Can you be certain it wasn't someone removing paintings?" Reilly asked.

"N-no, sir, I can't be certain," she said nervously, still twisting her apron, "but sometimes a body just senses things."

"I get that, Mrs. D.," I said, "because I sense that you're basing your conclusion on something tangible, like a voice, a familiar footstep, a smell . . ."

At the word *smell,* the housekeeper shut her eyes and shook her head, setting her chins to trembling. "I don't remember."

Reilly and I exchanged glances. Mrs. Dunbar knew who it was — and so did I.

"If you have any information that could help with this investigation," Reilly said, "you need to let us know now. I mean, you need to let *me* know." He frowned at me as though his blunder was my fault.

She picked up the dishcloth and began wiping the kitchen counter, making tight little wet circles with it, her lips pressed firmly together.

"If we find out you withheld information," Reilly said, "you'll be charged with hampering our investigation. You don't want that to happen, do you?"

"Please, Mrs. D.," I said, as Reilly's young partner swaggered over to join us. "Work with us. The person you heard leaving the house could be involved with the art theft or the murder, or both. You'd be a big help if you could give us more information."

"It'll go much easier on you if you do," Junior added.

"I smelled perfume!" she blurted, then covered her mouth, as though she couldn't believe she'd let it out.

"Where?" Reilly asked, taking notes.

She shook her head.

"Mrs. Dunbar," Reilly said with a frown, "where?"

"Right here," she said. "When I came out of my room, I smelled perfume right here."

"Whose perfume?" I asked.

"I don't know," she said, and began wiping the counter again, her motions extremely agitated. "I didn't want to know. It wasn't my place."

"You don't have to protect anyone now, Mrs. Dunbar," Reilly said. "Your loyalty was to your employer. You don't owe these people anything."

"I can't," she cried, scrubbing viciously.

I took Reilly's arm and led him out of earshot. "Go easy on her," I whispered. "She wants to keep her job."

"She can't withhold information," he whispered back.

"Then let me handle her." I walked back to where she was now cleaning the stainless-steel sink with a scouring pad. "I understand your dilemma, Mrs. D., so let me make this easy. I know whose perfume you smelled."

Her head jerked around and she stared at me openmouthed.

"It was Juanita's," I said.

"I never said I smelled her perfume," she cried.

"You didn't have to. I was just with Juanita and Virginia, and I couldn't detect any perfume on Virginia, but I caught a whiff of Juanita's from the opposite end of the hall —"

I stopped.

If Juanita had been in the sitting room, I would have smelled that strong musky scent when I crossed the room to get to the French doors. But there was no perfume in the air. So the mystery whisperer must have been Virginia. Or . . . Mrs. Dunbar?

It couldn't have been the housekeeper.

She wouldn't have mentioned hearing beeps if she'd been the one to open the door. Plus, I didn't get any negative vibes from anything she'd said, only nervousness.

I did a mental head scratch, trying to sort out the information. If Virginia was talking to her accomplice on the phone, then she must have been the one to give him access to the house. Yet Mrs. Dunbar had smelled Juanita's distinctive perfume after hearing the beeps, so either Juanita was in on the theft with Virginia, or she was merely sneaking out to meet her lover.

Given Juanita's flirtatious behavior with Marco, my choice was obvious. She had a lover. It would also explain why Virginia hadn't seemed alarmed. However, it would make perfect sense that Constance Newport would be furious. Her daughter-in-law was cheating on her son.

Had Constance threatened to tell Burnsy? Had the two women argued a third time, after Mrs. Dunbar had gone to the garden, and it had ended with Constance's death?

"Is Abby right?" Reilly was saying to the distraught housekeeper when I tuned back in. "Did you smell Juanita's perfume?"

Mrs. Dunbar shrugged three times, sniffling loudly as she reached for a tissue from the box on top of the refrigerator.

"Answer yes or no," the junior partner said, trying to sound official.

She hesitated, then finally whispered, "Yes."

"Did you smell Juanita's perfume on the morning of the murder, too?" Reilly asked.

After blowing her nose, Mrs. Dunbar nodded again.

"Will you sign a statement to that effect?" Junior asked.

"A statement?" she cried. "Oh, I couldn't! Please don't tell them I said anything. I don't want to lose my job. I need my job." Pushing past us, she fled the kitchen, sobbing.

"Now look what you did," I said to both cops. "I was handling it just fine until you butted in."

"What *we* did?" Reilly sputtered. "Who's handling this investigation anyway? Wait. Where are you going?"

"To find Marco so I can get back to Bloomers. I've been away too long." I walked to the back door and opened it, pausing when I spotted the keypad. It was tan, the same color as the wall. How had Marco noticed it?

I walked through the courtyard and had to resist the temptation to check out the rosebushes, which were starting to bud.

234

Okay, where had Lolita taken my man?

To my left was the long, long garage; to my right, a grape arbor; and at the far back of the property, the hedge that surrounded the garden. I saw no sign of Marco and Juanita, but I did see Guy Luce. He'd finished loading his truck and was about to close it.

*Hmm.* Just what I needed, a potential eyewitness to all the sneaking going on. "Hey, Guy," I called, trotting toward him.

He pulled the metal rolling door down with a loud *thunk.* "Yeah?"

"Did you hear the news about Mrs. Newport's art collection?"

"No," he said, wiping sweat from his forehead with the back of his sleeve. "Something happen to it?"

"Some of her paintings were stolen and copies put in their places."

His eyes widened in surprise. "Are you sure? Because I don't understand how that could have happened. Someone is always here during the day, and the alarm is set at night."

"It did happen, Guy. The appraiser discovered the theft just now, and Mrs. Dunbar said that on a number of mornings this past month, she heard beeps, as though the system was being disarmed; then she heard the sound of the back door opening."

Guy pondered that for a moment. "So someone in the house must have disarmed the security system."

"That's what it looks like."

He put one foot on the bumper. "Wow. That'd be awful if one of Mrs. Constance's kids stole her art. Really awful." He shook his head. "You know, when the lawyer read that part in the will about Mrs. Constance wanting everything appraised right away, I was surprised, because it made it seem like she didn't trust her family. I guess she might have been right."

Gorgeous Guy had a brain after all. "Can you think of anyone in this family that Mrs. Constance didn't trust?"

He rolled up his shirt cuffs. "All I know is that she trusted me."

"Did she tell you that?"

"Sure did. She said, 'You're probably the only one around here I can trust, Luce.' "

"When was that?"

"Couple of weeks back."

"Set the stage for me."

"Set the stage?"

Okay, maybe I'd been too hasty on the brain judgment. "What were you doing when Mrs. Constance told you that?"

"Driving her to see her lawyer."

Now I was getting somewhere. "What was the appointment for?"

"I'm just her driver. I don't ask questions."

"I thought maybe she offered."

"Nope."

"Okay, think back to Monday morning. When Mrs. Constance came out to tell you she didn't need you, did she go straight back to her house?"

He scratched his ear. I was beginning to suspect ear mites. "Seems like I remember her going to the far end of the garage."

"To do what?"

"Probably to see Mr. Griffin. I wasn't really paying attention. I just went back to working on my Harley."

I was hitting a dead end with that line of questioning. "It would be really helpful to know if you've noticed any unusual activity in the past month, like unfamiliar cars or vans parked in the driveway, strange sounds during the night — that sort of thing."

He put his foot down and placed the other one on the bumper. "Can't say that I have, but I'm a pretty heavy sleeper."

My cell phone chirped, and as much as I wanted to ignore it, I was afraid it might be Lottie or Grace with news about her case. I opened the phone and saw a text message from Jillian: *If u want 2 find the cat brglar look 4 the person who's nrvus as a cat. LIKE THE MOVIE. It wrkd 4 Cary Grant. It can work 4 u.*

I texted back: *Putting phone on silent works even better.* I changed the settings, stowed the cell, and looked up at Guy. "Has anyone taken a car out early in the morning?"

He used his sleeve to wipe his forehead again. "Like I said, I'm a heavy sleeper."

"But living over the garage, even a heavy sleeper would be able to hear a garage-door motor grinding as the door rolled up, right?"

"I guess."

My gut told me he was telling the truth, yet something felt wrong. I looked around for inspiration and spotted Juanita's red Porsche in the third bay, which would be directly below Guy's apartment. "Are you positive you didn't hear Juanita take her car out early on any mornings in the past two weeks?"

He started to reach for his ear, then seemed to catch himself and stuffed his hand in his pocket. "Positive."

I was stumped. Could Mrs. Dunbar be wrong? Had she smelled Juanita's perfume because Juanita let someone *into* the house? Like the art thief? Would a professional thief risk moving art around that close to dawn?

"I need to get going," Guy said.

"Okay. Sorry for holding you up."

I noticed suddenly that both of Guy's ears were bright red. What would cause that? Not an itch certainly, because I'd only seen him scratch the right one. So unless he really did have ear mites, I was guessing that I had said something to cause that embarrassment. I went back over our conversation but couldn't come up with a reason.

Nervous as a cat?

Then a thought popped into my head. Guy was quite a hunk — no comparison with my hunk, of course, but definitely someone who would attract women. Was Juanita having an affair with *him?*

"Guy . . ." I began.

"You know," he said, "now that I think back on it, I do remember seeing something unusual. There were muddy shoeprints running along the driveway here going straight up to the back door."

*Way to change the topic, Guy.*

I heard a door close and turned to see Marco striding across the courtyard toward us.

"Hey, what's up?" he said to me, giving Guy a nod.

"Guy was just telling me about some muddy shoeprints he saw on the driveway heading toward the house." I took out my notepad and pen and turned back to Guy. "Can you give me a time frame?"

"Seems like I started seeing them about a month ago."

"When was the last time you saw them?" I asked.

He went to scratch his ear and I nearly grabbed his hand. "Maybe last week."

"Was there something unusual about the prints that made you notice them?" Marco asked.

"Yeah. They just seemed to start in the middle of the driveway, like someone drove halfway up to the garage, parked, then got out of the car and walked up to the back door. In muddy shoes. And this mud was caked, man. Like clay. Took a shovel to get rid of them."

"Do you think the prints came from someone living here?" Marco asked.

"Are you joking? People in this family drive straight into the garage. They don't leave their cars parked outside. And they wouldn't be caught dead with mud on their shoes."

"How many times have you seen the prints?" I asked.

"Like nine or ten times." He shrugged one shoulder. "It just seemed kind of strange that someone would get out of a car with mud on his shoes. Where had he been, you know?"

"Was there just one set of prints?" Marco asked Guy.

"One set."

"Man-sized or woman-sized?" Marco asked.

"Big man-sized." Guy raised one leg so I could see his yellow work boot. "Bigger than my shoes would make."

"Where did the prints start?" Marco asked.

Guy led us down the driveway about twenty yards. "Right around here."

What professional art thief would come to steal a painting with mud-caked shoes? It made no sense. I glanced at the surroundings. "The evergreens bordering the east side of the driveway are mulched," I said to Marco. "No mud there. And there's only grass on the other side."

"The only place we have dirt is in the garden," Guy said, "but that's all black loam. I'm telling you, the guy drove here with mud on his shoes."

"Were they going in just one direction?" Marco asked.

"Yep. From right here up the driveway and around to the back door."

"Wouldn't someone have seen those same prints inside the house?" I asked Marco.

"He probably removed his shoes," Marco said. Then to Guy, "Did you mention the shoe prints to anyone in the house?"

"Sure did. I told Mr. Griffin about them."

"How long ago?" Marco asked.

"Maybe a week ago."

"Did he seem concerned?"

"All he did was ask me to clean them up."

I could feel my cell phone vibrating against my hip. Did I dare not check?

After another round of vibrations, I answered quickly. "Hello?"

"Second tip," Jillian said. "You have to catch the cat burglar before he knows you're after him. That's from the movie, too."

My blood did a fast boil. "Listen to me, Jillian. If you bother me one more time, you'd better pray I don't catch you!" I ended the call and turned to see Marco and Guy staring at me.

"Sorry," I said. "Where were we?"

"I was just leaving." Guy started up the driveway, calling back, "Nice talking with you both."

"Ready to go?" Marco asked me.

"There's something else I wanted to ask Guy, but Jillian interrupted me and now I can't remember what it was."

"You can think on the way to town. I need to get back to the bar."

"Oh, wait, Marco. I just remembered." I took off after the chauffeur, calling, "Hey, Guy, hold up a minute."

He stopped and turned, but didn't look happy about it. "What?"

"You'd like to keep working here, right?" I asked, as Marco caught up with me.

"Well, sure," Guy said.

"Have you talked to anyone in the family about staying on?"

"Yeah."

"What were you told?" I asked.

"That I'd get a call when a decision was made," he said.

"Who did you talk to?" I asked.

"Ms. Virginia."

"If they haven't made a decision, why were you asked to move out? Why didn't they wait until they knew for sure so you wouldn't have to move twice?"

He started to answer, then stopped, scratched his ear, which I fully expected to start dripping blood at any second, and said, "I don't know the answer to that, but I do know that I need to get my boxes to my parents' house and return the truck by four o'clock."

"Sorry to keep you." As he climbed into

the cab of his truck, I said to Marco, "He knows more than he's saying."

"I suspect it's all about staying employed."

"And to stay employed, he has to protect someone in that family." I watched Guy drive past us. "I know who it is."

My cell phone vibrated. I was betting I knew who that was, too.

# CHAPTER FIFTEEN

"What now, Jillian?" I answered sharply, as we headed down the driveway toward Marco's car.

"This is the best tip yet, Abs. Cats don't like water. Try flicking a little water on each of the Newports and see who reacts. Voila! Your cat burglar."

"Seriously, Jillian, if I walked around the room flicking water, I would expect them all to react by sending me directly to jail or to a mental institution. This is not a movie set. This is a real-life crime scene, so stop it. I'm really turning off my phone now. Goodbye."

"What's wrong with Jillian now?" Marco asked.

"She heard about the art theft, so of course she thinks she can solve the case because she knows the movie *To Catch a Thief* by heart."

"You're supposed to flick water on

people?"

"It's really not worth going into."

"Good. So tell me who Guy's protecting."

"It's just a gut feeling, but I'll start with what I learned from Mrs. Dunbar while you were escorting Lolita around the grounds."

"You're doing that Lolita thing on purpose, aren't you?"

"Always trying to keep you on your toes, Salvare. Anyway, Mrs. D. said that on several occasions over the past month she heard someone deactivate the alarm and open the back door. This always happened very early in the morning, and she even heard it on the day of the murder. She wouldn't name any names, but she did say that when she came into the kitchen a short time later, she smelled perfume.

"So the conclusion I came to, after having been around the women who live in that house, including Mrs. Dunbar, is that Juanita is the little sneak because she's the only one of the three wearing perfume."

"The only one wearing it *today*." Marco opened the passenger side door for me. "Remember what I've said about jumping to conclusions?"

"So I shouldn't conclude that Juanita was panting over you?"

Marco grinned as he closed my door. Two

points for the redhead.

I waited until he was in the car, then said, "Guy told me that a few weeks ago, while on her way to see her lawyer, Constance told Guy that he was the only person she trusted. I'm guessing that was the day she had her will changed. Then I asked Guy if he'd heard anyone taking a car out of the garage early on any mornings in the past month, and he said no. But then he added that he wouldn't have heard it anyway because he's a heavy sleeper, which I didn't buy at all. Can you figure out why?"

"I'm sure you'll tell me."

"Did you notice that there isn't a finished ceiling in the garage? Think about how loud those garage-door motors are, Marco. And the bay where Juanita keeps her Porsche is right below his apartment. How could he not hear a door lifting?"

"I'm with you so far."

"And when I questioned Guy further about Juanita, his ears turned red. That was when it hit me that maybe he was telling the truth about not hearing the garage door open because Juanita hadn't used her car to meet her lover. She wouldn't need to if she were having an affair with someone on the estate."

Marco stopped for a red light. "You based

this on his ears turning red?"

"Do you remember our first conversation with Guy? How he carefully avoided answering questions about Juanita? And then Virginia's remark to her about her not being discreet? Then toss in Guy being asked to move out. Doesn't it add up? I think she's having an affair with Guy."

"Back up, Sunshine. I can buy your conclusion about Juanita having an affair, but you can't assume it's Guy. It could be Griffin. Yes, I know he's her stepson, but it happens. And there *is* the cost factor, Abby. They didn't receive the large inheritances they were expecting, so maybe they decided they couldn't afford him."

"Or maybe Burnsy found out about Juanita doing the tabletop tango with Gorgeous Guy and wanted him tossed out. The others might not have agreed, hence the delay on the decision."

"You realize that none of this matters unless we can tie Juanita's alleged affair to the murder. Let's go over everything at dinner. That'll give us time to process all the information."

"Speaking of information, what did you learn from Juanita, besides that she's self-absorbed and has terrible taste in perfume?"

"Remember Grace saying she thought that

248

Virginia had broken off her relationship with the art professor? Not so, according to Juanita. When I asked Juanita who she thought might be involved in the theft, she said I should check out Virginia's boyfriend. I asked who she meant by boyfriend, and she said the art professor."

"If that's true, Marco — and considering the source, it could go either way — then I'll bet that's who Virginia was talking to in the sitting room."

"I think it's time to find out more about Professor Francis Talbot."

"Did you learn anything useful from Reilly?"

"Nothing. They dusted for prints on all the forged artwork and the front and back doors, and that's about all I could get from him. Were you able to get a look at the murder scene?"

"Reilly wouldn't hear of it."

"I'm not too concerned about that. Ultimately, it'll come down to trapping someone in a lie."

Marco's cell phone rang. He glanced at the screen then handed it to me. "It's my brother. Would you take it? I'm trying to keep my blood pressure down."

I flipped open his phone. "Hey, Rafe, how's the bar business?"

I could barely make out what Marco's younger brother was saying. He was tending bar at Down the Hatch and even beyond the background noise, seemed to have a really bad connection. "Is Mar — com — ack soon?"

I stuck my finger in my other ear to block out the street sounds. "If you're wanting to know when we'll be back, we should be there in five minutes. Any messages?"

"Rep — tal — beer."

"Okay, I'll pass that along, Rafe. Ciao." Then I handed the phone back. "Rafe said something about beer."

"That was helpful." Marco slid the phone back into his shirt pocket.

"Do you think Rafe will be ready to take over managing the bar for you in September?"

"That's over four months from now. I hope Rafe has a handle on it by then. Any word from Grace or Lottie on how things are going at Bloomers?"

"Not a peep. Everything must be running smoothly."

Just to make sure, I pulled out my cell phone, turned it on, and saw that I had four messages, every single one from the flower shop. I dialed the shop and got Grace.

"We have something of a situation," Grace

said in her understated way. In the background I could hear a woman shrieking and a small dog barking. "Hurry, dear."

When I opened the yellow-frame door and stepped inside Bloomers, what I saw looked like something from a disaster movie. A wicker bench was lying on its side, a plant stand was upended, and potted lilies, hyacinths, tulips, and miniature roses lay tipped over onto the floor, their petals strewn about like confetti, with black soil everywhere. In the midst of this debacle stood Mrs. Dobbins, one of our regular customers, plump hands pressed against her heart, as though she expected it to stop at any moment, watching with a horrified expression as Lottie ran around the shop with a broom, trying to corner Mrs. Dobbins's barking Chihuahua, Booboo.

Customers who had fled to the coffee-and-tea parlor to escape the chaos were watching from the doorway, afraid to make a dash for the front door lest the incensed pooch turn on them. So naturally, when the dog saw me, he went straight for my ankles.

"Get behind me!" Lottie yelled, using the broom to stave off the dog so she could back me behind the cashier's counter.

"Booboo isn't usually like this," Mrs. Dobbins cried. "How do I make him stop?"

"Take off your coat, Mrs. Dobbins," Lottie yelled. "Get ready to toss it over Booboo."

Somehow Lottie managed to hold the frenetic canine down with the broom long enough for Booboo's jittery owner to gather him up in her green spring coat. Hugging the dog against her chest, Mrs. Dobbins apologized profusely, then turned and scuttled out of the shop.

Lottie leaned against the broom and wiped her brow. "What a day."

"What happened?" I asked, righting the overturned pots.

"That's what happened." She pointed to the top of the armoire, where Simon sat on his haunches calmly watching us. "That little fiend sprang out from behind a plant and pounced on Booboo, scaring the little yapper out of a year's growth." She shook her finger at Simon. "Yes, I'm talking about you! And stop your smirking."

Simon did indeed seem pleased with himself. "I'm so sorry, Lottie. There's a Chihuahua that lives across the hall from our apartment that Simon detests." I paused to greet customers filing past. "Hello. Nice to see you again. Thanks for coming in. Sorry about the mess. Please come back."

"You're gonna have to do something

about Simon, sweetie," Lottie said. "We can't let him scare off our customers or ruin our flowers."

I scooped dirt into a pot and pressed it firmly around the bulb end of the lily to secure it. "Maybe I can talk Marco into taking him back to his apartment for a few days. Where's Grace?"

"She's on the phone with our supplier, trying to have flowers overnighted. We got in seventy-five orders for the Newport funeral, and the viewing starts tomorrow at one o'clock."

"Seventy-five orders?" I could almost feel my bank account swelling even as panic set in. "It's going to be a late night, Lottie."

"We have enough stock on hand to do about forty arrangements if we work all evening. My boys are coming in after basketball practice to deliver the orders to the funeral parlor as we get them done. I'll also have them finish cleaning up this mess. Your niece Tara said she and a friend would come in to handle ribbons and cards."

"Lottie, you are amazing. How can I ever thank you?"

Lottie gave me a sheepish look. "By forgiving me."

"For what?"

"I accepted help from someone else, too."

"Please tell me it's not Jillian."

"It's not Jillian."

That was a relief. My cousin had volunteered to help make arrangements when I was in a bind once, but every order came out looking identical to a painting on her dining room wall.

"Is it my mom?"

"You're getting close."

At that moment, the purple curtain parted and Marco's mother walked through the doorway, a green bib apron tied around her black sweater and slacks. "Abby, bella! You're back. Now the party will really get started, no?"

# CHAPTER SIXTEEN

"Forgive me?" Lottie whispered, as Marco's mom headed back to the workroom.

Being in a state of shock, all I could do was nod.

"Good, 'cause there's more. Your mom will be here at four o'clock."

The nightmare had only just begun. And there went my dinner with Marco, too.

I dumped pieces of a clay pot into the trash can behind the counter. "It's a good thing I gave Miss Sea 3PO a makeover this morning. Mom would have been crushed to see the damage Simon caused. I don't suppose we were lucky enough to sell any sea glasses."

"Did you look in the window?" Lottie asked.

I glanced at the bay, but there was no manikin in it. "Oh, Lottie, please don't tell me Simon destroyed Mom's head again."

"It's about the only thing Simon didn't

destroy. A group of college girls was passing by the window at lunchtime and spotted the display. They bought the entire lot to give away at some kind of sorority function. They thought the glasses were janky, whatever that means."

"That's great news. No more sea glasses! Why are you making a face?"

"Think about it, sweetie. Won't that encourage your mom to make more?"

Way to rain on my parade, Lottie.

To my relief, Francesca Salvare was a genuine asset that afternoon. She pitched in to help prepare the stems, place wet foam in the containers, and clean up after us as Lottie and I put together one arrangement after another. She even brought in appetizers that she'd whipped up that morning, made with only the freshest ingredients, she'd reminded us. She stayed until five, when she sailed off to cook supper for her daughter's family, still looking as fresh as when she'd arrived. I, on the other hand, looked as wilted as a two-week-old rose.

My thirteen-year-niece Tara and her friend Dana came in at three thirty and quickly mastered the art of bow-making, as well as tagging all the arrangements with signature cards. Then my mom arrived at four to take care of customers in the shop, leaving Grace to tend to the parlor. We were quite a team.

However, as Lottie had predicted, when Mom learned that her sea glasses had sold out, she instantly made plans to produce more. And what were the odds that another sorority would happen by and want all of them?

At five, just as we closed up shop for the day and turned our focus to making arrangements, Lottie's seventeen-year-old quadruplets showed up. We put Jimmy and Joey in charge of cleaning the floor, while Johnny and Karl began delivering arrangements to Happy Dreams Funeral Parlor.

At six o'clock, I had four large pizzas brought in, and everyone stopped to eat. Marco took a break from the bar to come down and join us, and then it did seem like a party, especially when Francesca returned with platters of cannoli. When had she found time to make them?

The only person not in a partying mood was Grace. Instead of joining us, she busied herself cleaning out the coffee machines in the parlor.

"Aren't you going to eat?" I asked.

"I'm not much in the mood actually. But thank you for inquiring."

"Is there anything I can do for you?"

She paused in her cleaning. "There is one thing. Would you mind telling me what you learned from your visit to Connie's house?"

"I'm sorry. I should have filled you in sooner."

"It's fine, dear. We haven't had a minute to breathe, have we? Did it go well, then?"

"We were able to interview most of the people on the estate, starting with Guy Luce. He was packing up to move out because he doesn't know if he'll be asked to stay on."

"Because of the cost?" Grace asked.

"That's what Marco thinks."

"Is Mrs. Dunbar's job in jeopardy as well?"

"She hasn't been let go yet, and she's really hoping it doesn't happen."

"The poor old thing probably doesn't have much in the way of retirement funds."

"But here's the big news, Grace. While we were talking to Mrs. Dunbar, the art appraiser announced that a number of the Newports' valuable paintings had been removed from the house and replaced with forged copies. If we can tie that in with the murder, there is no possible way the police can believe you're involved."

I waited for a look of relief. Instead, Grace merely sighed as she put the espresso machine back together. "I hope you're right, dear. My nerves are in a terrible state."

"Grace, please don't worry. Marco is a smart guy, and I'm not so bad at this myself."

She said nothing, only gazed at the countertop forlornly. This was so unlike Grace that all I could do was give her a hug. She hung on tightly for several moments, then, sniffling, said, "Dave called this afternoon, Abby, and I'm afraid the news is rather discouraging. It seems the detectives interviewed Mr. Duval, the estate lawyer. Apparently when Connie went to see him to have her will changed, she told him it was at my suggestion."

"There's nothing wrong with advising a friend to see a lawyer, Grace."

"Unfortunately, that's not all Connie said. She told Mr. Duval that I had advised her to cut her family out of the will and put the bulk of her estate in a trust fund for Charity — to be administered by me."

I pulled out a chair and sat down. "Why would Connie make up such a ludicrous story?"

"Ever since Dave's phone call, I've gone over and over my last conversation with Connie. Other than offering some helpful quotations, I would never presume to tell her what to do with her money."

"Do you recall the quotes?"

Grace sat down across from me and folded her hands on the table. Normally, this was a gesture of her serene state, but now I could see that she was pressing her fingers so tightly together that her knuckles had turned white. "The first was by George Eliot. 'One must be poor to know the luxury of giving.' This was after Connie had complained about her children's selfishness. The other was" — she sat back suddenly — "oh, dear! I think I see the problem."

"What was the other quote, Grace?"

"It was from Oliver Wendell Holmes. 'Put not your trust in money, but put your money in trust.' "

Oh, dear, was right. Those two pieces of advice had undoubtedly been misconstrued by the distraught dowager, and, unfortunately, could now be used by detectives looking to make a stronger case against their number-one suspect. It could be the last piece of damaging information the chief prosecutor would need to indict Grace.

I was really worried now, but I didn't want Grace to know that. "They're just quotes, Grace. I'm sure Dave can clear it up."

She gazed at me briefly, but it was long enough to see the look of fear in her eyes.

She knew I was putting on a good front. "I'm sure you're right, love. Run along and have your pizza before it gets cold." Then she went back to the counter and began polishing the stainless-steel coffeemaker.

When I got back to the workroom, Marco was nowhere to be found, so I checked the galley kitchen at the back of the shop and saw him washing his hands. I slipped up behind him and put my arms around his waist, needing the reassurance of his solid body.

He turned with a smile. "Hey, here's my fireball. Where did you disappear to?" Seeing the expression on my face, he said, "What happened?"

I gave him a rundown on Grace's situation, then said, "I tried to be encouraging, Marco, but frankly, I don't feel like we're even close to finding the killer."

Marco put his arms around me and pulled me close, rubbing my back. "It'll be okay, Abby. We'll figure it out."

I breathed in his clean scent and hugged him tighter. "I hope so, Marco."

"Ah, here you are," Francesca said, coming into the kitchen. And with a kitchen that size, it was now officially crowded.

I turned to see her holding a large binder in her arms. "I brought the book of sample invitations from the printer," she said. "As soon as we finish with the flowers, we can sit down, have a glass of wine, and pick out your shower invitations."

"I have to get back to the bar, Ma," Marco said. "We'll do it another time."

"Marco, you work too much," Francesca said. "Go on, then. Abby and I will pick out the invitation ourselves. Yes, bella?"

*Go to your happy place, Abby. Go to your happy place.*

Rats. The workroom *was* my happy place.

"Ma," Marco said, "Abby has a long evening ahead. Let it rest, okay?" He lifted my chin and smiled into my eyes. "I'll see you later."

I gave him a grateful smile. "If you insist."

Glass shattered somewhere in the shop. Muttering something about the devil in the white fur coat, Lottie grabbed a broom and ran off to find Simon.

"Why is there a cat here?" Francesca asked.

"It's a long story," I said. "In a nutshell, I'm taking care of a cat with a broken leg at my apartment, and Simon doesn't get along with other animals, so I brought him here."

"Come down from there!" I heard Lottie say. "I know you broke that vase. Don't give me that innocent look."

Francesca shook her head. "This will never do."

"I don't have a choice," I said. "Grace and Lottie can't take him, and my mom —"

"I have a pet," Mom chimed in.

"A llama in the garage," I said.

"Taz doesn't live in the garage," Mom said to Francesca with an embarrassed laugh. "He has his own heated living space *attached* to the garage. And as I told my daughter, I've cared for many house pets over the years. I'm over that."

I gave Francesca a shrug. "As I said, I have no choice."

"There are always choices, bella," Francesca told me. "I will take the little cat with the broken leg, and you can take Simon back to his home where he belongs."

I blinked several times, trying to figure out what to do.

"Is that okay with you, Abby?" Marco asked, as though to say, *Do you want my mom more involved in your life?*

On the other hand, would taking care of an injured cat keep his mom out of my hair?

I threw my arms around his mother and gave her a big hug. "Yes! Oh, yes."

After putting in a fourteen-hour day on Wednesday, I would have loved to sleep in the next morning, but a shop owner has certain responsibilities. And with at least thirty-five more funeral arrangements waiting to be done, I even managed to drag myself out of bed an hour earlier — grumpy, yes, according to Marco — but still eager to get started.

Marco had shown up at my door bright and early to pick up Tabitha and take her back to his sister Gina's house, where his mother was staying. Gina had a lower-level guest suite that gave Francesca all the privacy she needed. My fear was that it would also encourage her to stay in New Chapel. While I really liked Marco's mom, dealing with my strong-willed mother was difficult enough. Dealing with two such mothers would be a real headache.

I couldn't very well complain, though. Both my mom and Francesca had been a huge help in getting the arrangements done, and today Nikki had volunteered to help, then cart Simon home before her three o'clock shift at the hospital.

Meanwhile, Tabitha had learned to manage fairly well with her leg in a cast. She'd even filled out a bit, and according to Nikki, was still refusing all but the best cat food. Amazing how picky a homeless cat could be. But with her calm disposition, sweet little meow, and clean fur coat, I knew someone would want to give her a home eventually. Who knew? Maybe Francesca would fall in love with her and decide to take her back to Ohio. Soon.

"You'd better read this," Marco said, unrolling the newspaper as I sat down to coffee and toast slathered in peanut butter and honey. He slid the front section across the table.

The headline read: Missing Cat Worth Millions.

I scanned the article below the fold with growing horror. It began with the news that the vast Newport fortune had been left to Constance Newport's cat, and that a one-thousand-dollar reward was being offered for her safe return. The cat was described as a gold-and-white domestic shorthair wearing a bright pink collar. Again, I paused to wonder at the coincidence of my finding a golden tabby. Still, the time line was all wrong.

"Get to the part yet about Grace?" Marco asked.

"Just getting to it . . . Oh, great. She's named as the cat's guardian. Where could the reporter have gotten that information?"

"Someone from the family must have leaked it. I'm certain it didn't come from the estate attorney."

"It doesn't make sense. Why would the Newports want the whole town to know that the cat got their inheritance?"

"Jealousy, vindictiveness — who knows?"

My cell phone rang and I jumped up to get it. "Hey, Lottie. What's up?"

"Did you see the article about the missing cat on the front page of the newspaper this morning?"

"I was just reading it."

"Well, brace yourself, sweetie. I don't know if you got to the part yet about Grace working at Bloomers, but it says that anyone who finds the missing cat should bring it to the shop so she can identify it. The same news has been on the local radio station all morning, and guess what? I just got to Bloomers, and at least twenty people are waiting outside the door."

"Don't tell me they all have cats with them."

"Bingo."

# CHAPTER SEVENTEEN

I parked in the public lot and used the alley entrance to get inside Bloomers. Then Lottie and I stood behind the purple curtain, peeking through the slit at the crowd out front, some of whom were peering through the bay window.

"Does Grace know about them?" I asked.

"I called her before I called you."

"The Newports have to be behind this, Lottie. They're obviously trying to make Grace's life miserable."

I heard the heavy fire door hinges squeak as Grace came in. She joined us in the workroom, where all three of us peered through the curtain.

"Poor sods," Grace said, removing her coat. "All hoping for that reward."

"Would you recognize Connie's cat, Grace?" I asked.

"I've seen Charity a few times, but I couldn't pick her out of a crowd unless she was wearing her pink collar."

"Lots of cats wear pink collars," I said.

"Not like this collar, love. It was studded with diamonds."

We let the curtain fall. "A diamond-studded cat collar?" Lottie exclaimed.

"I did mention the animal was pampered, didn't I?" Grace asked. "There must have been a dozen one-carat diamonds on that collar."

"No wonder Connie's family was jealous of the cat," I said.

"It isn't as if Connie didn't spoil them, as well." Grace peered through the curtain again.

"What should we do?" Lottie asked. "We can't leave them out there. They'll all come rushing in when we open."

"I suppose we could announce that unless their cat is wearing a diamond-studded collar, they needn't bother waiting," Grace said.

"But think about it, Gracie," Lottie said. "Who's gonna return a cat for a thousand-dollar reward when all those diamonds could be pawned instead?"

"Oh, dear, I hadn't considered that," Grace said with a frown.

"Would anyone even know that the sparkly stones on the collar were diamonds and not crystals?" I asked. "After all, there was nothing in the newspaper article about that. Besides, if someone did realize it and pawn them, they might try to collect the reward, too."

We peeked through the curtain again, and Grace sighed heavily. "One of those people out there could be holding the missing heiress."

"Here's a thought," I said. "Let's take photos of any cat that matches the description, and then show them to the Newports. Someone will be able to identify Charity."

"Considering their animosity," Grace said, "I wouldn't want to rely on the Newports for identification. They'd rather she not reappear, I'm sure."

"What other choice do we have?" Lottie asked. "Those people aren't going to go away. If we're lucky, one of those cats will be wearing a diamond collar."

"Luck!" Grace said, as though struck by an idea. "That's the ticket. As Francois de La Rochefoucauld once said —" She stopped, a look of uncertainty on her face. She cleared her throat and started again. "As Francois de La Rochefoucauld once said . . ." Her eyes filled with tears. "Oh, dear."

She couldn't remember. I'd never seen

Grace forget a quote before.

"Take your time, Gracie," Lottie said. "It'll come."

Grace balled her hands into fists, willing her memory to function. " 'Nature creates . . .' " She faltered yet again, then squared her shoulders. " 'Nature creates ability; luck . . .' "

I crossed my fingers behind my back.

" 'Nature creates ability; luck provides it with opportunity.' "

I sighed with relief as we clapped for her. Still looking shaken, Grace smiled in gratitude.

"If we were really lucky," I said, trying to make light of the moment, "opportunity would be knocking right about now."

Someone pounded on the front door.

We exchanged looks of amazement. I took a peek through the curtain and saw Juanita standing outside, a furious expression on her face.

"See?" Grace asked. "Knock, knock."

"What is the meaning of this?" Juanita said, shaking the newspaper at me as I opened the door to let her in. Immediately, the crowd behind her swelled forward, all shouting for attention, while the cats in their arms struggled to get free.

"I'll be right out," I called to the growing line of people.

Juanita pushed past me, so I started to close the door, but another woman said, "Wait! I'm with her!" and squeezed inside. I quickly closed and locked the door, then turned to see Juanita and her friend straightening their disheveled clothing.

Mrs. Newport's hot-tempered daughter-in-law looked like a fashion plate in a cropped brown tweed-and-leather jacket, tight brown leggings, and thigh-high leather boots with killer heels. Her long black hair was abundantly curled today and pushed back to reveal large, double-hooped gold earrings. Over her shoulder was a bright orange patent-leather purse with a gold chain for a strap.

"Tough crowd," her young friend said to me with a smile. She was a bright, bubbly contrast to the scowling Juanita. She wore a three-quarter-length fitted red twill coat that I would have given my eyeteeth for, with a pair of faded-wash blue jeans, and a red-and-blue-striped scarf looped casually around her neck. Her hair was a honey blond that curled softly at the ends and her eyes were more green than hazel. She also appeared to be closer to my age than to Juanita's.

"That crowd," Juanita said angrily, "is here because of the newspaper article. I demand to know why the press was told about the cat."

Grace held one edge of the curtain aside. "Do come back here, please, Juanita. We don't need any more of a spectacle than we have already."

"You!" the furious Juanita cried, pointing at Grace. "You are responsible for this!"

I watched her march through the curtain; then I turned to her friend. "Sorry. Juanita didn't introduce us. I'm Abby Knight. I own Bloomers."

"I know," she said with a big smile, and shook my hand. "I've read all about you. You're very brave. I've heard good things about your assistants, too. Lottie and Grace, right? Anyway, I'm Lindsey —"

We heard a thud; then Juanita cried, "Look at this newspaper! Look at it! This is your fault, you old —"

"Now, you listen here, missy," Lottie said.

"We'd better get back there," Lindsey said. "Juanita has quite a temper."

When I parted the curtain, Lottie had stepped between Juanita and Grace and was shaking her finger at Juanita. "You show some respect or I'll boot your sassy butt out of here."

With Lottie being taller and about fifty pounds heavier than Juanita, her words had the desired effect. "Fine," Juanita said in a cooler tone. "Then explain why you spread this around."

"I can assure you that I did not talk to the press," Grace said. "I would suggest you poll the rest of your family to find your perpetrator."

Juanita put her hands on her hips. "My per— What?"

"Tattletale," Grace said.

"You think one of *us* told the media?" Juanita cried, splaying her bejeweled, pink-tipped fingers against her breasts. "That is a ridiculous statement. I have told no one!"

"She hasn't," Lindsey whispered to me. "I didn't know myself until I read the paper this morning."

And she apparently harbored no ill feelings from it either.

Grace cleared her throat loud enough to scrape her tonsils. "I didn't reveal anything to anyone, and the information certainly wouldn't have come from your mother-in-law's estate lawyer. So who does that leave? The people mentioned in the will."

Juanita narrowed her eyes at Grace. "We are *not* the only ones who know." Then she swung toward me. "*You* know, too!"

I noticed she left Marco out of it.

"Did you not see the mob outside, Juanita?" I asked her. "Do you think I'd blab to the media and willingly bring that situation on? I have a business to run here, not an animal shelter. Besides, as an investigator's assistant, I'm obligated to keep anything I learn during an investigation confidential until the case has been solved."

Mental asterisk: with the exception of Lottie and Grace and Nikki, who wouldn't dream of revealing anything I told them in confidence.

Juanita tossed her head. "Then I don't know who is to blame. But *someone* is."

Brilliant deduction.

"Why are you so determined to know who leaked the news?" Grace asked. "It won't matter now that it's out, will it?"

"She's embarrassed," Lindsey whispered, having apparently been brought along as Juanita's personal thought translator. "She's been telling all her friends how much money she got from Constance, and now they know she lied."

"Someone obviously did it to hurt me," Juanita said, tossing her hair. "And in the Garcia family, when someone hurts us, we get angry. Very angry. And then we get even."

Lindsey nodded emphatically. "They do — trust me."

Lottie, Grace, and I exchanged glances, and I knew they were wondering the same thing: Had Juanita gotten even with Constance Newport?

I pulled out two wooden stools and invited them to sit. "Maybe I can help you figure out who it is."

Juanita gave me a skeptical glance. "You would help me?"

"You bet I would. But first I need a little help from you."

"Attention, please," I called over the shouts from the crowd, until word spread that I was about to make an announcement, and then the noise quickly died.

"This is Mrs. Newport's daughter-in-law," I said. "She'll be walking down the line looking for the missing cat. Please wait your turn."

"I don't like doing this," Juanita whispered to me, even though I could tell she enjoyed being the center of attention.

I walked alongside her as she inspected each cat, even checking inside their ears. Many of them had the gold-and-white stripes of a tabby, but none, apparently, were the real deal. Some were so far off that

I had a hard time believing anyone would even attempt to bring us such a feline. I didn't say anything, but Juanita had no brakes on her mouth. She reminded me very much of my cousin Jillian.

"Do you think gray is the same as gold?" she asked one woman. "Go home."

To another, she said, "Really? You would bring a black cat here? Really?"

By the time she reached the end of the line, she had eliminated all of them.

Back inside the shop, Juanita, Lindsey, and I sat at a white wrought-iron table in the parlor with a pot of Grace's gourmet coffee and a plate of cinnamon-pecan scones, while my assistants prepared for the day. Grace seemed to be throwing herself into her work, no doubt to keep her mind occupied.

"Okay, Juanita, I have half an hour before the shop opens. Tell me about Virginia's art-professor boyfriend."

"First you have to promise to find out who leaked the information," she said.

"I promise."

"Then what do you want to know?" Juanita asked.

"Is Virginia still seeing him?"

"I can't swear to it," Juanita said, "but I did hear her talking to him on the phone last week. She stopped when I came into the room, but I knew who was on the other end. I heard her making silly cooing sounds. Like a dove, you know?"

"She was talking to Professor Talbot?" I wanted to be sure we were talking about the same person.

"Yes," she said. "Francis Talbot. Really. Who names a son Francis?"

"What do you know about him?" I asked.

"He's a nerd," Juanita said. "He wears a blue bow tie with a gray pullover sweater and has no sideburns." She made a dismissive gesture with her hand. "That's all I have to say about him. He deserves nothing more."

I glanced at Lindsey, but she merely shrugged.

"That's not much to go on," I said.

"He talks, talks, talks all the time about art," Juanita continued. "Constance invited him to dinner once, and I wanted to drown myself in my soup — and that was only during the first course. So instead I used wine. I can tell you that he got better looking as the evening wore on, but no more interesting."

"What did your mother-in-law think about him?" I asked.

"She was impressed with his knowledge,"

Juanita said. "She fawned over him. Is that the right word? Fawn? Isn't that a baby deer?"

Lindsey rolled her eyes at me. "Sometimes she struggles with English."

"I understand that at some point your mother-in-law stopped fawning," I said, "and wanted Virginia to break it off with Talbot."

Juanita toyed with a curl as she glanced around the parlor, as though bored. "I didn't really listen. All Constance and Virginia ever did was argue."

"You must have heard something," I pressed. "Weren't you curious as to why your mother-in-law wanted Virginia to stop seeing him?"

"All I know is that Constance told her to break it off or she'd be cut out of the will. So she broke it off. Or so she said."

"Did Constance find out that Virginia hadn't broken it off?"

Juanita shrugged, then took a sip of coffee.

"Is that a yes?" I asked.

Juanita shrugged again.

"It's an *I don't know*," Lindsey whispered, trying to be helpful.

I knew better. It was a sign Juanita knew more. But there didn't appear to be any love lost between the sisters-in-law, so why wouldn't she want to tell me everything? Was Juanita afraid that if she said too much, it would get back to Virginia, and that would cause a repercussion of some kind? Or was I jumping to conclusions again?

I decided to probe further.

"Where were you on Monday morning?" I asked Juanita.

"Now you're going to interrogate me as if I am a suspect?" Juanita asked, her eyes blazing with indignation. "This is ridiculous. Everyone knows your assistant did it."

Grace was standing behind the counter, filling the coffee machine with water. At Juanita's statement, she froze.

I leaned toward Juanita and said in a low voice, "If you're innocent, then you won't mind answering my questions, will you?"

Juanita drummed her fingertips on the table, then sighed sharply and refilled her coffee cup. "If you must know, I went out for a drive in the country."

"What time did you leave the house?" I asked.

"Early," she said, stirring sugar into her cup. "I like to drive before the streets are busy."

And yet Guy claimed he hadn't heard the garage door open. "How early?" I asked.

Juanita shrugged. "Eight o'clock? What does it matter?"

"Mrs. Dunbar heard someone shut off the burglar alarm and leave the house before dawn."

"It wasn't me," Juanita said.

"She smelled your perfume when she got to the kitchen."

Juanita met my gaze defiantly for several long moments, then looked away. "Perhaps I did leave before dawn that day. Who can remember from one day to the next?"

I glanced at Lindsey, but she was breaking tiny pieces off her scone, obviously wanting to stay out of it.

"Is there anyone who can verify that you went driving that morning?" I asked.

"How would I know that?" Juanita snapped. "Anyone could look out the window and see my red Porsche go by."

No witnesses. Convenient. "What did you and your mother-in-law argue about on Monday morning?"

Juanita put down her cup with a hard clink. "That is *none* of your business."

"It's a sore subject," Lindsey added sheepishly.

Juanita pointed a bright pink fingertip at me. "You told me you wanted to know about Virginia's boyfriend, so I told you.

Now it's your turn."

"But you didn't tell me everything," I said.

"Are you calling me a liar?" Juanita asked, shoving back her chair. "Because if you are, I will walk out of here right now."

"Are you having an affair with Guy Luce?" I asked.

Juanita's eyes grew wide. "First you call me a liar and now you accuse me of that? I will not answer such an insulting question." She huffed loudly, then tossed her hair. "Guy Luce? How ridiculous. He drives cars for a living." At a cell phone's beep, she began to search through her enormous purse.

"She's not having an affair with Guy," Lindsey said quietly.

I studied Juanita as she returned a text message. If she wasn't seeing Guy, maybe Marco was right about Griffin, as disgusting as that thought was. Maybe Constance had suspected what Juanita was up to and confronted her daughter-in-law at breakfast.

Had Constance threatened to tell Burnsy about the affair? Had Juanita gotten angry enough to push her mother-in-law to her death?

"Are you having an affair with Griffin?" I asked Juanita, as she shut her phone.

"That's it!" Juanita cried. "I am through

answering your ridiculous questions."

"Okay," I said, sitting back. "Find the tattletale yourself."

Juanita gasped. "Are you going backward on your word?"

"Going back," Lindsey whispered, "not backward."

"You broke your promise," Juanita said, ignoring the correction. "That makes me very angry."

"Here it comes," Lindsey whispered.

Juanita got up, put her bag over her shoulder, then pointed at me. "You know what happens when a Garcia gets angry."

*Gulp.*

# CHAPTER EIGHTEEN

"That didn't go well, did it?" Grace asked, coming over to clean up the table after Lindsey and Juanita had gone.

"Juanita has a hot temper," I said. "Don't pay any attention to her."

Grace emptied the tray before answering. "I had another dream last night. I saw the letter *g* written on a chalkboard. That was all. Just the letter *g*. I knew it meant something to the murder investigation, but I wasn't sure what until I overheard Juanita's threat just now. Perhaps the *g* refers to the name Garcia."

"Grace, the *g* could be referring to you, too."

"No, I'm sure it has some other significance. Perhaps you should run it past Marco. He called a bit ago, so I told him you were interviewing Juanita."

"Run what past Marco?" Lottie asked, coming into the parlor.

"Just an idea I had," Grace said. "Are we ready to open the shop?"

"In ten minutes," Lottie said. "I wanted to mention two things to Abby. Remember the stalker I thought we had but we didn't really? The guy who ordered a single flower each week? I just came across that stack of his orders I'd clipped together, and it dawned on me that he hasn't been around lately. I think we finally got rid of him."

"That's a relief," I said.

"And the flower shipment arrived," Lottie said.

"Super," I said. "We can get busy on those remaining orders."

"Already underway," Lottie said.

"Is Nikki here?" I asked.

"Marco's mom. She came in with the deliveryman, so I put her right to work."

"I thought she was going to stay home to take care of Tabitha." That had been my hope anyway.

"I don't know anything about that," Lottie said. "All I know is that I can use the extra pair of hands because you have other things to do. Come take a look."

I followed Lottie out of the parlor and into the shop, where I saw another group of people had gathered, all holding wiggling bundles of fur. "Wonderful," I said with a sigh. "More cats."

"I'm reminded of a quote by the ancient Roman playwright Plautus," Grace said, "who said —"

What a relief to see Grace back to her old self.

But then she stopped, and I could see that she was struggling to remember. "Who said," she began again. She took a deep breath. " 'Patience . . .' "

Lottie adjusted the pink barrette in her hair. I pushed back my cuticles.

" 'Patience,' " Grace said forcefully, " 'is the best remedy for every trouble.' "

"There you go!" Lottie said, and we both hugged her.

The curtain parted and Francesca stuck her head out. "Abby, bella! Here you are. Did Grace tell you I brought bruschetta and homemade gelato for lunch? Come. Hurry, hurry. We have a lot to do. After we get these arrangements done and delivered, we have to look at the invitations; then I have to run back home and finish Marco and Raphael's laundry."

"You do their laundry?" I asked.

"What's a mother for, eh?" Francesca replied, then glided back to the workroom.

"Patience," Grace said softly.

As it worked out, Marco saved me yet

285

again from having to pick out shower invitations with his mom. We had worked like fiends to finish the orders by noon so we could get them delivered in time for the one o'clock viewing, and then Marco swept in like my knight in shining blue jeans to pluck me away for a surprise. Luckily, Nikki had come in as promised, so she could fill in for me while I was gone.

"What's my surprise?" I asked, as we buckled ourselves into Marco's car.

"We're going to waylay Burnett Newport."

Yippee?

"I tried to get him to agree to meet with me," Marco continued, "but that wasn't successful, so I thought we'd catch him in his usual habitat."

My ears perked up. "The racetrack?"

"Yep."

"Oh, Marco, I love horses. I've always wanted to go to the races."

"I thought you'd like that. Now tell me about your conversation with Juanita this morning."

I filled him in on the hothead's denials, lies, accusations, and subsequent vow to get even, which Marco dismissed summarily. "Even if Juanita did kill her mother-in-law, she wouldn't risk anything that would draw more attention to her, like harming you."

286

It took almost an hour to get to the racetrack across the border in Illinois. We parked in the last row of a giant parking lot, then headed for the two-story brown brick building adjacent to the track.

"Remember this morning when I told you about the dream Grace had, where she saw the letter *g*?" I asked, as Marco opened the door for me. "Grace thought it might refer to Juanita's maiden name, but as I pointed out, it could also refer to Grace. Or for that matter Guy Luce or even Griffin. But you know what else that *g* could mean? Gambling."

"You're reaching, Sunshine."

Inside, we made our way through a crowd and walked to the wall of plate glass that overlooked rows of stadium seats facing the oval track below. "How are we supposed to find a man we've only seen on TV?" I asked.

Marco took out a stack of color photos of Burnett Junior and handed them to me. "I took footage off the cable news's Web site and broke it into separate frames. You can get a better idea seeing him from different angles."

I shuffled through the photos, then searched the crowd behind me while Marco looked at the people in the seats. But after ten minutes, I was ready to give up. "It's a needle in a haystack," I said glumly. "We're better off trying to see him at the Newport mansion."

"He can avoid us there. He can't here. Keep looking. We'll see him eventually."

Eventually? What did that mean? Hours? Months?

I got tired of standing on my tiptoes trying to see over people taller than me — which was just about everybody — and sat on a bench under the glass instead. The rectangular, brightly lit area resembled a hotel lobby and bustled with people hurrying back and forth from the seats outside to the betting windows. How would we ever spot one pudgy, balding middle-aged man in a room full of them?

On the far end of the room, I caught sight of a petite blonde who reminded me of Juanita's friend Lindsey. She was even wearing a long red coat with blue jeans, and a red-and-blue-striped scarf around her neck. She was darting in and out of the six lines of people waiting to place their bets as though she were looking for someone. Was that Lindsey? Was Juanita here, too? Maybe if I found her, I'd also find her husband.

I jumped to my feet and was about to go after her when I spotted Burnsy waiting in line at the third betting window some distance away. I dashed back to Marco and grabbed his arm. "I found Burnett. Come with me." I took him to where I'd been standing and pointed. "He's just about to place a bet. See him?"

"Let's go."

We plowed through the crowd and waited at the back of the third line until Burnsy walked by. We followed him out into the stadium and watched him walk down three levels, then sidle down the row of spectators.

"There's a vacant seat next to him," Marco told me, "and several in the row behind him."

"You should sit next to him," I said. "I'll take one behind him."

While Marco made his way along one row, I scooted along the row one level up and took a seat behind Marco. Burnsy had a cardboard coffee cup in one hand and a pair of small binoculars in the other. He raised the binocs to his eyes and focused on the horses that were being led toward the starting gate.

Marco had picked up a tip sheet inside and now folded it so he could see the stats for the fourth race.

"Any sure bets?" Marco asked.

Burnsy didn't even look around. "If there

are, I haven't found them."

"Sounds like you haven't had a good day today," Marco said.

"I should probably call it quits, but you know how it goes. Never know when a horse will surprise you."

"I hear you, man, but after a day like I've had, I could really go for a cold beer. How about you? I'm buying."

Burnsy lowered the binoculars and turned to give Marco a long look. "Do I know you?"

"Ever stop by Down the Hatch?"

"Never even heard of it." Burnsy turned back to the track and resumed his scrutiny.

"How about this, then?"

Burnsy sighed to show his irritation and looked over again. "How about what?"

Marco displayed his wallet ID. "How about answering a few questions?"

Burnsy squinted to read the name. "Marco Salvare? Is that supposed to mean something to me?"

"If you've listened to any of the three voice mail messages I've left you, it should. I'm investigating your mother's death."

"Which is the reason you didn't get a return phone call," Burnsy said, turning away. "If you have questions for me, see my attorney."

"I don't think your attorney would have

answers for these questions," Marco said.

"What a pity," Burnsy said, and raised the binocs.

"Questions such as where your wife was Monday morning, who she was with, why she snuck out of the house before dawn."

Burnsy's fleshy face turned deep red, highlighting the veins in his nose. He glanced around to see if anyone was listening, so I quickly shifted my gaze to the jockeys who were trotting their nervous, prancing horses toward the gate.

"Look," Burnsy said in a low growl, "I don't owe you any explanations about anything, so get out of my face."

"In my line of work," Marco said, "when people won't talk to me, it's almost always because they have something to hide. Do you have something to hide, Mr. Newport?"

I hadn't thought it would be possible to see Burnsy's face get any redder, but he proved me wrong. "Don't treat me like a fool," he snarled. "I know how the game is played."

"I don't play games," Marco said in a deadly serious voice. "I'm telling you straight out, if you have nothing to hide, answer a few questions and I promise I'll get off your back. Otherwise, I'll stick around to enjoy the races today . . . tomorrow . . . and the next day."

"You harass me and I'll call security."

"And say what? The guy sitting by me keeps asking questions? They'll tell you to find a new seat. Of course, if you do have something to hide, I can understand your reluctance to talk to me. But just so you know, that kind of behavior usually guarantees that I'll have to tail you."

Burnsy started to argue, then closed his mouth, pressed his lips tightly together, and turned away, clearly fuming. Marco glanced back at me and gave me a wink. He knew he'd wear the man down.

While Burnsy sat there weighing his options, an announcement over the loudspeaker told us that the next race was coming up. That started a buzz of conversation around me. The anticipation was high. I could feel it in the air. Was there something special about this race? A new Seabiscuit?

I spotted a tip sheet someone had left on the seat beside mine and, purely out of curiosity, picked it up to look at the names of the horses. As I skimmed down the list, I saw that a pencil line had been drawn under one of the horses. The name circled was Abby Rose.

Wait. What? A horse named Abby Rose? How cool was that?

Burnsy still hadn't said a peep, so I glanced around at a big digital clock on the wall behind me and saw that there were five minutes before the start of the race, probably just enough time to place a bet, if I were so inclined. But who had money to lose? Not me.

A sneeze caught me by surprise, so I reached into my jeans pocket to get my emergency tissue and felt a folded piece of paper. To my amazement, it was a ten-dollar bill.

I looked at the tip sheet again, then at my newfound money. Was it a sign?

*Nah.* I'd never won anything in my life.

But with a name like Abby Rose, could that be a coincidence? And it was ten dollars that I didn't know I had and wouldn't miss if I lost it. I turned to tell Marco what I was going to do, but he and Burnsy were moving up the row, probably heading for the bar.

I jumped up and hurried along the row, trying not to step on toes or get kneed in the thigh. Inside, I ran to a betting window and slapped down my ten dollars on Abby Rose to win. I glanced around to see if I could spot Marco, but there was no sign of him or Burnsy.

Another announcement came over the

loudspeaker. Two minutes till race time. Where was the bar? Could I find it, locate Marco, let him know what I was doing, and get back in time to see the race? Just ahead I saw a man with *Staff* written on the back of his red shirt. He'd know where the bar was.

One minute to go.

No time to hunt for Marco now. I didn't want to miss the race.

I ran to the plate-glass windows overlooking the track and watched as the horses balked and snorted as their trainers pushed them into their starting positions at the gate. Which one was Abby Rose?

The tip sheet was clenched in my hand so I had to smooth it out to read it. I was so excited I could hardly focus. *Abby Rose, where are you?* There she was! Position seven.

"Oh! You're beautiful," I whispered to the sleek black beauty with white stockings. She seemed more delicate than the other horses, but I could see how eager she was to run. And her jockey was wearing yellow, too, my favorite color. "You can do it, Abby Rose," I called.

"And they're off," came the voice over the loudspeaker.

I pressed my hands flat against the glass

and watched excitedly as the horses shot out of their gates. *Number seven, come on!*

*Woo-hoo!* Abby Rose was in fifth place and gaining ground. I was practically jumping up and down as she slowly caught up to the horse in the fourth spot. When she passed number three, I hooted and slapped the window, causing people around me to sniff and cast disparaging looks my way. I stuffed my knuckles in my mouth as Abby Rose began to overtake number two. But there she stayed, one length behind the lead horse, a bigger, more powerful animal by the name of First String.

By the time the race was into the final lap, I couldn't watch any longer. My nerves were shot. There was no way Abby Rose would be able to catch up. I turned to look for the guy in the red shirt and saw him picking up empty drink glasses.

"Excuse me," I asked him, "where is the bar?"

He pointed to the far end of the long room. "See the sign that says that way to bar? See the arrow below it pointing to the doorway?"

"Okay, thanks. I can take it from there." I could have done without his sarcastic eye rolling, too.

I started toward the doorway and then

heard over the loudspeaker, "It's Abby Rose in a spectacular win!"

I stopped dead in my tracks. *My* horse won?

With a whoop for joy, I ran to the nearest betting window to gather my winnings.

# CHAPTER NINETEEN

After collecting my fifty dollars, I pocketed the money and made my way through the throng to the doorway at the other end of the long room. Inside, I saw a long, polished wood bar with at least two dozen barstools lined up in front of it, and lots of dark oak tables and club chairs. Marco and Burnsy were at one of the tables, so I walked over to see how Marco was coming along with the interview.

He was laying out the case, explaining everything we had learned, obviously trying to convince Constance's son that he should work with us. Burnsy, however, sat with his arms folded, a scowl on his face, not looking convinced.

Not wanting to interrupt, I glanced around to see who else was in the bar area, hoping to catch a glimpse of Juanita and Lindsey. Then I heard the announcement on the loudspeaker that there were five minutes left to place bets before the start of the fifth race. At that, a number of people got up and left, no doubt heading for the betting windows.

That was when I noticed a tip sheet on the floor next to my shoe. Just for fun, I picked it up and scanned the names of the horses. There wasn't anything close to Abby Rose, but there was another name that caught my eye. Sunshine.

I tuned back in to Marco's pitch, but my thoughts kept returning to the horse. I glanced at the tip sheet again. Twenty to one odds. Anyone crazy enough to bet on that was sure to lose. Still, the horse and I *did* share a nickname. And if Abby Rose won, why not Sunshine?

I fingered the fifty dollars in my pocket then glanced at the clock on the wall behind the bar. Three minutes. I still had time. And that money would go a long way toward wedding expenses.

"I'll be back," I whispered to Marco, then dashed out of the bar to place a twenty-dollar bet on Sunshine to win. I couldn't bring myself to use the whole fifty. I wasn't brave enough to go for broke. But even at twenty bucks, I stood to make a quick four hundred twenty dollars' profit.

My cell phone beeped to indicate an

incoming text message. I was almost certain it was from Jillian, yet that niggling fear that it was news about Grace made me open it.

*OH NO! OH NO!! Hurry! Call me now!!!*

I glanced from the line at the betting window to my phone. With Jillian, it could be life threatening or it could be nothing, and the only way to know was to call.

"Oh, Abby, thank goodness!" she said when she heard my voice. "Can you program your DVR remotely? I forgot to set mine for the Grace Kelly retrospective on cable TV this afternoon."

"Jillian, I don't have a DVR. Can't you have Claymore set it?"

"Claymore can't set the clock on the microwave, Abby. You have to help me."

"There are Web sites that play television programs for free. Do an Internet search for the show."

"I hire people to do computer work for me, Abs. What else have you got?"

I saw the betting window close and figured it was probably for the best. "Check the cable-TV guide. Those shows always repeat. Anyway, I don't see what your urgency is. You already know everything there is to know about Grace Kelly."

"How do I know, Abby, unless I watch this one?"

Hard to argue with that logic. "Where are you?"

"Still in Chicago. Hey, if you get a chance, mention my name to Virginia Newport. I would so love to take her shopping. Last time I saw her out in public, she looked like an escapee from a hippie commune. So, anyway, as long as I'm here, I'm still available to select your dress for the shower."

"Good-bye, Jillian."

I put away my phone and heard over the loudspeaker, "Would you look at that? Talk about a horse rising from the ashes. To think that little filly hasn't won in three years."

No way. It couldn't be.

"It's Sunshine by a nose!" the announcer shouted.

"Abby?" Marco said, coming up to me. "Why are your hands balled into fists?"

"I was just thinking about noses — and how much I wanted to punch one."

"Tell me on the way to the car."

"What happened with Burnsy?" I asked, after filling Marco in on my win and miss. "Did he get angry and stamp out?"

"Not at all. I would imagine he's standing in line to place a bet. Interesting guy. He seems to have no idea how the world works. He's never held a real job and doesn't have a clue as to what he's going to do when his money runs out."

"I thought he managed the Newport rental properties at one time."

"I'd define the word *managed* loosely. I think Burnsy played more than he managed. He freely admitted that he has a gambling addiction, but he doesn't consider it a problem. His problem, as he tells is, is how to make enough money to keep on gambling, which is one of the reasons I'm putting him at the bottom of our suspect list. There's no way he would kill the cash cow."

"Not even during an argument?"

"I couldn't find a single trace of animosity toward his mother. I even pressed him on the issue of losing his inheritance to a cat to see if I could get a rise out of him, but he said his mother's actions hadn't surprised him all that much."

"I have a hard time believing that, Marco. Wouldn't you be struck dumb to learn your mother had left everything to her pet? And didn't Grace tell us the family was shocked when the will was read?"

"They may have been shocked by where the money was going, Sunshine. According to what Burnsy told me, his mother had called them together about a month and a half ago and told them she was fed up with their lack of industriousness and didn't want them sponging off her any longer. Her edict was for them to earn an honest day's wage or she would change her will."

"And that didn't motivate Burnsy to look for employment?"

"He considers his winnings to be earnings, believe it or not. And he said his mother had made similar threats before. He figured it was simply a matter of time before she followed through on one of those threats."

"What was your other reason for putting Burnsy on the bottom of our list?"

"He gave the detectives ticket stubs that prove he was right here on Monday from eleven a.m. until four p.m., and had witnesses sign affidavits."

"Then I'd call this a successful trip. We've eliminated one of our suspects, and I finally picked a winner." But for Jillian, two winners.

Marco gave me a quizzical glance as he opened the car door for me. "Finally?"

"That came out wrong. I meant that I picked a winning horse on my first try."

"Thank you."

It had taken me *two* tries to pick a winning man.

As we headed back to New Chapel, Marco

said, "I quizzed Burnsy about the other members of his family, but he was tight-lipped about his sister and his wife as well as about Guy. He acknowledged that Guy was competent, but then he clammed up. They only new information he gave me was that he once witnessed the housekeeper pocket a valuable crystal figurine from his mother's collection."

"I can't picture Mrs. Dunbar doing anything that would jeopardize her job, Marco."

"Burnsy told me he didn't think it was her first time either."

"What makes him think she's taken other things?"

"He said the curio cabinet used to be full of the bird figurines his mother had collected for years. Now the collection is half of what it was. He would have thought his mother was giving them away except that he caught Mrs. Dunbar in the act."

"His mother still might have given some away. Maybe that's why Mrs. Dunbar helped herself. She seems so loyal and kindhearted, I just can't imagine her stealing."

"Trust me, Abby. Employee theft isn't unusual and doesn't mean Mrs. Dunbar didn't like her employer, only that she has sticky fingers."

I watched the flat farmlands whiz by, letting my mind relax so I could absorb the events of the past hour. "Did Burnsy happen to mention whether his wife was at the races at all today?"

"No, why?"

"I could have sworn I saw her friend in the crowd. Anyway, what's next on our list?"

"A trip to Chicago to talk to Professor Francis Talbot. When I was searching for him on the Internet this morning, I came across an article from a Chicago newspaper about a man by the name of Frank Talbot who was suspected of fencing a valuable piece of stolen art. I couldn't find anything about him being charged with the crime, so I'm guessing there wasn't enough evidence to make anything stick. But the fact that a Frank Talbot was involved in any kind of art theft makes me suspicious."

"How do we find him?"

Marco pulled a folded paper out of his jacket pocket. "White-pages listings. There are two Francis Talbots in Chicago proper and twenty Frank Talbots. We'll start with the Francises and see where that takes us."

When I got back to Bloomers, I was relieved to see it was business as usual. Lottie was assisting a customer in the flower shop, and Grace was serving tea and scones to three full tables. There was no cat on the armoire, no manikin head in the display window, no mess on the floor, and not even one pair of funky sunglasses to be found. As long as there was no Francesca either, all was right in my world once again.

I gave Lottie and Grace a wave, then headed straight back to the workroom, pausing at the curtain to listen. Hearing no sounds from the other side, I peered in. No Francesca, but she had been there. A plate of chocolate biscotti sat on the worktable. I took one and bit into it, savoring the slightly sweet, crunchy chocolate flavor. Then I checked the spindle on my desk and saw that there was only one order waiting. Where had all my business gone?

"Hey, sweetie," Lottie said as she headed for one of the big walk-in coolers, "have any luck at the racetrack?"

"Yes, but not in the way you mean. I took a chance on a horse named Abby Rose and won fifty bucks."

"Wow, sweetie. Aren't you the lucky one?"

"Finally!" I pulled the order from the spindle to study it.

The arrangement was for a customer's mother's birthday, so I started gathering my tools and supplies while Lottie loaded up a basket with roses and daisies from the cooler to restock the display case out front.

The customer wanted a spring basket, so I pulled pink amaryllises, hyacinths in hues of pink, purple, and a peachy beige, bicolor tulips in orange sherbet and yellow, glory lilies in white, and long pussy willows for added texture and dimension.

Next I hunted for a basket, scouting the shelves on the back wall until one seemed to jump out at me, a flat, lime-green colored one with a broad handle. The green matched the broad leaves of the bicolor tulips.

"Were you able to interview Connie's son?" Lottie asked, closing the cooler behind her.

"Yes, and we've moved him to the bottom of our list."

"I didn't think Burnett would harm his mother," Grace said, gliding into the room. "He's really an old softie."

Clearly a side of him we hadn't seen.

"Were you able to learn anything useful at all?" Grace asked.

"Only that Mrs. Dunbar stole a crystal figurine from Connie's collection," I said.

"That's not sporting of her, is it?" Grace asked. "I suppose this only proves what William Shakespeare said . . ." Grace paused, then shook her head. "I can't remember."

"Don't push yourself, Grace," I said.

She cleared her throat and stood taller. "As William Shakespeare said, 'Beauty provoketh thieves . . .' " Her mouth opened, but no words came out. She pulled out a stool and sank onto it, holding her head in her hands. "I simply can't remember."

"Gracie, how do you know all those quotes, anyway?" Lottie asked. "I can't tell you what I ate for breakfast."

Grace drew a shaky breath and lifted her head. "It happened when I was stationed in Germany in the 1960s. I had one book in my possession — a book of quotes — that I read to pass the time. One tends to remember something one reads several hundred times . . . or so I've always imagined."

Lottie patted her shoulder. "Once this case is solved, you'll be back to normal."

"I'm not so sure, Lottie, but thank you for your kind words." She straightened her shoulders. "Let's talk of other things, shall we?"

"Here's a topic," Lottie said. "Have you noticed that those mysterious orders stopped arriving?"

"I'd forgotten all about them," Grace said.

"Seems like our *stalker* moved on," Lottie said with a wink. "Maybe he didn't like our flowers."

"Or his secret love affair with the woman

at the old Donnelly house cooled down," I said.

"Or the woman's sons went after him," Lottie said, chuckling.

"Demanding a shotgun wedding," I added, making us both laugh.

At Grace's sad sigh, I said, "I'm sorry. We were just having a little fun."

"Don't mind me, love. I just can't focus on much else these days."

"We'll find the killer soon, Grace, I promise. In fact, Marco found an article in a Chicago paper mentioning a Frank Talbot in connection with some kind of art theft, so we're going to Chicago this evening to see if we can locate him."

Grace merely sighed again.

"And here's more good news," Lottie said. "Marco's mom promised to bring in veal and mushroom risotto for our lunches tomorrow."

Yippee?

"I'll tell you, sweetie," Lottie said, "that woman really knows her way around a kitchen. And I have to say, Abby, I enjoyed working with her this morning. I like a woman who will roll up her sleeves and dig right in. I think she's going to make you a real good mother-in-law."

"I like her, too, Lottie. I'm just afraid she's

going to take control of our wedding plans."

"She can't take it from you," Lottie said. "You'd have to give it up first, and you won't let that happen. Just tell her flat out that you'll handle it."

"We've tried that," I said with a sad sigh. "She doesn't seem to take the hint."

"As the great Khalil Gibran wrote," Grace said, " 'Love has power that . . . that . . .' " She sighed sharply. "What I'm trying to say is that you have to show Marco's mum the love and she'll come around to your way of thinking."

"I thought I was showing her love," I said.

"Try just a bit harder, Abby," Grace said. "You'll be amazed at the result."

The bell over the door jingled, so Lottie said, "We'd better get out there, Gracie."

"Right behind you," Grace said.

And then I heard, "Yoo-hoo! Abigail?"

Lottie came to a stop inches from the doorway, causing Grace to put out her hands to keep from smacking into her back.

When Lottie turned, she had a sheepish look on her face. "I forgot to pass along a message from your mom. She'll be dropping off more sea glasses today."

Every winning streak had its end.

# CHAPTER TWENTY

I was just finishing up the basket arrangement when Mom stuck her head through the curtain. "I thought I'd find you back here. Guess what I brought with me?"

"More sea glasses?" I asked, trying to appear happy about it.

"More sea glasses!" she sang out as she came into the workroom holding a box. "What a pretty basket, Abigail. Did Lottie help you?"

For some reason Mom still saw me as a florist-in-training. "It's all my doing, Mom. How many pairs of glasses did you make?" I tightened my stomach, girding myself for her answer.

"Three dozen."

Three what? Okay, no amount of girding in the world could have prepared me for thirty-six pairs of cheap sunglasses covered with hunks of colored glass.

"And I worked half the night to finish

them," she said. "Thank goodness I've had enough practice so that the process moves along quickly."

"Let's hope they sell fairly quickly, too," I said. *Please, God, make them sell quickly — like now.*

"To tell you the truth, Abigail, I'm tired of making them. I need variety. I need —"

My cell phone beeped to signal an incoming message. "I need to answer this. Excuse me just a minute." I checked the text. It was from Marco: *B ready @ 5 pm 4 trip 2 Chi.*

"Is that written in code?" Mom asked, reading over my shoulder, another bad thing about being short.

"It's texting shorthand," I said. "We're going up to Chicago —"

"Maureen," Lottie said, sticking her head through the curtain. She motioned for Mom to come quickly.

I sent Marco a quick reply, then hurried into the shop. What I saw floored me. Mom was surrounded by half a dozen young women, all talking excitedly as they passed around pairs of her glasses. I sidled up to Lottie and whispered, "What's going on?"

"Remember the college girls who bought the first batch?" she whispered back. "Well, those glasses were such a hit, the girls want to buy them all and resell them to other sororities."

I was too stunned to reply.

When Marco picked me up at five o'clock, he told me there'd been a change in plans. We weren't going to Chicago after all.

"To make sure we didn't waste our time driving to Chicago," he said, "I tried phoning the two Francis Talbots I'd located earlier. One number belongs to an elderly woman in an assisted living facility, and the other phone number has been disconnected. I got the address for the disconnected line — a condominium high rise in the Gold Coast area — called the management office there and gave them a story about needing to inform Mrs. Talbot of an inheritance she'd received. They told me that Mr. Talbot was currently out of the country on a business trip, and that Mrs. Talbot had been visiting relatives in Indiana for the past two months, and that they didn't know when either was expected back."

"Francis is married? I'll bet Virginia doesn't know that."

I was distracted by the sight of three young women striding along the sidewalk on Lincoln Avenue. They wouldn't have been remarkable except that they were wearing Mom's sea glasses, and judging by the scowls on their faces, they weren't happy about it, either.

"Then I struck gold," Marco said, jerking me back to the conversation. "They gave me Mrs. Talbot's forwarding address. And guess where that address is? Right here in New Chapel. Quite a coincidence, isn't it?"

"There seem to be a lot of coincidences lately. And that noise you hear is my stomach growling."

"We'll eat right after we check out the Talbots. I don't want my fireball to go hungry."

"You're too good to me, Marco."

"I know I am, but someone has to spoil you."

I could live with that. Him. Okay, both.

Marco turned onto County Line Road, the same two-lane road that ran past the old Donnelly place. But instead of passing it, he pulled into the gravel driveway and turned off the motor.

"This is where the Talbots are? Marco, this is the house where we delivered the arrangements that Lottie thought the stalker was sending."

"Are you sure?"

"Yes, I'm sure. I made one of those deliveries."

"Remind me again about the stalker."

"According to Lottie, about twice a week, first thing in the morning, she'd find an envelope filled with cash stuffed through the mail slot. Within ten minutes a man would call in an order but wouldn't leave his name. He was specific about what he wanted and the money he left always covered the cost of the flowers. And this is where he had them sent every time. That can't be a coincidence."

"I'm having a tough time believing that someone who lives in a condo in Chicago's Gold Coast area would rent this house, Abby. It doesn't make sense."

"Neither does the woman having an African American son whose hair was as gray as hers."

"Did you get Mrs. Talbot's first name?"

"Dorothy, but she asked me to call her Dot."

"The condo manager referred to her as Dorothy. Are you still getting those orders?"

"Nope. They've stopped. Right after Mrs. Newport's death. Another one of those coincidences, right?"

Marco opened his car door. "Let's go see if Dot and Francis are home."

We walked across the weedy stubble and carefully climbed the five steps to the front door. Marco pushed the doorbell, then

314

knocked. This time I didn't hear any footsteps at all and no one answered the door.

Marco tried the handle, but the door was locked tight. We trudged around to the back door and found it locked as well. We peered in dusty windows, but saw only empty rooms.

I told Marco what Dot had said about her sons and about the black van with the tinted windows parked behind the house. We circled the garage and peered through the one dusty window there, too. Once again, the space was empty.

"These tire tracks aren't fresh," he said of the heavy marks in the gravel. "They've packed up and moved on. That's clear. It would be helpful to know when."

"I'm getting a strong gut feeling that this is connected to the Newport murder case."

"So am I. Not just to the case, but to one specific Newport — Virginia. Let's stop at the bar and grab a sandwich, then head over to the mansion to have another talk with her."

Eating dinner at Down the Hatch was always a dicey proposition because there were a hundred things that could crop up to pull Marco away from a meal. But this time he gave his brother, Rafe, strict orders that we were in a hurry and not to be bothered.

Rafe, who was a ten-year-younger version of Marco without all his common sense, had only one comment when he stopped by our booth to deliver beers. "You owe me."

"Why do I owe you?" Marco asked, as we wolfed down hot Italian ham and Manchego cheese sandwiches. "I'm training you to take over the bar."

Rafe glanced over his shoulder, then whispered, "Mom is driving me crazy. She made me look at shower invitations because you and Abby weren't around. What do I know about shower invitations? What do I know about any invitations? She said it's good practice for when I get married." He folded his hands. "I'm begging you, please, make Mom stop pestering me."

I looked at Marco. "Tomorrow, Rafe. We promise."

Before we left, Marco printed out a photo of Frank Talbot from the online archives of the Chicago newspaper; then we headed for the Newport Mansion. We got as far as the gate, where Marco buzzed several times and got no response. I called Grace, got Connie's home phone number, and was able to reach Mrs. Dunbar.

I put her on speakerphone. "This is Abby Knight. Marco and I are outside at the gate. We were hoping to talk to Virginia. Is she available?"

"Oh, miss, I don't dare bother Ms. Virginia when she's working in her studio. She closeted herself up there this afternoon and has only been down for something to eat. She's in a frenzy of painting with an exhibit coming up soon."

Marco motioned for me to move my phone closer. "Mrs. Dunbar, this is Marco Salvare. I have a photo I'd like to show you that might help with the investigation into the art theft. It won't take more than five minutes."

In the background, I heard Juanita say sharply, "Who are you talking to?"

There was a whispered reply; then Juanita said, "I will handle this." And then in a sultry voice she said, "Hello, Marco, you bad boy. Are you here to see me?"

"Sure am," Marco said, then held his finger to his lips to warn me not to speak.

There was a loud buzz, and the gates swung slowly open.

"Come on in, Marco," Juanita purred.

"Thanks," Marco said, and ended the call. "Sorry, Sunshine, but I figured she'd be more likely to let me in if she thought I was alone. And I'm still hoping we can see Virginia, but we may have to get creative. Keep your eyes open for an opportunity."

He drove up the long driveway and parked in front of the garage; I followed him along the brick path to the courtyard. The wind was picking up and the night air had a bite to it, so I pulled my jacket tighter and stayed behind Marco, using him as a wind shield.

The back door opened and light spilled out onto the courtyard. "Welcome, Marco," I heard Juanita say in a voice that gushed with delight.

Then I stepped out from behind him, and her smile, as the saying went, turned upside down.

Juanita was wearing a revealing white halter top and clingy bright blue yoga pants that showed off every curve. She had arranged her black curls into a messy bun on top of her head held by a huge blue clip encrusted with crystals. She moved back to let us enter, pressing her lips into a pout as I passed by.

Mrs. Dunbar was standing by the table, dressed in a white flannel robe covered in a print of tiny rosebuds, with open-toed slippers in powder blue. At our greeting, she dipped her head respectfully.

"Why this unexpected visit?" Juanita

asked, casting Marco a flirtatious glance.

"We're hoping you can help us identify someone." Marco took the printed picture out of his inside jacket pocket and showed both women. "Do either of you recognize this man?"

Mrs. Dunbar put her hand over her mouth.

Juanita tapped the man's face. "That's him. That's the professor I spoke about. Do you see what I mean about his sideburns? This is an old photo, though. His hair isn't slicked back now, and he has gray at the temples."

"Mrs. Dunbar?" Marco asked. "Do you know who he is?"

She nodded. "That's Professor Talbot."

"When was the last time you saw him?" Marco asked.

Juanita shrugged carelessly. "I can't remember. Mrs. D., when did he come to dinner?"

The housekeeper got a deer-in-the-headlights look. "Three months maybe?" She looked at Juanita for verification.

"I don't have a clue," Juanita said, looking bored.

Clueless. Who knew?

"Was that his only visit?" Marco asked. "The only time you saw him here?"

"Yes, sir."

"Me, too," Juanita said.

Marco paused, and I guessed that he was trying to figure out how to question Virginia without barging into her studio.

"Are we finished?" Juanita said, and at Marco's hesitation, she moved to the center of the room and posed with one foot on the calf of the other leg, her arms outstretched, maintaining perfect balance. "Do you know what this is?"

A blatant display of her body?

"Or this?" She bent over at the hips, buttocks in the air, hands flat in front of her.

"I'm hoping they're yoga poses," I said.

Ignoring me, she straightened and slipped her hand through Marco's arm, smiling coyly. "Since I answered your questions, now you have to come watch my yoga class. My students are upstairs in the exercise room. I promise you'll like our moves. We're very" — she slanted her eyes at him — "flexible."

Good for her, because if she made any moves on Marco, I was prepared to tie her into a pretzel. "Actually," I said, glancing at my watch, "we can't stay."

"Long," Marco cut in. "We can't stay *long*, but we can watch for a while."

What was he doing?

"Come with me," Juanita said, smiling triumphantly. As an afterthought, she turned back to me and added, "You can come, too."

Marco handed the photo to me but held on to it a second longer than necessary. I looked at him to see why, and he lifted his eyebrows and glanced toward the ceiling. Puzzled, I gazed upward, too.

*Duh.* Obviously this was the opportunity he'd been watching for. Now it was up to me to make it work.

I gave him a quick nod and slid the photo in my pocket as I followed Juanita and Marco out of the kitchen and to a door that led to a back staircase. The stairs were narrow and steep but thickly carpeted, so our footsteps didn't make a sound. Helpful, I thought, for anyone who wanted to sneak out the back door.

On the second floor, I followed them up a wide, carpeted hallway and stopped at a door that opened onto a spacious exercise room. The room had floor-to-ceiling mirrors on one long wall, two treadmills, a weight-lifting bench, and a Nautilus on one short wall, and an open area in the middle that would accommodate at least half a dozen students. I leaned in just far enough to see that there were indeed other women in the class; then I ducked back to the staircase and followed it to the third floor. Juanita would never miss me.

It wasn't difficult to find Virginia's attic studio because there were only two doors off the third-floor hallway. One was open and, fortunately, the nickel-plated lamps on the nightstands on either side of her bed were on, giving me a good view of an immense bedroom decorated in the golds, oranges, reds, and browns of the desert.

Oil canvases of clay pottery and pueblos painted in desert colors filled every available wall space. There was a painting leaning against the wall just near me, so I checked the signature in the bottom corner and saw *Virginia Newport-Lynch* written in thin strokes. This had to be her bedroom, then.

I stepped inside and glanced around. In front of me was a king-sized platform bed flanked by nightstands. Opposite the bed was a long dresser with a mirror above it. On one end of the room was a sedate sitting area done in browns and oranges, with two upholstered chairs facing a fireplace flanked by bookcases. On the other end of the bedroom was a hallway that I was guessing led to a master closet or bathroom, or both.

Hearing faint strains of music, I went back

outside and put my ear against the closed door. From behind it came the rousing sounds of Beethoven's Fifth Concerto. I turned the knob and eased the door open just far enough to press one eyeball to the crack. There stood Virginia in her white artist's smock and long skirt, an easel in one hand, a thick brush in the other, painting as she swayed to the music turned up full blast.

At her feet were canvases that she'd completed and shoved aside. More canvases stood on the floor all around the room, all in the same colors and with the same desert themes. It was as if she had never left Taos.

I stood there wondering how to approach her and decided that interrupting Virginia now could be counterproductive. Still, I hated to let this perfect opportunity to investigate slip away. I eased the door shut, then glanced around. What else could I do?

*Hmm.* Her bedroom door *was* wide open.

After a quick glance over my shoulder, I slipped inside and took a longer look around. If Virginia and Frank had been lovers, surely there would be some evidence of it. And since her mother had frowned on their association, I was betting Virginia would have taken pains to hide anything Frank had given her.

I started with her nightstands, but found only a few paperback novels, pens, a notepad, and cough drops. I went through her top dresser drawer, but it contained only sweaters. The second drawer was filled with thick socks, and the third held lingerie — if you could call white cotton underwear lingerie. I slid my hands under the garments and felt a thick cardboard envelope. I pulled it out and discovered a package of Spanx.

That was surprising. Virginia hadn't seemed the *Spanx* type to me.

I started to put the package back, but suddenly realized there was something small and square in there. I pulled out the black girdle inside and a flat, black velvet jewelry box fell to the carpet. I opened it up and saw a brooch pinned to a black velvet backing. The brooch was in the shape of the letter *g* and covered in what appeared to be diamonds.

Another *g*? Was that some kind of cosmic joke?

I removed the pin from the backing and flipped it over. Engraved on the back was: *From F T with love* — and a date. I covered my mouth to suppress a gasp. Someone had received the brooch one week before Constance Newport died. But who was *g*?

I heard a noise. Someone was coming.

With a racing heart, I stuffed the jewelry box back inside the package, stuck it in the bottom of the drawer, eased it shut, then tiptoed to the doorway and peered out.

There stood Lindsey, gazing at me with a knowing smile.

# CHAPTER TWENTY-ONE

"I think I'm lost," I said.

Lindsey covered her mouth to stifle a laugh. She was clearly amused by my lame attempt to defend myself. "You're not lost. You were snooping."

"Snooping is a rather harsh word. I'd prefer *investigating*."

"Call it whatever you want. We need to get away from here before Ginny comes out."

"Ginny?"

"Virginia. That's her nickname." She took my wrist and practically dragged me to the staircase. "Trust me. You don't want to talk to her when it's time for her evening cocktail. She'll eat you alive."

"I really need to talk to her."

"Not here. Now, come on. Hurry."

We ran down the steps like schoolgirls heading out to recess. Not a moment later, I heard a door open and then Beethoven's

Fifth filled the hallway above. "That was close," I said breathlessly.

"I told you so."

When we came out on the second-floor landing, Lindsey said quietly, "Yoga is over. Everyone is getting ready to leave. Go down to the kitchen and wait for Ginny there if you want to talk to her. Just don't tell her you were in her room. Now, go!"

She hurried off toward the exercise room, so I turned and ran down the next flight of steps, coming out in the hallway near the kitchen. There was no sign of Mrs. Dunbar, and I could hear footsteps on the stairs behind me, so I sat down at the kitchen table, pulled out my cell phone, and pretended to be talking to someone.

Virginia came around the corner and stopped dead in her tracks when she saw me.

"What on earth are you doing here?"

I signaled for her to wait a minute, then said into the phone, "I'll call you about this matter in the morn—"

My phone rang. I was so startled, I pulled it away from my ear and stared at it.

Jillian's name was on the screen. Fuming silently, I hit END and slid it into my pocket. "That can wait."

Virginia folded her arms over her chest

and sneered. "Just exactly how did you get inside? We have gates to keep people like you out."

People like me? That did it. I'd had enough of Virginia's snooty attitude.

"Don't worry, *Ginny.* I didn't break in. Juanita let us in. In fact, Marco is upstairs talking to her now."

"Did you just call me *Ginny?*" she snarled.

"That is your nickname, isn't it?"

"You have some nerve using a familiar name with me," she said, looking me up and down. "I've never seen such rude behavior."

"How about this man?" I opened up the piece of paper with the photo on it and held it out. "Have you ever seen him?"

Virginia snatched it from my hand and gave it a cursory glance. "Never." Suddenly her eyes seemed to sharpen their focus, and she drew it closer. Her breathing became fast. Then, with one strangled gasp, she fainted dead away.

She really had to stop doing that.

Marco and Juanita entered the kitchen at the very moment she collapsed. *"Madre de Dios!"* Juanita said, standing with her hands on her hips. "What happened now?"

"All I did was show her the photo," I said, as Marco and I crouched beside her.

"Well, no wonder she fainted," Juanita snapped, standing with one hand on her hip. "It's a ridiculous picture." Turning away, she yelled, "Mrs. Dunbar! Virginia fainted again. Bring her smelling salts." She swung back around to blow Marco a kiss and then she sashayed out of the room as though she hadn't a care in the world.

Mrs. Dunbar came rushing in with a bottle of salts, her hair in curlers, and white cream slathered all over her face. She knelt down beside Virginia and waved the uncapped bottle beneath her nose.

At that, Virginia's eyes snapped open. She sat up abruptly and glanced around, slowly realizing what had happened. She got to her feet and straightened her clothing, clearly angry at herself for showing such weakness. "What are you staring at," she asked me, "and why are you still here? Mrs. Dunbar, get the police on the line. These people are not welcome here and are, in fact, intruders."

I opened my mouth to protest, but Marco said, "We were just leaving. Have a nice evening."

On the way to the car, he said, "Sorry to cut you off, but I learned a long time ago not to throw stones at an angry dog."

"She'd be even angrier if she knew what I

found buried in her underwear drawer."

"You snooped in her underwear?"

"Must everyone refer to what I do as snooping? When you do it, people call it investigating. Why is that?"

"Okay, let's start again. You *investigated* Virginia's underwear drawer?"

"I saw my opportunity and went for it, Marco. You would have been so proud. Virginia was painting in her studio with the door shut, and right across the hall was her bedroom with the door open. And voila! I found a diamond brooch with the letter *g* on it, which just happens to be the first letter of her nickname.

"And wait, it gets better. The initials *FT* and a date were engraved on the back — and the date was last week. There's our connection. High five!"

Marco gave me a high five and then kissed me, which I found much preferable. "Great work, Abby. Now we need to figure out how to connect the dots between Frank Talbot, Virginia, and the art theft."

"Okay, I've been thinking about that. Remember the flowers Lottie and I delivered to the Donnelly house? They were very specific arrangements sent to a woman who we now believe is Mrs. Talbot. So were those arrangements merely gifts from a kind son,

330

or were they some kind of code?"

"I hear another theory brewing."

"Something is brewing, but it's just beyond my grasp. Let me work on it awhile longer. You haven't told me about the yoga session. Did you like watching Juanita flex and stretch and bend?"

"If I'm going to watch a woman flex and stretch and bend, Fireball, it's going to be you."

*Aw.* Marco was so adorable. And wise. Very, very wise. "If you're lucky, Salvare, you might get your chance for some flexibility tonight."

"Exactly what I had in mind."

It was not flexibility Francesca Salvare had in mind, however, as we discovered when we got back to the bar.

"Here you go," Rafe said, handing a thick binder to Marco. "Mom says you and Hot Stuff here have to pick out a few invitations tonight, and she'll help you narrow it down tomorrow when you meet her for lunch."

I turned toward Marco. "We have a lunch meeting?"

"It's news to me, Abby," the adorable wise one said.

"She's bringing Filetto alla Rossini," Rafe

continued. "You'll love it, Abby. Won't she, bro?"

"I'm sure I will," I said wearily, plunking my chin on my hand.

"And," Rafe said, "she said to tell you both no more stalling. If you don't pick an invite for the Salvare shower, she will."

Marco tucked the binder under his arm and ushered me toward his office. "Looks like we'll have to be flexible with our plans tonight, Sunshine."

Wait a minute! No way was his mother going to ruin our evening. "I think we'll find a way to do both," I said with a smile.

"Both what?" Rafe asked from behind, startling me.

We swung around in surprise. "What?" Marco asked.

"What else do *you* have to do?" Rafe asked. "*I'm* running the bar."

Marco and I exchanged glances. "Yoga," we said together.

"Yoga?" Rafe glanced at us skeptically, then turned and walked away. "Whatever. I've got work to do."

It took us ten minutes to pick out an invitation we both liked. Lucky for us, our tastes were very similar. Even luckier, we snuck out the back way and had the rest of the evening to ourselves . . . to practice our yoga poses.

One of these days, I'd have to sign up for a class.

*Friday*

On the way to Bloomers the next morning, I kept pondering the puzzle of those flower arrangements, wishing I had an answer. It seemed to hover right at the edge of my mind, just out of my grasp. I parked the car in the public lot and was walking toward Franklin Street when I saw two of the college girls who'd bought Mom's sea glasses hurrying across the street toward me.

"Remember us?" one of the girls asked. "We bought those janky sunglasses from you."

"Do you have any left?" the other one asked. "We need twenty more pairs."

Twenty more? I was stunned. Then the image of the two young women I'd seen wearing Mom's sea glasses popped into my head, giving me an uneasy feeling. Before I committed Mom to making more, I needed to find out why.

"I'm all out at the moment, and I hope you don't think I'm being nosy, but what makes them so popular?"

"We make sorority initiates wear them,"

333

the first girl said with a giggle. "It's part of their hazing."

"We're stocking up now for next semester," the other girl said. "So when will you get more in?"

My stomach dropped. Poor Mom! There was no way I was going to sell her glasses to be used as instruments of torture. Mom would be crushed if she found out.

"Unfortunately," I said to the girls, "the artist just retired."

Now I had to figure out how to stop Mom from making more.

When I got to the shop, I saw Grace in the parlor, setting up for the day. I stopped to say good morning and spotted a large, coffee table–sized book lying on a nearby table. It was covered in burgundy leather and inscribed: *The Language of Flowers* by Leticia Goodwin.

"That was Connie's gift to me, love," Grace said. "I brought it for you to see."

"What a nice remembrance," Lottie said, coming in behind me.

I ran my fingers over the book's textured surface. It felt like smooth pebbles and smelled of old paper and leather.

"Just look at the illustrations," Grace said, turning pages. "You'd swear they were photographs. But what I found intriguing is the flower dictionary. One can look up a name of a flower and find the meaning that was in vogue at that time. Look here."

She pointed to a name and read aloud, "Alyssum. Worth beyond beauty."

My inner antennae began to rise.

"Amaryllis," she read. "Splendid beauty. Isn't that lovely?"

The antennae were up and waving, and I suddenly remembered the art appraiser talking about the forged paintings.

"*First we have* Splendid Beauty," Mr. Ventury had said, "*portraying a single red amaryllis —*"

It was coming back to me.

"— *then* Magnificent Beauty *portraying —*"

"*A white calla,*" I had said. At Ventury's quizzical look I had told him that I was a florist.

"Lottie," I said, "would you look up the meaning of a calla?"

She turned a few pages. "Here it is. Calla means magnificent beauty."

"And hibiscus?"

"Delicate beauty."

Just like the paintings in the Beauty collection.

Lottie glanced at the clock on the wall.

"Ladies, we'd better get ready. We open in twenty minutes."

"May I borrow your book?" I asked Grace.

While my assistants prepared to open the shop for the day, I returned to the workroom and pulled the Donnelly house orders from the filing cabinet where Lottie had stowed them.

A single tiger lily in baby's breath.
One red hibiscus with thyme leaves.
One iris in statice.
An amaryllis in palm leaves.
One primrose — not an evening primrose
— with oleander.

Researching the meanings of the flower combinations, it became apparent that Frank had used the first flower in each arrangement to name one of the Beauty paintings. But what had the other part of the arrangement meant?

I put in a call to Marco, got his voice mail, and left him a message to call me back. Maybe he would have an idea.

"Abby," Lottie said, coming through the curtain, "I hate to interrupt, but I went to open up and saw a bunch of people with cats waiting outside."

"As if our day wasn't busy enough," I said

336

with a sigh.

"There's good news, though," Lottie said. "Francesca called to say she was coming in. I'm sure she'll be glad to lend a hand."

That was good news?

"Just show Marco's mum the love, dear," I heard Grace say from the other side of the curtain.

"Thank you, Grace."

# CHAPTER TWENTY-TWO

I glanced through the big bay window and saw people gathered outside the door, holding cats in their arms, waiting for the shop to open.

"Okay, here's what we'll do," I said. "Grace and I will handle the shop, and Lottie, would you go outside and take pictures of the cats with our digital camera? I'll print them out; then Marco and I can take them to the Newport mansion at noon and see if Juanita will help us again. We need to find that missing feline so these people will stop coming around."

"Sounds like a plan," Lottie said. "I'll hand out business cards, so maybe we'll even get some orders out of it."

While Lottie worked with the crowd, I put in a desperate call to Marco at Down the Hatch. Fortunately, this time he picked up. "Hey, how's my gorgeous redhead? Sorry I didn't call you back right away, Buttercup. I got your message and —"

"Never mind about that, Marco. How quickly can you bring that invitation book down here?"

"Let me guess. My mom is on her way."

"You got it."

"On my way, too," the wise, wise man of my dreams said.

As luck would have it, when Marco stopped by, we were swamped with customers. I ducked into the workroom just long enough to get the invitation binder and a kiss and give him a condensed version of my code theory.

"It's a solid theory, Abby. I like it."

I beamed. "And I have a great excuse to get us back inside the mansion." I showed him the photos I'd printed out. "Cats!"

"Awesome, babe. Now I've got to concentrate on finding Frank Talbot."

"See you at noon?"

"I've got a meeting with Dave at eleven, and I'm not sure how long it will take, so let's play it by ear."

We paused as the front door jingled. I heard Marco's mom call a greeting to Grace.

"You'd better go out the back way," I said, "unless you feel like looking at those invitations again."

Marco hugged me, then started walking backward, heading toward the kitchen. "For that you're getting a foot massage tonight."

"Make it both feet and you've got a deal."

As usual, Francesca looked fantastic. Hair soft and flowing, jacket and scarf draped just so, making me wish I'd taken more time with my appearance that morning.

She set down a huge pan in her hand to give me a hug and to kiss both my cheeks. "Bella, you look tense this morning. Too much work, eh?"

"Something like that."

"Don't worry. I am here to help. I came early because my daughter asked me to babysit at noon. And I've brought my famous *Filetto alla Rossini,* made with the freshest, grass-fed, organic beef, so you needn't worry about lunch, either. I had to hunt all over for the beef, but nothing is too good for my family. Now, let's see what you've decided about the invitations."

Over Francesca's shoulder, I caught sight of Grace standing in the parlor doorway. She mouthed, "Show her the love."

I took a deep breath. "I was wondering . . . if you'd found any that you liked."

Francesca gave me a puzzled look, so I

handed her the binder. "Would you show me?"

"Yes, of course." She placed it on the cashier's counter and began to flip through the samples, finally tapping her finger on one. "This one would be perfect for the Salvare shower."

She was taller than me, so I couldn't see her selection until she stepped aside. Then I did a double take. "*That's* the one you like?"

A wrinkle creased her brow. "You don't like it?"

"No, I *do* like it!"

"Really?"

"Really." And that was the absolute truth because it was the same invitation Marco and I had picked out, a beige linen look with darker-colored deckled edges. "I love it, Mrs. Salvare. You have excellent taste."

I saw movement in the parlor doorway and glanced up see Grace give me an encouraging thumbs-up.

"And," I said, "I think it's perfect for the Salvare shower."

With a delighted laugh, she hugged me so hard she lifted me off my feet. "Abby, bella, thank you! It makes me so happy that you're pleased with my choice. Maybe you should use the invitations for the Knight shower, too, yes?"

"Sure. I can do that."

Then she laughed, a light, tinkling sound that was pleasing to the ear. "My Marco was right. You don't hide your emotions well at all. I know you want one big shower, Abby, and if that will make you happy, then that will make me happy, too. One big shower for both families."

I hugged her. "That will make me *very* happy, Mrs. Salvare."

She held me by my arms and gave me a serious stare. "Now we will get one more thing out of the way. No more Mrs. Salvare. It's Francesca. Say it with me. Fran. Ches. Ka. Yes?"

"Yes, Francesca." I felt my face go hot all over. It felt odd to call her by her first name, but I supposed in time I'd get used it.

"Later on you will call me Mama." And with that, she went into the back room to hang up her coat.

With Francesca helping out, I had a little window of free time in the late morning, so I decided to use it to see if I could find the missing cat. I called Marco to see if he could go with me to the Newport mansion, but he was still in his meeting, so I went alone.

Fortunately, the gates were open, so I drove straight up the long driveway and parked in front of the garage. As I headed toward the courtyard, I caught sight of Mrs. Dunbar in her gardening clothes and rubber shoes, with a basket over one arm, walking toward the back of the property. I called to her, but she didn't hear me, so I kept going.

I knocked on the back door and waited, hoping someone would be in the kitchen. After a few minutes, I tried the door and found it unlocked, so I peered inside. "Hello?"

Getting no answer, I stepped into the house and called again, but all was silent.

*Hmm.* Wasn't this how Grace had started out?

I glanced at the door to the basement, but it was closed and no light showed beneath it. *Whew.*

Hearing a door open behind me, I spun around and saw Lindsey just coming in from the outside. She had on jeans and that red coat I lusted after, her blond hair pulled back in a swingy ponytail.

"Hi, Abby," she said, as though seeing me in the Newports' kitchen was an everyday occurrence.

"The door was open, so I kind of let myself in." I shrugged sheepishly.

"Mrs. Dunbar has a habit of leaving it

unlocked. Don't worry. I let myself in all the time. Are you here to see Juanita?"

"Yes. I brought more cat photos."

"She should be here in about fifteen minutes. She had a mani-pedi appointment."

Drat. Fifteen minutes of valuable time wasted.

"I know what Charity looks like," Lindsey said. "Want me to look at the photos?"

"That would be great." I pulled the photos out of my purse and handed them to her.

Lindsey went through the pile one by one, shaking her head. She paused at one, then said, "Nope, not that one either. Sorry. None of these are her. I hope they aren't strays. I'd hate to think of so many cats being homeless."

"Me, too. But thanks for your help."

"I'd better get moving," Lindsey said. "I help Juanita teach a Shakti yoga class on Fridays, and I have to get the room ready."

"I'll see myself out."

I opened the back door just as Griffin came up the walk. When he saw me, he stopped in surprise that instantly turned to irritation. "What are you doing here?"

"I came to see Juanita to show her some new cat photos."

"Juanita is clearly not here, as evidenced

by the empty garage bay."

Never one to waste an opportunity, I said, "Actually, maybe you could help me. I'm looking for information about Virginia's boyfriend."

"I have said all I'm going to. So, nice seeing you again. Good-bye."

I hated to be blown off. It brought out my Irish temper.

"I know about your affair, Griffin," I blurted.

# CHAPTER TWENTY-THREE

Griffin's smile froze. "What did you say?"

"I know about your affair?"

"I think you'd better leave right now."

"Okay, if you don't want to talk about that, could you tell me about Virginia and Francis Talbot?"

He seemed flustered by the change in subject. "What?"

"Your aunt and her boyfriend. Are they still seeing each other?"

He made a dismissive motion. "I don't keep track of my aunt's activities."

"Then what do you know about the forged paintings?"

"My dear girl, where do you get such deluded ideas? I didn't learn about the forgeries until Ventury discovered them."

"Then you and Juanita weren't in on the scheme?"

"What scheme? I knew nothing about what my aunt was up to. I thought she gave up on her crazy idea, so before you start trying to link me to the crime —"

"You're already linked, Griffin. So if you're not involved, talk to me."

"I really don't have time for this."

"Do you have time for the police to start investigating you? Because I know enough to make them very interested in you as a suspect."

He studied me for a long moment. "If I do tell you, what's in it for me?"

"My silence. I can keep my mouth shut when I want to, but I've got to have a reason to want to." Wow. I sounded just like Marco.

His forehead wrinkled, as though he didn't know what to make of me. He opened his mouth to speak, then shut it again, as if totally perplexed. I often had that effect on people.

"So, if I tell you about my aunt's so-called scheme, you'll stop making me look like a suspect?"

I smiled in relief. "Sounds like we have a deal."

"Shall we sit in the courtyard?" Griffin led the way to a stone bench, took out a freshly ironed handkerchief, dusted off one end of the bench, and offered me a seat.

Putting his foot up on the bench and taking his chin in hand, he leaned toward me, as though waiting for a signal to begin.

"First, tell me how Virginia's plan was supposed to work."

He thought for a moment. "Picture this, if you will. Grandmother gathers us together to warn us that unless we become a credit to our family and get involved in her pet charities, she will cut us out of her will. Just imagine our reaction to that news. The next thing I know, here comes Virginia with this outlandish idea to sell off the art collection, determined not to be cheated out of her rightful inheritance. We thought she had gone completely off her rocker and refused to go along with her. In truth, I couldn't have cared less about any inheritance because I earn a tidy income all on my own. At any rate, I heard nothing more about it and assumed my aunt had dropped the idea."

"Did your aunt say who was going to help her get rid of the collection?"

"No. I would suppose the professor had a hand in it, but I know nothing more than what I've told you."

"What can you tell me about this professor?"

"I met the man at dinner once and thought him a bore."

At that, I showed him the photo Marco

had printed out that was still tucked into my purse. "Is this the professor?"

"A bit younger, I would say, but yes. That's him."

"This is a picture of Frank Talbot, a suspected art thief."

Griffin's eyes widened. "Does my aunt know about that?"

"I don't know what your aunt knows. When I showed her this photo, she fainted."

"She tends to do that when she's stressed." Griffin glanced at his watch, then straightened, as though he were about to leave.

I got to my feet. "Is it possible your aunt was letting Francis into the house to steal the paintings?"

"Anything's possible, but I really don't know. Look, I need to get back to my writing. I have a deadline coming up."

What a champ. Griffin was more concerned about his deadline than with the fact that he'd just ratted on his aunt. Seriously, was making a deadline *that* important?

"One more quick question. Did your grandmother visit you Monday morning?"

He glanced at his watch again and said hurriedly, "She came to say good morning, as she always did."

"Why did she cancel her manicure that morning?"

"I didn't know she had, and that's two questions, not one."

"Sorry, I'm terrible at math. So your grandmother came to see you right after her argument with Juanita?"

Griffin's Adam's apple bobbed as he swallowed. "She what?"

"Didn't she come to tell you she knew about your affair?"

"That's beyond absurd. Once again, where do you get these ideas?"

"Come on, Griffin. Your grandmother found out Juanita was sneaking over to your apartment, so she canceled her appointment to have a talk with you, to ask you to call it off. But you must have denied the affair; either that or you told her you wouldn't call it off —"

"Not true!"

"— because at lunchtime, she had another argument with Juanita, and shortly afterward was pushed to her death."

His face drained of color.

"Did Juanita push your grandmother down the stairs, Griffin?"

"No!" he said in a choked voice.

"Can you prove it?"

"I don't have to prove her innocence."

"Okay," I said. "We'll let the cops do that. I'm sure Juanita will love knowing you wouldn't defend her." I turned, as though to walk away.

"Wait!" He put one hand on his forehead, as though he didn't know what to say. Then, after a heavy sigh, he said, "Juanita was with me."

"I need details, Griffin." Remembering another one of Marco's favorite lines, I added, "I can make this go easier on you and Juanita both if you talk to me."

He sank onto the bench and put his head in his hands. For several minutes, he sat there shaking his head, as though he couldn't believe what he was about to do. Finally, in a small voice, he said, "Nita came over after lunch, all upset, saying my grandmother had threatened to tell my father if we didn't stop seeing each other. Nita's fear was that my father would divorce her and she would be poor again, so I told her I would support her, but she said we couldn't afford to take that chance. Then she took off in her car and didn't come back until after the police arrived.

"Yes, it's true Grandmother treated her like a child, but not in a bad way. Grandmother wasn't happy with my father when he married Nita, but she accepted her."

"Just not as your lover."

He seemed to sag inwardly, as though the

weight of his guilt was too much. "It was wrong, and I knew it. Grandmother pleaded with me to stop seeing Nita, but I denied that anything was going on. She left angry and disappointed, so very disappointed, in me — and that was the last time I saw her."

He put his hands over his face and turned away, his shoulders shaking in silent sobs.

I left him there to mourn privately.

What an afternoon. I'd gotten a lot more information than I'd expected and couldn't wait to tell Marco about it.

When I got to Down the Hatch at five o'clock, the concerned frown on Marco's face was enough to make me forget all the exciting news. "What's wrong? Did something happen?"

He began to massage my shoulders. "Did it go all right with my mom? She didn't give you a hard time about the invitation, did she?"

"Not at all. It went surprisingly well."

The worry lines between his eyebrows disappeared and then he lifted me off my feet in a bear hug. "That's great, Abby."

"Were you really that concerned?"

He scoffed. "Not at all."

Yeah, right. That was the way Marco always reacted to good news. "Why don't we sit at our booth and I'll tell you about my amazing afternoon," I suggested.

"You can tell me in the car. We have to take a field trip to Chicago this evening to track down the elusive Professor Francis Talbot. With a little luck, Abby, we may be able to wrap up the art-theft case tonight."

"And clear Grace's name, too?"

"Let's hope so."

"Awesome. And yes, that's my stomach growling again."

Marco picked up a large brown bag. "I have sandwiches packed. We can eat on the way."

"What spurred this field trip?" I asked, folding back the wrapper on my sandwich as we headed north to the interstate.

"Three things. First, after making a lot of phone calls to various former employers this afternoon, I was able to track down a cell phone number for Professor Francis Talbot. Then, after some serious arm-twisting and promises of free beer, my source at the cellular provider e-mailed me Talbot's records for the last thirty days, and it appears he's been in England for part of the month. But there was one call on the list made to a cell phone registered to Virginia, and that establishes enough of a connection for us to talk to her again."

"If Francis has been in England, then he obviously directed the operation from there."

"That's what I was thinking. After more phone calls, I found out that Mrs. Talbot is back in residence, so I figured we should get up there tonight and see if she can verify that Francis is our man Frank."

"Perfect timing, Marco. Let me tell you what I found out this afternoon. You will be so amazed."

I went through the whole story from beginning to end, feeling quite proud of myself, and then opened the floor to questions.

"I have one," Marco said, taking a swig of water to wash down the last of his sandwich.

Only one? I must have done a better job of explaining than I thought. "Go ahead, please."

"What the hell were you thinking, Abby?"

He was a lot less amazed than I'd imagined.

"Breaking into their house? Putting yourself in jeopardy? Did you think any of it through beforehand?"

"Well, to tell you the truth —"

"What if Griffin was in on the art scheme with his aunt?"

"I'm pretty sure he's not."

"With Juanita, then? What if he's our killer? What if Griffin decided to make sure you couldn't tell anyone else? Can you even begin to imagine the danger you put yourself into? Why didn't you at least let me know where you were going?"

Way more than one question. "In the first place, I wasn't there alone, Marco. Virginia was up in her studio and —"

"Virginia was up in her studio on Monday morning, too, Sunshine, if she's telling the truth. It's not the same as someone having your back."

"But I got answers."

Marco sighed so deeply, clearly frustrated, that it seemed to start at his toes. "Abby, Abby."

Merely by the way he said my name I could tell how disappointed he was, and that was much worse than his being angry with me. Disappointing Marco made me feel awful.

"I'm sorry, Marco. I got caught up in the moment."

"You let your ego take over, Sunshine. That's how private investigators get themselves killed."

I wanted to argue, but the little voice of conscience in my head said, *He's right. You were on such a roll, you threw caution to the wind.*

Did consciences always talk in clichés?

At least Marco was still calling me Sunshine. "You're right. I knew better. I promise I'll try not to let that happen again."

He reached over to take my hand. "I do my best to protect you, babe, but I can't protect you from yourself. Just be aware of the signs that your ego is taking control and stop it immediately, okay?"

"Okay."

"Good. Now, tell me what happened with my mom today."

*Think positive, Abby.*

"Your mom was a big help in the shop, Marco. And get this! She liked the invitation we picked out and wants us to have one big shower instead of separate showers for each side of the family."

"Are you sure this is my mom you're talking about?"

"Yep. And she asked me to call her Francesca."

Marco sighed again, but this time it was a sigh of relief and came from the belly region. When he stopped for a red light, he leaned over to give me a kiss, then pulled back to gaze into my eyes. "I love you, Abigail Christine Knight."

He remembered my middle name! And that made *me* sigh, but mine started at heart level.

It was still light outside when we got to the Gold Coast neighborhood where Francis Talbot lived. There was no public parking lot in the vicinity, so Marco had to circle the block for fifteen minutes before we finally found a parking space along the curb. Inside the high-rise condominium building, a doorman in a blue blazer with black braids on the sleeves asked us to sign in at the reception desk. Marco wrote down our names, then displayed his ID to the security guard behind the counter.

"I'm Marco Salvare," he said. "This is my assistant, Abby Knight. Are you William?"

"Yes, sir, that's me," said the sixtysomething man with salt-and-pepper hair.

"I spoke to Maryann at the management office today," Marco said. "She told me she'd let you know I was coming this evening to meet with Mr. and Mrs. Talbot."

"Yes, sir, she did say you were coming in to see them. This is about an inheritance, isn't that right?"

"That's right," Marco said. "Our job is to make sure we have the right Francis Talbot before the legal department can proceed any further in processing the inheritance. And along those lines, would you identify the man in this photo please?"

Marco held out a copy of the newspaper picture of Frank Talbot. William glanced at it briefly, then nodded. "That's Mr. Talbot, all right. It's an old photograph, but that's him. I'm sorry to say that Mr. Talbot is out at the moment, Mr. Salvare, but Mrs. Talbot is here. Do you want me to ring her?"

"That would be helpful," Marco said. "She's in the penthouse, right?"

"That's right, sir."

As William picked up a phone at his desk to call the Talbot apartment, I whispered, "How did you know they live in the penthouse?"

"I didn't, but I figured he'd tell me which floor if I was wrong."

"They must be doing well financially."

Marco held his finger to his lips as the security guard began to talk.

"Mrs. Talbot? This is William. I've got a gentleman here by the name of Marco Salvare. He wants to see you about an inheritance. Do you know anything about that?" He listened a moment, then said, "No, ma'am. Yes, ma'am. Thank you, Mrs. Talbot."

He replaced the receiver in the cradle,

then looked up. "She said to have a seat and she'll be right down."

Wow. I couldn't believe Mrs. Talbot had bought our story. Maybe she was unaware of what her husband had been up to.

We looked around the spacious waiting area and decided on an upholstered sofa on the far side of the room, out of view of the bank of elevators. The reception room had a black marble floor and four long baby-blue sofas, with a beautiful silk centerpiece on a large, white marble-topped table in the center. Obviously this was a building for tenants with money.

I heard an elevator ding, and a minute later, a woman came around the corner. She was an attractive older woman in her mid-seventies with white hair cut in a blunt bob, with thick silver hoops in her ears.

I recognized her at once and grabbed Marco's arm, whispering, "It's her! It's Dot, Marco, the lady who was renting the Donnelly house."

"She can't be Frank's wife, Abby. She's too old. She must be his mother."

Dot looked very elegant in an apricot silk blouse and matching wide-leg pants with silver flats. When she spotted me walking toward her with Marco at my side, I saw a glimmer of recognition in her eyes, but she calmly turned and went back to the elevator. Before she could get inside the cab, however, Marco stopped the door from closing. He waited for me to enter, then let the door slide shut.

"Mrs. Talbot, I presume?" Marco said.

# CHAPTER TWENTY-FOUR

"Open that door at once!" Dot said in an authoritative voice.

As the elevator began to ascend, Marco put his finger on a large red button. "Okay, but that means pushing the emergency button, and that could trap us here for a while."

Her eyes shifted from side to side, as though calculating her next move. Dot's clothing and accessories spoke of money, yet she had the sly glances and quick movements of a pickpocket.

Lifting her chin, she said, "I don't know who you think you are, but you have no right to hold me prisoner in this elevator!"

"We'll go up to your apartment and talk, then," Marco said.

She studied us both for a moment, then tried the innocent routine again. "You tricked me! This isn't about an inheritance."

"Not your inheritance," I said. "Not Frank's either."

"Who," she asked haughtily, "is Frank?"

"Your son," Marco said, "also known as Francis."

Dot burst out laughing. "Francis? I don't know anyone named Francis — or Frank, for that matter. You've got the wrong Talbot, mister."

"Then why did William downstairs identify the man in this photo as Francis Talbot?" Marco asked, showing her the copy.

Dot said nothing, only pressed her lips together and lowered her eyebrows.

When the elevator doors opened, she kicked off her shoes, shot out of the cab, and ran up the long hallway, her arms pumping as hard as they could as she tried to reach the open door at the end. But Marco was faster, and when she dashed inside, he was right behind her.

"Help!" she cried, trying to shut the door on him. "Call the cops!"

"Why don't you do that, Mrs. Talbot?" Marco said, motioning for me to step inside. "In fact, let's call the New Chapel Police, too. I think they'll be very interested in that painting behind you."

Dot swung around to look as Marco pointed to a large oil painting hanging on the wall of her foyer above a gorgeous red Chinese chest. The painting was of an amaryllis in a glass vase sitting on a round table covered with a blue tablecloth.

*Splendid Beauty*! It certainly wasn't a coincidence that it was hanging in her condo. But was that the original or another forgery?

She scowled at us but finally indicated a sitting room to my left. "Have a seat, then."

"Thanks," I said, eyeing a comfy-looking sofa facing a gorgeous, pale green marble fireplace.

Dot suddenly sprinted up the center hallway toward the back of her unit.

"Sprightly for a woman her age," I said to Marco, as we ran after her.

Dot ran into her kitchen and seemed to be heading for a knife block full of black-handled blades, but she slipped on her polished marble floor and nearly collided with her massive, stainless-steel refrigerator. Marco caught her as she staggered backward.

He ushered her to her kitchen table and sat her down. "Now, let's have a talk, and if you cooperate, maybe I won't have to call the New Chapel Police."

She crossed her arms over her chest and pouted. "You, mister, are going to be in big trouble. I'll have you charged with kidnapping."

"And you, Dot," Marco said, swinging a

363

chair around to straddle it, "are going to be charged with aiding and abetting a criminal."

"How dare you insult me!" she cried. "I don't know who Dot is, and I certainly don't know any criminals."

Marco put the printout of Frank Talbot on the table in front of her. "You know him."

She shoved it away and said nothing.

"Tell me about your sons again," I said, taking a seat across the table from her. "The ones I saw when I delivered your flowers."

She gave me a contemptuous look. "I've never set eyes on you in my life."

"I'm the florist, remember? You told me about your three sons, and how only one of them was successful. That'd be Frank, right? A successful art thief?"

"You, missy, are mistaken. I've never even been to New Chapwick."

New Chapwick. Dot was good. "Who sent you all those arrangements?" I asked. "Frank?"

"Frank who?" she said stubbornly.

"What were you supposed to do when you got the arrangements?" I asked.

She tapped her fingers on the table. "You're making no sense whatsoever."

"When is Frank due back?" Marco asked.

"How many times do I have to tell you —

364

I don't know a Frank!"

"That's okay," Marco said. "We can wait until he gets here."

She shifted her eyes back and forth again, obviously trying to find a way out. Then, with a gasp, she put her hand over her heart. "I'm getting palpitations. I need to call my doctor."

She started to get up, but Marco blocked her. She sat down again with a hard *plop* and folded her arms, scowling at both of us. "You'll be sorry when I keel over dead."

"Look," Marco said, "just tell us how Frank worked the heist, and we'll leave."

"Oh," she said in a quivering voice, fanning her face with her hand, "I'm feeling faint."

Marco sighed sharply, then rose and motioned for me to follow him. Once we were far enough away that she couldn't hear, he whispered, "We're not getting anywhere, and we can't interrogate her all night. I'm not even sure Frank is coming back here. So I'll stall for a few more minutes while you see if you can find anything that would connect Frank to the Newports or to the art theft."

"What about that painting in the foyer?"

"She could say she got it as a gift or found it in the alley, for that matter. We'll need something more concrete."

I nodded and left the kitchen.

"Where is she going?" Dot demanded. "She can't just walk about as she pleases."

"She needs to use the washroom," Marco said.

I didn't hear the rest of the conversation. I had reached the first bedroom and was doing a fast search, but the masculine-looking room that I assumed was Frank's was Spartan, with no personal effects whatsoever. In the closet I found a row of identical navy raw silk suits and another row of white shirts. Four pairs of navy leather shoes were beneath. The one chest of drawers contained underwear and socks and nothing more.

In the second bedroom, a decidedly feminine room, I found lots of women's clothing, shoes, purses, and hats, but again, no photos. In the dresser I found undergarments. On her bedside table was an Agatha Christie novel and a phone. I checked the phone and memorized the number.

The bathrooms held the usual shaving and bathing supplies, with one cabinet full of cosmetics in the bathroom off the second bedroom, but nothing of interest to our investigation. I did pocket a brown tortoiseshell comb in the man's bathroom that could prove useful for DNA.

I was in the sitting room when Marco came striding toward me. I was just about to tell him I'd given up the search when I spotted a large book propped beside an upholstered chair.

"Let's go," Marco said. "We're done here."

"Just a minute." I ran to the chair and picked up the book. The title was *The Language of Flowers.* It was by the same author as the book Grace had given me, only a more modern edition. Could it be merely a coincidence? My gut told me no.

Marco was holding the door for me, so I replaced the book and dashed out after him. As we trotted toward the elevator, I heard the door slam behind us. "Is Dot going to call the cops?" I asked.

"I doubt it. She doesn't want more trouble. I left her my card and told her I could make it go much easier on her if she'd work with me. I'm sure she and Frank will be spending the rest of the night trying to decide on their next move. Let's hope it's not getting out of town."

"They keep that place clean, Marco. No photos whatsoever, or any bills or statements that I could find. Who doesn't have some kind of mail lying around on a table or in a drawer? The only thing I found almost too coincidental was that gigantic oil painting in the foyer that I would swear is identical to one in the Newport mansion, and a book on the language of flowers by the same author of the book that Constance left Grace."

"The cops would be less than impressed. Dot could claim it was left there by previous owners."

"What about the doorman who identified Frank in the photo?"

"Unreliable eyewitness. I'm telling you, the Talbots knew what they were doing, Abby. They're pros. I've read about these types of art-theft rings before. Those two men you saw when you made the delivery were part of the team. One collected the paintings; the other was the master forger. Dot acted as their cover, and Frank directed the whole scheme from a safe distance."

"And they used those floral deliveries as a code, Marco. I'm sure of it. This morning I made a list of the flowers we'd delivered and matched them to the meanings in Grace's book. All of them corresponded to the paintings in the Beauty collection. So when Dot received the flowers, it had to be a message as to which painting to steal."

"If only we had airtight proof," he said with a frustrated sigh.

Marco was silent as we walked out to his car, no doubt sorting through all the information we'd gathered, trying to find the answer. To lighten the mood, when he opened the car door for me, I said with a coy smile, "If you play your cards right, when we get back to Bloomers, I'll show you my list."

Marco put his hands on the roof on either side of me and leaned in, giving me that quirky, sexy half smile that always drove me wild. "Is that all you're going to show me?"

My bad boy was back. "Come closer and I'll whisper what else."

At that moment, I spotted a black minivan with tinted windows driving slowly up the street. It couldn't be another coincidence.

"Marco, it's them!" I grabbed his shoulders and pulled him to a crouched position. "It's their black minivan, the one I saw at the Donnelly house."

Marco raised his head to look, then, still crouched, led me around to the back of the car. "They're parking. Stay down until I give you the word, then take a quick look and see if you recognize them."

I waited, my heart racing, until Marco said, "Now."

I raised my head and saw the two men

about five yards past us, moving rapidly toward the condo building. "It's them, Marco," I whispered. "Those are the men Dot claimed were her sons."

Marco had already pulled out his pocket camera and was snapping photos. "They probably won't be good enough to use in court, but I wanted a record of it anyway."

We watched through the long expanse of glass as Dot's so-called sons nodded to William, then headed toward the elevators, and as soon as they stepped inside the cab, we returned to the security counter.

"William, I forgot to thank you for your assistance," Marco said, handing him a fifty-dollar bill. "You were a big help."

"Thank you, sir," he said with a pleased smile. "Thank you very much."

"I've got a few more quick questions for you." Marco held up another fifty. "Those two men who just went by — would they be going up to the penthouse?"

William eyed the money. "Yes, sir, they would."

"Know their names?"

"Johnny and Eamon is how I know them, but let's see." William pulled out a clipboard and looked through a list. "Here it is. John Talbot and Eamon Talbot. Family members."

"They don't have to sign in?" Marco asked.

"Not if they get clearance from the owners, no, sir."

"Thanks. That's all I needed to know." Marco gave him the money and we left.

Outside, he took down the minivan's license plate number and phoned it in to Sean Reilly, leaving the message on his voice mail. "Hey, Sean, Marco here. I might have a break in the Newport art heist for you. Run this plate and I'll explain when I talk to you."

Within ten minutes, Reilly returned the call, so Marco put him on speakerphone.

"Hey, guys," Reilly said. "I have to make this quick. The van in question is registered to a John J. Cole. He was released from prison six months ago for — get ready for this — art theft."

"Thanks, Sean. That's just what I needed to know. I'll call you as soon as I have more information."

Marco put in a call to his former army commander, now a vice president at Prairie Communications, who had turned to Marco for help after he'd been falsely accused of a crime, and was assured the necessary phone records would be faxed to him as soon as possible.

Back at Marco's bar by nine o'clock, we went straight to his office to pick up the faxes, then headed down the block to Bloomers. I made coffee, a poor imitation of Grace's, sadly, and we sat in the parlor poring over cell phone records for Francis Talbot and Eamon MacShane. We struck out on Cole because there was no listing under his name, but what we did learn was that Talbot hadn't called either his men or Dot, further confirming my belief that he'd communicated through the flower arrangements.

The key, Marco said, was finding out who the inside person was and getting him or her to talk. That person was the only weak link in a very slick art heist.

"It's Virginia," I told him. "She knew Frank beforehand. She was in love with him. He was probably sizing up that art collection the evening he came to dinner, figuring out how to steal them. I'll bet Connie sensed something about him and that's why she tried to get Virginia to stop seeing him."

"Don't forget, Abby, that Frank met other family members at that dinner. He could have made contact with any or all of them later. After all, we have only Griffin's word that the family turned down Virginia's plan. They might have said no initially, but had a change of heart later."

Marco's cell phone rang. He answered with his usual "Salvare," then listened for a minute before holding his hand over the speaker. "It's Sean. I'll take it in the other room."

While Marco was talking to Reilly, I took another look at the list of flower arrangements Frank had sent. It was just too much of a coincidence that the orders had stopped when Connie died. It was also hard to believe that professional thieves would make a mistake and leave two forged copies of *Splendid Beauty.* What had happened? Had Constance noticed the missing painting? Had that discovery led to her death?

"Abby," Marco said, coming through the curtain, "you'll never guess what Constance Newport had clutched in her hand when she died."

"Would a piece of paper with the name of her killer on it be too much to hope for?"

"Cat fur."

# CHAPTER TWENTY-FIVE

"Say that again," I said, trying to shift gears.

Marco straddled a chair across from me. "Forensics found cat fur in Constance's hand."

"Does that mean she was holding on to Charity when she died?"

"No, but it indicates that her fingers were curled around an object, possibly a leash, when she fell, and there were faint marks on the insides of her fingers, as though the leash had been pulled through them. Reilly said the detectives are trying to come up with a scenario that fits the evidence. He was very interested in what we learned in Chicago, by the way. He said he'd pass it along to the detectives and that we'll probably get a call from them."

He covered his mouth for a yawn. "Sorry. Long day. I see you've been working on your list. Did you make any progress?"

I gave him a rundown on my missing

painting theory, only to have Marco yawn again.

"I'm sorry, Sunshine. It's not you. I was up late last night working on this. It sounds like you're onto something, though."

I knew Marco needed his rest, and that if he came home with me, he'd be distracted, so I said, "Let's call it quits and work on this tomorrow, Marco. I'm exhausted, too. Go home and get some sleep."

When I got to the apartment, Simon was there to greet me, giving me that innocent meow and rubbing against my legs just like the sweet little white cat I used to think he was.

"You're not fooling me, boy-o. I have your number now."

Simon stood up on his hind legs and reached way up with his front paws, as if to say, "Hold me. I missed you."

I picked him up to cuddle him, and he rubbed his cold pink nose against my chin.

All was forgiven.

When I got to Bloomers the next morning, Grace met me at the door with a worried frown. "Abby, come with me, please."

I followed her into the parlor and sat down in front of a cup of her delicious java. "Did something happen?"

She sat down across from me with a cup of tea. "I had a call from Dave Hammond yesterday evening, and it wasn't good news."

No wonder she wanted me to have coffee first. A shot of Jack Daniel's in it would have worked even better.

Grace took a deep breath, then said, "The chief prosecutor has called for a grand jury." Her hand shook so hard, she had to put down her cup. "I know they're going to indict me, Abby."

"Grace, we won't let that happen. We're making progress on the case. Let me tell you about our evening."

Fifteen minutes later, Grace's tenseness had eased. "Oh, my! To think that an art-theft ring was operating right under Connie's nose! And, moreover, that one of her children was involved. She must have feared a plot was brewing, Abby, to have wanted an appraiser to come in immediately. Poor thing. What a dreadful shame."

"And then you walked into the mansion and became the perfect patsy, Grace."

Grace sighed sadly. "I did, didn't I?"

"Morning, ladies," Lottie said, coming in to pour herself a cup of coffee. She sat down at the table, saw our somber faces, and her sunny smile turned to concern. "What happened?"

Lottie listened closely as I gave her a quick update on the previous day's events; then she got a refill for her cup and sat back down. "They're making good progress, Gracie. And I've been doing some thinking on this myself. Let me tell you what came to me in the middle of the night.

"First of all," she said, "I agree with you that Virginia is the most likely inside person. And I'd bet any money she was responsible for her mom's death. Now, about your duplicate painting theory, Abby. Think way back to when those orders came in. Do you remember me telling you I had to substitute a red amaryllis for the hibiscus?"

"Vaguely."

"If your hunch is right," Lottie said, "then by substituting the amaryllis, we told the thieves to copy a different painting than what they were supposed to."

And suddenly I saw the whole picture — or rather two pictures. Because of our error, two paintings of the same subject showed up at the house. And if I'd noticed them, they'd have been very obvious to Connie.

"But the arrangement with the substituted amaryllis wasn't completely identical to the other one," Grace said. "One was accompanied by thyme, and the other by palm leaves. Wouldn't that have told the thieves something?"

"What if the greenery that accompanied the flower was a different type of message?" I asked. "For instance, according to your book, thyme can mean strength or courage. Palm leaves can mean victory or success. Perhaps they functioned as green lights."

While I was explaining, Grace had gotten up to get *The Language of Flowers,* and was now poring over entries in the dictionary. "Abby, you're definitely onto something. The last order we received included oleander, which means caution or beware."

"That was a red light," I said. "I'll bet Frank found out that Connie was onto him and had to warn his men."

"So what do we do now?" Lottie asked.

"Find out who the inside person is," I said. "I think it's time to confront Virginia."

"Not alone," Lottie said. "You get on that phone and call Marco. I don't want to find you lying under a suit of armor — unless Marco's inside it. Okay, ladies, it's time to open the shop. Positions, please."

Back in the workroom, I called Marco to tell him what we'd concluded.

"Let's head to the Newport house at noon," he said. "If Virginia is involved, I have a feeling that we have everything we

378

need to make her crumble."

"So lunchtime, huh?"

"I'll have sandwiches waiting for us when we get back. Ham and Swiss with spicy mustard and tomato for you, right?"

"Right." Actually, it was turkey and Swiss, but he was too adorable to correct.

Juanita was just driving out of the gates when Marco and I arrived at the mansion. She pulled even with him, ignored me, and blew him a kiss. Marco pretended to catch it; then, as she sped down the road with a roar of her powerful motor, he sailed up the driveway and parked behind the garage.

"Now do you see why I let Juanita flirt with me?" Marco asked.

"No comment."

When we presented ourselves at the back door, Mrs. Dunbar seemed surprised to see us.

"We'd like to speak with Virginia," Marco said.

"I'd be afraid to disturb her, sir," the housekeeper said with a worried frown.

"Tell her we spent yesterday evening with Dot," he said. "She'll see us."

The housekeeper hustled off to deliver our request, and a few minutes later, Virginia came striding into the kitchen with her braid slapping against her back. As usual, she was wearing her artist's smock over a long skirt, and her cork-bottomed sandals.

She came to a halt with her feet splayed like a goose and glared regally at us. "What is the meaning of this? I don't know anyone named Dot and I resent this interruption."

"I think you know Dot as Dorothy Talbot," Marco said.

She paled, but maintained her pose. "I don't know who that is either."

"Memory tweak," I said. "She's Francis's mother."

"I've never met his mother," Virginia said with a lift of her chin. Still with those prickly chin hairs. Didn't she have a magnifying mirror?

Marco leaned one hip against the kitchen counter and folded his arms over his chest. "We had a long chat with Dorothy yesterday, Virginia. She told us all about her stay at the Donnelly place."

"We know about the flower code, too," I said. "And about Eamon MacShane and John J. Cole, and how you let them in to steal and replace paintings."

With each declaration, Virginia seemed to shrink back more.

"You were talking to Frank Talbot on the phone in the sitting room," I added. "I overheard you tell him you should have gotten rid of the duplicate painting."

"I don't know what you're talking about," she said, but this time with very little conviction. "Mrs. Dunbar, show them to the door."

Fearing Virginia would walk out of the kitchen, I said, "We know about the scheme you and Frank devised, *Ginny.* Sell the paintings, replace them with forgeries, and reclaim your inheritance. Griffin told us all about your plan."

Virginia grabbed her throat. "Griffin told you?"

"Then your mother found out," Marco said, "and your scheme fell apart."

"Did she threaten to call the police?" I asked.

Her mouth opened but no sound came out.

"You must have had quite an argument over the paintings," I said, "to get so angry that you pushed her down the stairs."

At that, Virginia collapsed into a heap on the floor.

"You were right," I said to Marco, as we knelt beside her. "She did crumble. Mrs. Dunbar, the smelling salts?"

We carried Virginia into the sitting room

and placed her on the sofa, then waited for her to regain consciousness.

"I don't think it would be wise to keep asking her questions," Mrs. Dunbar said, twisting her apron in her rough hands. "Not in the state she's in."

"We'll keep it short, Mrs. Dunbar," Marco assured her. "Would you make Virginia some tea?"

"Yes, sir," she said, and scurried out of the room.

Virginia moaned and put her hand to her forehead. Her eyelids fluttered; then her gaze focused on us. "Oh, for God's sake, did it happen again?"

"Talk to us, Virginia," Marco said. "We're not going away."

She stood up and walked to the fireplace, standing rigidly, her back to us. "Leave me alone."

"If that's how you want it," Marco said. "But we'll still have to turn your name and the names of your cohorts over to the police."

"Hasn't my family suffered enough humiliation?"

"You can make it stop," Marco said.

She swung to face us. "I'll pay you whatever you like. Just go away and leave us in peace."

"We're not here to blackmail you," Marco said. "We're investigating crimes committed against your mother. So why don't you have a seat and tell us about this plan to steal her art?"

"It isn't my mother's art," Virginia snapped. "It belongs to the Newport family. I have every right to sell whatever I like."

"Not against her will," Marco said.

"She had no right to take away our inheritances," Virginia cried, pounding the mantelpiece. "The artwork was my father's! I know he wouldn't have left it to a *cat*."

"It was your mother's choice," I reminded her. "She must have been very hurt by what you did."

Virginia stared at us for a long moment; then her lower lip began to tremble.

Sensing that she was weakening, Marco said, "If you talk to us, Virginia, I can make it go better for you when it comes time to make your statement to the cops. And you *will* be talking to the cops."

Good line! I made a mental note to add that to my growing repertoire.

Virginia sank onto a nearby chair and put her hands over her face. "How did I get myself into such a mess? How? I loved my mother. I never meant to hurt her. I didn't know those paintings meant so much to her."

Mrs. Dunbar came to the doorway with a cup of tea, glancing at us uncertainly. I motioned for her to put it on the table. She hurried in, set it down, and hurried back out.

Virginia drew a shuddering breath. "I know what everyone will think of me, but I really did try to stop Francis. After my mother confronted me with her suspicions, I told him I couldn't go through with it any longer, but he said Mother's suspicions meant nothing without proof. Trust him, he said, and when I said I was too afraid to continue, he threatened me."

"Threatened you how?" Marco asked.

"He didn't come out and say it, but I feared he would kill me. I knew then that Francis was no longer the man I fell in love with. He was ruthless and cruel, and I truly believed I had no choice."

"Tell me how the plan worked," Marco said.

She pulled a tissue out of her pocket and dabbed her eyes. "A flower arrangement sent to the house Francis had rented told his men which painting to copy. Dot would call me from a disposable cell phone, and that night I'd let J.J. into the house to take the original. When the duplicate copy was completed, Francis would send another arrangement to let them know the next painting he wanted. Then J.J. would return to the house with the forged copy, and take the next original."

"How did Frank decide which painting he wanted?" Marco asked.

"I'd foolishly given him a catalog of the art," she said in a defeated voice. "He found the buyers."

"You told me there was no catalog," I said.

Virginia said nothing.

"Did you know from the beginning that Francis was Frank Talbot, a professional art thief?" I asked.

"I had no idea, and neither did anyone else here. When Francis came to dinner, Mother was so impressed with him that she showed him the art collection. I'm sure that was when he started planning the theft, but he didn't say anything to me at that time. Mother must have sensed something because the next day she told me to stay away from him."

*Wow.* I'd hit the nail on the head. I glanced at Marco and he gave me that little flicker of a grin. Score another for the redhead.

"I voiced my concerns to Francis," Virginia continued, "but he assured me that she'd never catch on. According to him, he'd had an acquaintance in a similar situation who had sold off valuable art and replaced it with exact replicas. He said no one had ever found out, and all I had to do was leave everything to him."

My cell phone rang, momentarily distracting all three of us. Not wanting to stop Virginia's confession, I slipped out of the room as I answered in a whisper, "Hello?"

"Abs, I watched *To Catch a Thief* again last night and came up with the perfect solution for you," Jillian said. "If this doesn't help you catch the cat burglar, nothing will."

"I'm in the middle of a very important conversation, Jillian, and your interruptions are not helpful."

"This one will be, I promise. First, take each family member, individually, into the art room. Then ask, 'Doesn't it make you nervous to be in the same room with all these paintings?' "

"What will that do?"

"An art thief in a room full of art? He'd give himself away immediately."

"Nope, not helpful. I have to go now. Please don't call again."

She sighed in exasperation. "Well, I was hoping it wouldn't come to this, but it looks like I'll have to take matters into my own hands."

"Whatever." I closed my phone and returned to the sitting room, where Virginia was saying vehemently, "I hope Francis rots in jail for this. I hope he and his two men and his mother all rot in jail."

A lot of rotting for one jail.

"You said you apologized to your mother about the stolen art," Marco said. "So she knew about all the forgeries?"

"No, she knew only about *Splendid Beauty.* She came to me with her accusation and said if I didn't get it back, she'd go to the police."

"When was this?" I asked.

"Last Sunday."

"Walk me through the events on Monday leading up to your mother's death," Marco said.

Virginia picked up the cup of tea and took several sips, as though collecting her thoughts. "I saw Mother briefly at breakfast on Monday, and again at lunch. We didn't talk much. She was very distracted because of the situation with Juanita and Griffin." Her gaze flickered over to Marco. "I suppose you know about that, too."

"We know," I said.

"How did your mother find out about

their affair?" Marco asked, not missing a beat.

"She saw Nita sneaking across the yard to Griffin's apartment."

"Were you aware of their affair?" Marco asked.

"Yes," she said wearily.

"Did your brother know?" I asked.

"Burnsy? He couldn't care less what Juanita does as long as it doesn't interfere with his gambling."

"Why was Guy Luce told to leave his apartment?" I asked.

"Griffin wants to rent out both garage apartments. He thinks we'll be able to keep the house that way." Virginia scoffed. "Next he'll want to open the lower level to the public as a museum."

"You said your mother was distracted because of Juanita and Griffin," Marco said. "Were you present when she argued with Juanita at lunch?"

"Briefly. I took my food and went back to my studio."

"How do you think your mother died?" Marco asked.

"She was pushed to her death, as you well know. And if you think I had anything to do with it, you're dead wrong. The only possible person is Grace Bingham." With a scowl, she sipped her tea.

Marco motioned for me to meet him at the doorway for a conference. "Keep her talking. I want to call Reilly and get the cops out here to take her statement."

"Will they arrest Virginia?"

"*Nah.* She'll call her lawyer and he'll keep her out of jail. She may be indicted later, but my guess is that she'll remain free."

"I think she's telling the truth about not pushing her mother, Marco."

"I think so, too, but let's work on one thing at a time."

"Good, because I'm hungry."

"You're always hungry."

"Yet you love me anyway."

"That goes without saying." He turned my shoulders to face the sofa, gave me a light nudge, then stepped out of the room to make his call.

I sat in a chair adjacent to the sofa and waited while Virginia blew her nose with a big honk. I wouldn't have been surprised to see geese peering in the windows.

She glared at me. "What now?"

"I believe you, Virginia. I don't think you caused your mother's death."

"I don't much care what you believe."

No doubt about it. Virginia was just not a nice person.

Marco came back into the room and said, "Virginia, the detectives are on their way here to get a statement from you. This would be a good time to call your lawyer."

"I assumed that was coming." She set down the cup and waved us away. "See yourselves out."

As we walked to the car, Marco told me that two other detectives were heading up to Chicago to talk to Dot and Frank and, with any luck, MacShane and Cole, too. With Virginia's admission, the police were certain to get a confession from one of them.

But there was still a murderer to be found, and our suspect list had grown short. However, we made a pact not to discuss anything related to the Newports until after lunch, and instead, turned our attention to the upcoming nuptial event — namely the big fat Italian-Irish-English bridal shower. We'd pick up our investigation at dinner.

"We're right on schedule," I said. "We've chosen the invitation. I'll provide the flowers. My dad said he'd reserve the Fraternal Order of Police hall for us. All we need to do is to decide on food and guests."

"Let's decide right now that there won't be any games," Marco said. "If I have to attend this thing, I'm not playing games. I've heard your horror stories and that's enough for me."

"No games," I promised. "But for food, how about finger sandwiches, potato salad, coleslaw, a wine punch, a selection of teas and coffee, and a chocolate sheet cake?"

Marco smiled.

"What?"

"I was just picturing my mother's reaction."

"And?"

"You know she'll want to make the food and serve lots of Italian wine."

"But it's our shower, remember?"

"Have you ever attended an Italian family event, Abby? There are certain expectations."

"Come on, Marco. We're not in Tuscany."

He seemed about ready to counter that, but instead said, "Okay. Whatever you want is fine with me."

Why did I get the feeling the battle was not over?

At three o'clock, Francesca showed up with Tabitha the cat wrapped in a baby blanket. "Abby, bella," she said, "we have a problem."

Francesca put little Tabitha on the worktable, cooing to calm her, and then unwrapped the blanket.

There was no cast on the cat's leg.

"What happened?" I asked.

"She chewed it loose and somehow — I do not know how exactly — got out of it." Francesca threw her hands in the air. "I cannot believe it. I told you I would care for her and now this! And look. The poor little creature got pink paint on her leg."

"Pink paint?" I looked at the injured leg, and sure enough, there was a long streak of hot pink color that had been hidden beneath the cast. "It looks like nail polish."

Francesca held out her hands. "And see? I don't wear polish."

*Hmm.* Pink nail polish that looked a lot like the color Juanita wore. On a stray cat. A stray *tabby* cat. My inner antennae began to quiver. Was it possible that Tabitha was the missing heiress after all? But Grace had been told that the cat had escaped on Monday, and Tabitha had been missing for days longer than that.

*Maybe they lied about when the cat went missing,* a little voice in my head whispered. *If the cat vanished, they could contest the will.*

But there was a flaw in that idea. What would be the point of getting rid of Charity before Constance's death? The family hadn't known about the cat inheriting everything until the will was read.

Unless Constance had told them. That would be a powerful motive to do away with the feline. But was Tabitha really the missing cat?

"Do you want me to take her to the vet?" Francesca asked.

"Actually, I have to run an errand anyway, and I'll be going right past the veterinary clinic."

"But you're so busy, bella, and I have nothing else to do but make supper for my precious bambinos, those little angels, and drop off another load of laundry for my boys."

Nothing else to do? "In that case, would you mind giving Lottie a hand in the shop again?"

She clapped her hands together. "Yes! I love working here. It's paradise."

Yeah, *my* paradise. I'd have to make sure that Francesca didn't get too comfortable in it.

"I'll go tell Lottie now," Francesca said.

"Would you also ask Grace to come back here?"

Francesca nodded and sailed through the curtain.

"Who are you, Miss Tabitha?" I asked, petting the cat, who was looking around the workroom with interest.

"Yes, love?" Grace asked as she stepped into the workroom. "Oh, my! Where did that cat come from?"

"This is the cat I found, Grace. Francesca brought her in because she chewed her cast off. What do you think of her? Does she remind you of Charity?"

"Absolutely. But for the lack of her pink collar, she could be Charity's double." Grace scratched the cat beneath the chin, and as little Tabitha lifted her head for more, Grace exclaimed, "Abby, look! This cat had a collar at one time. See how her fur is matted?"

"That's not all." I pointed out the pink streak on the cat's hind leg. "This looks like the same color of nail polish Juanita wears."

Grace put on the half-moon glasses that she wore on a chain. "If this cat is Charity," she said, "then the family lied to me."

"Do you remember who told you that Charity had gotten out when the paramedics arrived?"

Grace tapped the side of her nose, thinking. "I seem to remember them all being in agreement about when she escaped, but Juanita was the one who said she'd heard the tires screech and thought Charity had been hit. And now that I think about it, I believe Juanita first suggested the idea of

Charity escaping during the rush of people coming in and out."

"Maybe that's what Juanita wanted everyone to believe. Do you remember the position of Connie's body when you found her?"

She sighed. "How I wish I could forget it."

"Was her right hand curled?"

"Yes, I believe it was. Why?"

"The investigators found cat hair in that hand, Grace, and evidence that she'd been holding on to something like a leash."

"It wouldn't have been a leash, dear. Connie never let Charity outside. There'd be no reason to have a leash." Grace suddenly put out her hand to steady herself. "Good heavens. I know what Connie was holding."

# CHAPTER TWENTY-SIX

"It has to be the cat's collar," Grace said. "I'd bet any money on it — were I the betting type. Find the collar and you'll find the killer, I'm certain of it."

"Gracie," Lottie said, poking her head through the curtain, "the parlor is filling up."

"I'll be right there, love." Grace turned back to me. "I suppose you're heading off to the mansion now to show them the cat? You will take Marco with you, won't you?"

I tucked Tabitha into the blanket, put her in my lap, and headed to the Newports to test Grace's theory. I'd phoned Marco and told him my plan, and he'd agreed to meet me there as soon as he could. Outside the gates, I rang the buzzer and the housekeeper answered.

"Mrs. Dunbar, I think I found Charity. She's in the car with me. I need someone in the family to identify her."

"Oh, my! I'll tell Ms. Virginia and Mrs. Juanita right away."

Marco had been right. Virginia hadn't been arrested.

The gates opened majestically and I drove the 'Vette through, winding up toward the house and parking as close to the courtyard as possible. It was a good thing I had the blanket wrapped snuggly around the cat, because she was struggling to get away.

"Hold on, Tabitha, or Charity, whoever you are. If I'm right, you're about to become the richest cat in New Chapel."

The back door was flung open by Virginia, still in the same outfit as earlier. "Let me see the creature."

"I'm afraid she'll get loose," I said. "Okay if I step inside?"

She glared at me, but motioned for me to enter. Behind her stood Mrs. Dunbar, wringing her hands anxiously. As though she'd been on her way to the garden, she was wearing a long-sleeved denim shirt, dirt-stained khakis, and rubber-soled brown slip-on shoes. Behind her stood Juanita, arms crossed over her bright orange tank top, wearing a pair of stretchy white yoga pants and a glare.

"Let's see the cat," Virginia demanded,

closing the door behind me.

"She's frightened," I said. "Let's do this calmly and politely, okay?"

"I've been closeted with two detectives and two attorneys for the past three hours," Virginia snapped, "so excuse my lack of civility."

*At least you're not in jail,* I wanted to say.

I gently eased the blanket back over the cat's face, talking to her in a soothing voice; then I brought the blanket out from under her thin body. Virginia immediately examined the cat's ears, causing poor Tabitha to tremble in my arms.

"It's Charity," she told the others in a disgusted voice. "Look at the inside of this ear. See the brown comma-shaped mark? Mother used to say it was a good luck sign — and I suppose she was right, wasn't she?"

Neither woman came forward to look.

"Well, we know who'll get that thousand-dollar reward now," Virginia said, looking at me as if I'd plotted it all along. I couldn't help but smile. I'd just made a thousand dollars!

"Wait a minute," Virginia said, turning an accusing gaze on me. "Where is her diamond collar?"

"She wasn't wearing a collar when I found her," I said.

"Or so you claim," Juanita said, drumming her fingers on each arm.

"Poor kitty," Mrs. Dunbar said, putting her hand out for the cat to sniff. "It's a wonder she survived on her own. Where did you find her?"

"She ran out from behind a shrub," I said, wrapping the blanket around the cat. "I nearly ran her over."

"What luck for us," Virginia said sarcastically.

"Are we finished here?" Juanita asked. "I have students coming."

"There's something I'd like you all to see first," I said.

With a sharp sigh, Juanita moved in closer.

"When I found the cat, her hind leg was broken," I said. "And see this streak of color? When the cast came off today, we found pink nail polish on her fur, as though someone with wet nails was holding on to her leg." I glanced at Juanita. "It's your color, Juanita."

"Don't be ridiculous," Juanita said contemptuously.

Virginia swung toward her sister-in-law and grabbed her hand. Holding it close to the cat's leg, she said, "It's a perfect match."

Juanita yanked her hand away. "Why would my nail polish be on Charity's leg?"

"Because with the cat gone," I said, "the will could have been contested."

"But we didn't know Mother left everything to Charity," Virginia said.

"Are you sure no one knew?" I asked.

Virginia glanced at Juanita only to have her look away. "Did *you* know?" she asked Juanita.

"I will not stay here and listen to such ridiculous accusations," Juanita said.

Virginia got up close and stared her in the eye until Juanita dropped her gaze. "You knew and didn't tell us?"

"Okay, yes, I knew about the change in Constance's will," Juanita said. "I overheard her talking to her attorney. But I did nothing about it. And that is all I have to say." She turned and marched toward the doorway.

"I swear to God, Nita," Virginia called, "if you pushed Mother down the stairs —"

"Ridiculous," she called in a singsong voice as she left the kitchen.

Virginia pulled out a chair at the table and sank onto it. "This is all too much."

"Oh, Ms. Virginia," the housekeeper said, fluttering around her, "you're not about to faint, are you?"

"No," she said wearily, waving her away. "Go about your business, Mrs. D."

The housekeeper hesitated, then said reluctantly, "I'll be out back, then."

She opened the door to leave, but before she could close it behind her, Charity jumped out of my arms and made a dash for freedom. As I ran after her, I met Marco coming through the courtyard.

"Marco, the cat got loose! I have to catch her. It's Charity. Don't let Juanita get away. I'll explain later."

I didn't stick around to see what Marco did. I just ran, and when I finally got to the opening in the hedge that surrounded the garden, I saw Charity digging in the dirt beneath one of the shrubs at the far end of the first row.

Knowing how easily cats could be spooked, I slowed down to a leisurely stroll and began to talk to her. "There's Charity. Aren't you a good girl? You know I won't hurt you, don't you? Yes, you do. What a good girl you are."

Charity was about five feet away from me and still digging. Then she stopped, glanced at me, and scampered away.

"Come back here," I called, and was about to go after her when I spotted something pink in the hole she'd dug. I stooped down to look and pulled out a dirty pink cat collar with bare rectangular areas all around it.

"Holy cow," I muttered. I'd found the collar — minus the diamonds.

"What do you have there?" I heard, and pivoted to see Mrs. Dunbar coming toward me, her basket over her arm.

"Charity's collar." I waited until she had reached me; then I showed her. "What do you want to bet the police find Juanita's fingerprints on it?"

"You'll be giving the collar to the detectives, then?"

She seemed almost alarmed at the thought. "Mrs. Dunbar, is there something about this collar that you need to tell me?"

"No, miss." She backed away. "I should get on with my work now."

I watched as she took her pruning shears out of the basket and started to clip the hedge. Something was definitely bugging Mrs. Dunbar, and that in turn bugged me. Did the thought of Juanita being accused of the theft bother her because someone else was guilty? And something else began to bug me. Why would Juanita hide the collar in the garden where Mrs. Dunbar would be likely to uncover it? Surely she was smarter than that.

Then I remembered something Grace had told us.

*"I ran upstairs to call for help and was talk-*

*ing to the police when Mrs. Dunbar came through the back door. She heard my end of the conversation, dropped the bundle of radishes in her apron, ran to the basement door, and would have charged straight down the steps had I not caught her in time."*

I looked at the housekeeper now, decked out in her blue shirt and khakis and rubber shoes. If she'd been working in the garden that day, why had she been wearing her dress and apron?

"Mrs. Dunbar," I said, walking toward her, "do you always wear these clothes when you work in the garden?"

She stopped snipping. "Yes, miss. Why do you ask?"

I picked up one of the clippings and plucked a leaf from it. "When you came back to the house Monday afternoon and found Grace Bingham in the kitchen, had you been working in the garden?"

She got to her feet. "Yes, miss."

"For how long?"

She squeezed the snippers so hard, her knuckles turned white. "An hour or so. I don't remember exactly."

I was about to question her further, but something had changed in the housekeeper's expression. Something flinty had entered it. It made me back up a step.

She held out her other hand. "Give me the collar, miss."

I took another step backward. "I can't do that, Mrs. Dunbar."

"You best give me the collar now, miss, if you know what's good for you."

Given that we were far away from the house, I had to make a quick decision — hand it over or run. But before I could make a move, she grabbed my wrist.

"You know, don't you? You know who buried this collar."

"Mrs. Dunbar, I don't really care who buried it. I'm more interested in who stole the diamonds. Would you let go of my wrist, please?"

"Look at Miss Juanita if you want to know who stole them."

"I'll do just that," I said, trying to placate her. "After all, why would you take diamonds when Mrs. Connie left you all that silver, right?"

Anger flashed in her eyes. "*All* that silver?"

Apparently not the thing to say to placate her.

"Do you know what the lawyer said that silver is worth? Maybe twenty thousand dollars."

"That's a lot of money."

"Try retiring on it." Mrs. Dunbar released

my wrist. "Mrs. Connie always promised she'd take care of me in my old age; then she turned on me, claiming she found that collar in my room. I told her she had it wrong, that someone must have put it there to make me look guilty, but she just kept shaking that collar in my face, saying she knew I'd been looting her crystal collection, so why would she believe I hadn't taken the diamonds?"

"Oh, Mrs. Dunbar, that's awful," I said, wishing Marco would come looking for me.

"I begged her to forgive me, but instead she said she was going to fire me. After all those years of faithful service, she was going to fire me over a few little glass birds and a cat's collar. The nerve of that selfish old bat."

At once, a big gold *g* flashed before my eyes, almost like someone had waved it in front of my face. I glanced at my surroundings, and the hair on my neck rose.

*G* was for *garden.* That was what Grace's dream meant. I was staring at the killer.

# CHAPTER TWENTY-SEVEN

Mrs. Dunbar was so worked up, she was trembling, and so was I. "I told Mrs. Connie I didn't have any money put away to speak of, and you know what she told me? That I could sell those crystal figurines I'd stolen and use that as my retirement fund."

I inched backward. "I can only imagine how that hurt, but once we explain all this to the police —"

Mrs. Dunbar gave me a hard shove that sent me staggering backward onto my rear. "You want me to sit in a prison for the rest of my life? You're just as cruel as everyone else. Who cares what happens to Mrs. Dunbar? She's only the hired help."

I crab-legged backward, but she kept advancing. "No one would've been the wiser if you hadn't found that stupid cat and brought her back here."

"Mrs. Dunbar, you don't want to compound your crime by hurting me."

With a crazed look in her eyes, she planted her heavy rubber boots on either side of me and raised the pruning shears. Apparently compounding her crime was not a concern.

I tensed my leg muscles, preparing to kick her in the knee as hard as I could. But suddenly her gaze shifted to something behind me and her arms froze. Before I could turn to see what had caused her reaction, she gasped and staggered backward, clutching her chest. She collapsed onto the ground, gave three loud gasps, and went limp, her head lolling to one side.

Stunned, I scrambled over to her to see if she was breathing. As I felt for a pulse, I heard someone coming and turned to see Lindsey hurrying from the far end of the row, carrying Charity in her arms.

"Lindsey," I called. "I think Mrs. Dunbar had a heart attack."

"Here, take Charity," she said, handing me the cat. "I've had CPR training. I know what to do."

She laid her head against the woman's chest, felt the pulse in her neck, then sat back on her heels. "That's odd. She's breathing fine and seems to have a strong heartbeat and a steady pulse. What happened?"

At that, Mrs. Dunbar moaned, blinked a

few times, and came to. As soon as she saw Lindsey, she began to tremble so violently, her teeth clattered. "I d-didn't mean to p-push Mrs. Connie," she whimpered.

Lindsey glanced up at me with a questioning look.

"*That's* what happened," I said.

"Why don't you tell us about it, Mrs. D.?" Lindsey said soothingly. "You'll feel better."

The housekeeper squeezed her eyes tightly shut. "I can't."

"Take a deep breath," Lindsey instructed. "Get it off your chest."

With a strangled sob, Mrs. Dunbar said, "If only she hadn't kept shaking that collar in my face, accusing me of stealing those diamonds, I wouldn't have lost my temper. I didn't realize how close she was to the stairs."

Mrs. Dunbar covered her face and began to sob. "When I saw what I'd done, I panicked and snatched the collar from her hands."

"Was she still alive when you ran out to the garden?" Lindsey asked.

"Yes," she wept. "God help me, she was. I buried the collar, but before I could get back to the house to get rid of the body, Mrs. Bingham arrived. Now what am I going to do?"

"Say a lot of prayers, Mrs. D." Lindsey rose and brushed off her knees. "Abby, I think you'd better get Marco now."

"Thanks for your help," I said, backing away. "I owe you."

"I'll hold you to that."

Clutching the struggling Charity against me, I hurried back to the house and saw Marco coming out the door.

"There you are," he said. "I thought you got lost again. I see you found the heiress."

"Marco," I said breathlessly, "Mrs. Dunbar just made a full confession. She pushed Constance down the stairs!"

"Where is she?"

"In the garden."

"Call the cops," Marco said, and ran.

Once the police arrived, Marco and I gave statements and answered questions for over an hour before we were able to leave. Marco phoned Dave with the news that the murder had been solved and was assured that the DA would be notified immediately.

We stopped at the vet to have the doctor examine Charity and ended up having to leave her overnight. On our way home, I called Grace to let her know Charity's situation, and she said she would make arrangements for the cat's care. I could tell by the tone of her voice that she had already heard from Dave, and at the end of our conversation she confirmed that for me in her usual inimitable way.

"Abby, love, no words can adequately express my gratitude."

I waited for a quote, but none was forthcoming, so after an awkward pause, I said, "Thank you, Grace."

"Please pass along my thanks to Marco."

"I'll do that. See you tomorrow morning?"

"Absolutely, dear. Enjoy your evening."

I glanced at the handsome man beside me and smiled. "I will, Grace."

It was after five o'clock when we stopped at Down the Hatch for dinner. We had purposely kept our plans for the evening private so we could relax and enjoy each other's company, but in the middle of our meal, Marco's mom, my mom, and Grace and Lottie came crowding into our booth.

"We heard the news," Lottie said, "and couldn't wait to get the full report."

"Grace knows what happened," I said.

"This is your story to tell, love," Grace said, thwarting my last-ditch effort.

"Your dad would have come," Mom said, "but he had physical therapy tonight."

"How did you know we were here?" I asked.

Francesca pointed toward the bar. I glanced over and saw Rafe lift his hand, a sheepish grin on his face. Marco signaled for him to come over to the table, and I thought his little brother was in for a lecture.

Instead, my hunky groom-to-be said, "Bring three bottles of Prosecco."

Then, over flutes of sparkling wine, the women got to hear about how Constance Newport had met her end, and my near-death experience in the garden.

"That explains the letter *g* that I saw," Grace said, and then had to tell everyone about her dreams.

"All I can say is, thank goodness for Lindsey," I told them. "She saved my life."

"Who is Lindsey?" Lottie asked.

"Juanita's friend," I said. At their blank looks, I added, "Cute little blonde about my age?" Still no recognition, so I said to Marco, "You saw her. She was with Mrs. Dunbar in the garden."

"There was no one but Mrs. Dunbar in the garden, Sunshine."

"That's impossible. She found Charity. You remember her, Lottie. She came to Bloomers with Juanita. About my height. Red jacket?"

More blank looks.

"Come on!" I said. "You have to remember when Juanita came storming into the shop. I was about to close the door when Lindsey slipped in after her."

"We were in the workroom when Juanita arrived, sweetie," Lottie said.

"But Lindsey was in the workroom, too," I said. "She came in with me."

They were watching me as though I was one floor short of a skyscraper. "Why are you staring at me like that? I didn't imagine her."

"Did Lindsey tell you her last name?" Grace asked.

"No. Why?"

"This is just a theory, love, but Mrs. Dunbar had an older sister who died when she was your age. Her name was Lindsey Ann, and from what I was told, she was quite an adventuress, always getting herself into some scrape or another. Perhaps that's who Mrs. Dunbar saw."

"What are you saying, Grace? That Mrs. Dunbar collapsed because she saw her sister's ghost?"

"Stranger things have happened," Grace said mysteriously.

"Hey, now," I said, starting to get annoyed, "I saw Lindsey up close. She was as real as I am."

"I'm sure you did, dear," Grace said. "What were the occasions when you saw her?"

"Well," I said, "there was the time she came to Bloomers with Juanita . . ."

*When Lindsey had warned me about Juanita's vengeful streak.*

"And then the time I thought I saw her at the racetrack . . ."

*Where her movements had led me straight to Burnsy.*

"And in the hallway outside of Virginia's studio . . ."

*Where she'd told me Virginia's nickname was Ginny.*

"And yesterday when I took the cat photos to the Newport house . . ."

*Where she'd helped me eliminate all the Charity wannabes.*

"And today in the garden."

*When she'd saved my life.*

"She certainly popped up at the right times, didn't she?" Grace asked. "Lindsey may have been your guardian angel."

Mom, Francesca, and Lottie nodded in agreement, while Marco swirled the wine in his glass, looking uncomfortable.

Time to change the conversation. "Marco, why don't you tell them about the rest of the Newports?"

Marco looked relieved, so I stuck my chin in my palm and let him fill them in. He started with the missing cat heiress and her diamondless cat collar.

"Juanita wasn't the least bit embarrassed about stealing the diamonds," he told them. "She said she wasn't about to be poor ever again. So in Juanita's struggle to remove the cat's collar, she grabbed Charity's hind leg and held on as the cat jumped off the counter. The cat ran out the door when the housekeeper came in from the garden.

"And since Mrs. Dunbar was a witness, Juanita made her promise not to tell Constance what had happened or else she'd reveal that the housekeeper had been stealing crystal birds, a little fact she'd learned from Burnett. Juanita then planted the stripped-down collar in Mrs. Dunbar's bedroom, where Constance found it. And you know the rest of that story."

"What a family," Lottie said. "Is Juanita going to be charged with theft?"

"I'm sure she will, but that's in the DA's hands," Marco said. "I expect charges to be brought against Virginia, too, for her part in the art theft."

"Will Mrs. Dunbar be charged with murder?" my mom asked.

"In some form," Marco said.

"That poor, tortured soul," Grace said with a sad sigh.

Suddenly, a tall, shapely copper-haired woman wearing a black spandex cat costume complete with ears and a mask squeezed onto the bench beside me. "What did I miss?" Jillian said, adjusting her tail so she wouldn't sit on it.

"Are you going to a costume party?" I asked.

"No, silly. We're going to stake out the Newport house tonight and catch that cat burglar. I've got it all worked out." Jillian glanced around at us. "What?"

"We caught the cat burglar," I said.

Jillian's face fell. "You mean I'm too late?"

"Yep," I said.

With a sharp huff, she pulled off the black mask. "Someone could have told me."

Grace cleared her throat. "Let us remember what Miguel de Cervantes wrote so eloquently in his masterful novel, *Don Quixote*, " 'There is a time . . .' " She hesitated; then a look of panic flickered across her face.

My heart jumped to my throat. I met Lottie's gaze across the table and knew she was as concerned as I was.

*Come on, Grace. You can do it!*

415

Grace drew a breath. Then she straightened her shoulders, and said forcefully, " 'There is a time for some things, and a time for all things; a time for great things, and a time for small things.' "

We all clapped. Relief flooded Grace's face. She was back!

"A time for small things," Jillian said to Grace. "You're talking about Abs, right?"

At that moment, a bartender rang the brass bell at the end of the bar to signal that he'd received a tip.

"Hey, sweetie," Lottie said with a laugh, "maybe that was your friend Lindsey earning her wings. Remember Clarence in the movie *It's a Wonderful Life*?"

"I love that movie," Jillian said with a sigh. "Jimmy Cagney was so good in it."

"Jimmy Stewart," I said.

"That's who I meant," she said. "I always mix them up."

"Right," I said. "They're so much alike."

"Girls," my mom said, "let's not fight. I might be forced to make you wear my sea glasses as punishment."

I stared at Mom in surprise. "What?"

"It's okay, Abigail," Mom said. "I know all about it. I saw several of the girls in town wearing the glasses and they told me. Frankly, I'm glad I don't have to make them

416

anymore. I was feeling a little burned out. Now I'm free to find new inspiration."

Grace lifted her glass. "And on that note, I would like to propose a toast."

That was more like it.

When all the glasses were in the air, she said, "Abby, Marco, thank you from the bottom of my heart for finding Connie's killer. Now that I've been cleared, I shall be able to sleep at night again. Cheers."

"Cheers," everyone said in unison, clinking glasses.

"I'd like to propose a toast, too," my mom said. "Here's to a successful, united wedding shower."

"Hear, hear," Jillian said.

We touched glasses all around.

"And now for our news," Francesca said, smiling at us. "Right, Maureen?"

*Uh-oh.* I grabbed Marco's hand beneath the table.

"Abby, bella," she said, "and Marco, my boy. You will be very pleased to know that Maureen and I have planned something very special for your shower."

My stomach gave a tiny lurch. "Are you talking about the menu?"

Our mothers giggled like naughty children. "No, honey," Mom said, "you wanted to select the menu, and we want you to do whatever makes you happy."

"Games, then?"

"No games," Francesca said, "just as you asked. You'll have to wait and see what our surprise is."

My stomach lurched harder. "You can't even give us a clue?"

"I'll tell you one thing," Jillian said. "You are going to l-o-v-e the bridal shower outfit I found for you. All I'll say is, think copper and think big."

I was thinking more about puking.

While I practiced my deep breathing, Marco tried to get more information out of them, but, as they seemed to be in on it together, they said good night and everyone scooted off.

"This is bad, Marco. Very bad. You know what my mom's surprises are like. Think dancing naked monkey table. Think giant bowling pin hat stand. Think of the many possibilities of how bad this could be."

"I've got a better plan. Let's go back to my place and think of ways to make it seem like a bad dream."

Best idea I'd heard all day. "And guess what? I still haven't collected on my bet."

"Your time is coming, baby," he growled, pulling me against him for a long, searing hot kiss. "That's just for starters."

■ ■ ■ ■

Before we headed to Marco's, I had to make a stop at Bloomers to retrieve my jean jacket that I'd left that afternoon in my rush to get to the Newports. While Marco waited outside, I shut off the alarm, turned on the lights, and then went through the purple curtain to get my jacket off the back of my chair.

I stopped in surprise. A three-quarter-length red twill coat was hanging on the back of my chair.

I glanced around but saw no sign that anyone had been there. I tiptoed to the kitchen for a look around, checked the bathroom, and came back to peer inside the giant coolers. It wasn't until I returned to my desk that I spotted a note.

Abby,
   I'm leaving this coat as a thank-you. Please know that you are never alone.

                                Love,
                             Lindsey

What was she thanking me for? I ran my fingers over the fine twill material. At least I had proof that Lindsey existed. Angels didn't wear coats.

I set the note aside and took the garment off the back of the chair, wondering where my old jacket had gone. I was about to try on the red twill when the bell over the door jingled.

*An angel just got her wings.*

"Hey, what's keeping you?" my impatient groom-to-be asked, coming into the room.

Ah! That was the reason for the jingling. I showed him the coat. "I told you Lindsey existed. She left this for me."

"She left you her coat?"

"Yes. She even wrote me a thank-you note." I turned to get it, but it was no longer on the desk. I got down to look underneath; then I crawled under the worktable and finally stood up and scratched my head. "I left it right here on the desk."

"Okay, Sunshine, let's get you home. It's been a long day and you've had a close call. I'll bet things will look better in the morning."

"I'm not making it up, Marco. I know what I saw. That note is here somewhere."

But ten minutes more of searching didn't produce it.

"I'll bet you picked up Nikki's coat by mistake this morning and forgot." Marco held up the jacket so I could slip my arms into the sleeves.

"This isn't Nikki's," I said. "Her sleeves would have covered my hands. Lindsey must have stopped by and left it for me."

But it had to be Nikki's. I mean, seriously. A guardian angel?

"Ready?" Marco asked, as I finished buttoning the front.

Ready for a cozy evening with my hot and hunky groom-to-be? He had no idea how much I was looking forward to it. I locked up the shop and took Marco's arm. "Okay, Salvare, time to put this case to rest and collect my bet."

"Whatever it takes, Sunshine," he said, smiling into my eyes.

What it would take was erasing all thoughts of forgeries and missing cats and possible angel sightings, and instead, focusing solely on Marco.

As we walked toward the street, I thought I heard the faint jingling of the bell inside the shop.

# ABOUT THE AUTHOR

**Kate Collins** grew up in a suburb of Hammond, Indiana, one block from the family home of author Jean Shepherd, whose humorous stories inspired Kate at an early age. After a stint as an elementary school teacher, Kate wrote children's short stories and historical romance novels before turning to her true passion, mystery. The author of the popular Flower Shop Mystery series, she lives in northwest Indiana and Key West, Florida.